The Catcher

Kerry Birds

For My Mum

Lost though not forgotten x

1

CELIA

I didn't want to kill him.

I didn't want to kill any of them.

But death happens. It's all about numbers. Predation. Resources. Life's stupid mistakes. Though he would die because he had hurt me, and for that he couldn't go unpunished.

He was the buff-tailed bumblebee which I kept in an old fish tank in the spare room. Purple clover grew in the soil-covered bottom and a glass jar filled with fresh dandelions and alliums sat in the corner.

I went to my bumblebee early that morning, before the bee could fight or fly. I watched it for a while, perfect and oblivious, preening its body and warming its clingfilm wings. Its face was furry, as black as my soul, and the stripes were yolk yellow. I had carefully trapped and nurtured my bee and had grown so very attached to it. Regardless, it stung me, and so it needed to suffer before the end.

After removing the tank lid, I swooped in with a pair of tweezers, plucked it out, and pinned it to the windowsill. For several minutes it seemed to rally, adjusting to its worsening predicament. The crumpled wing looked terribly untidy on the beautiful creature, so I snipped it off with a pair of silver scissors. Only after losing the wing, and with it the chance of freedom, did it finally give in. With the tip of my finger, I touched what remained of the bee. The soft hairs were like a money spider crawling across my skin. I held it to my lips and breathed across its desecrated body.

I had denied the bee of freedom, provoked and exhausted it, and made it suffer in every way. Its tolerance, however, had been remarkable – unlike those before it, which simply curled up and died.

Insects were just like people.

Yes, they absolutely were.

2

ELENA

I needed a name.

I had the new house, the new car, and the new start, but I didn't have a name that belonged. The journey from my maiden to married name came easily, the path marked by white silk and happy tears and a trail of confetti, but the way back had proved to be a different matter – an unconquered mountain of black ink and bitterness and regret.

Regret.

'I'm sorry.' That was it. All my husband of five years had to say on the matter. He offered no rambling apology or plea for forgiveness, and no explanation why another woman straddled him in our bed. Still, if a butterfly had the strength to fly a thousand miles, then I could survive the parade of eviction and divorce.

If only I could work out the right name.

I scanned the cardboard chaos in my show-home kitchen. Unpacked boxes waited everywhere, though my important paperwork was definitely in a bag. I rubbed my temples, then squeezed between two towers, wondering why on earth I declined the help offered by friends, family and a professional unpacking company – aside of the fact I was stubbornly fine.

The bag sat on top of the packaged microwave, miraculously balancing on its end. Inside the bag were, amongst other things, two passports. I skipped over the newest passport and opened the old one, the one with the snipped off corner. The pages were all stamped, though most of the words were indecipherable, the ink smudged. It was for the best. I didn't want to remember the happy holidays before we exchanged the rings.

And the lies.

I turned to the last page and stared at my old surname, the one I once shared with my parents. That wasn't right either. I lobbed the passport back in the bag and clutched the granite counter. 'Granite,' the estate agent told me; 'so hard-wearing they make it into headstones.' Which meant the granite needed to go. As soon as.

As I grabbed an over-filled banana box, a rap came from my open front door.

'Hello there.'

The Irish-tinged voice belonged to a man. With one hand on the back of his neck, he held out a small bouquet of flowers. Given the splattered rigger boots and worn utility trousers, he was obviously a builder and didn't work for Interflora. I looked between the man and the flowers.

'Hi.'

He waved a piece of paper marked Invoice. 'I was getting this when I saw somebody dump these flowers outside your gate. Didn't want the kids flattening them with a football.'

'Oh, erm, thank you.'

The water balloon holding the stems wobbled and bulged when I sifted through the carnations and roses and gypsophila, looking for the card. From afar, the flowers were bright, the blooms crisp, but up close, brown tipped the rose petals and the carnations appeared ragged. The non-descript card bore a cheap illustration and a printed message: 'Good luck in your new home'. Lucas had signed the back with a dot, a letter L and another dot: the kisses were long gone.

The builder folded his paper and flattened the crease. 'Secret admirer?'

'No. My ex-husband.' The thought of Lucas being at my new house, my new beginning, made my stomach tip with motion and gruel. 'Did he drop the flowers outside? He's got brown hair, glasses – drives a dark-grey Range Rover.'

'No. It was a red Fiesta. Only saw a woman.'

My hands quivered, shaking the flowers. 'What did she look like?'

He shrugged. 'Blonde hair. In her twenties. Tall, I think.'

The balloon of water hit the floor and exploded, sending beads of water up the front of my trousers and along the bottom of his. The thinner stems scattered, jaunty and crushed, whilst the thick ones, the thorny ones, remained trapped by the elastic band. I couldn't believe it. Lucas actually sent his new fiancé – the woman I caught gracing my marital bed wearing nothing more than a lace thong – to deliver a bunch of withered flowers into my new life.

I dropped to my knees, hot tears blobbing down my cheeks, and drew together the broken flowers and the sticky water with the sides of my hands. The builder dropped to his knees too and carefully picked out the gypsophila, the only flowers which weren't ruined by age or trauma. He brushed the crushed petals from my palms and handed me the perfect white flowers he'd collected.

'I'll chuck the rest in the green bin on my way past.'

Noticing his hands were chalky, the flower water drying on them, I said, 'Do you want to wash your hands before you go?'

'Yeah, suppose I should. Thanks.'

I nodded and then pulled on the cellophane hidden under his knee. There was no mistaking the words on the scuffed label. Reduced for quick sale. He winced, and I wanted to be sick.

The guy squirted the soap and turned on the tap and talked to me. He said something about hard water and shower heads, then laughed at himself for being boring. His warmth and kindness felt real.

It hit me then. The loneliness. The fact I had no husband, my friends and family lived miles away, and I couldn't even go into work to escape my isolation. I simply craved the company of another human, however brief, as pathetic as it was.

'Excuse me.' I passed him the hand towel. 'I know this is crazy – but you seem nice – I don't suppose you fancy a quick drink. It's fine if you're busy or whatever. I'm not coming on to you or anything,' I blathered. 'Gosh, sorry. I'm being silly. Forget I even mentioned it.'

My face felt warm and my eyes suddenly full.

The guy touched his lip. 'Are you alright?'

I stared into my glass kettle, avoiding his worried frown. 'Yes, I'm fine.'

I trotted out my worn-out line. I'm fine. Which, on the outside, I was. Yes, my new clothes were a size bigger than the old, and I shared the empty wine bottles between the bin and the bottle bank, but I hadn't malingered or cried, and it would be back to work, business as usual, once I'd taken my owed holiday leave. I hoped.

'Okay,' he said. 'I don't suppose a cuppa will do any harm.'

I turned my John Lewis mug tree, looking for my favourite, and a spotty cup flirted off. Bits of broken mug skittered everywhere, in front of my bare feet and between the rows of cardboard stalagmites, trapping me, separating me from what remained of my life. I didn't know what to do or where to go.

The builder meandered between the boxes, gathering jagged bits of pottery, with my trainers dangling from his fingers by the laces. 'Put these on so you don't cut your feet.'

Hands shaking, I took the shoes. 'Thank you.'

I dropped the trainers on the floor and lifted a foot. The world turned, and I clung onto my headstone counter.

'Seriously, are you alright?'

'No. I'm not.' I rammed my feet into my shoes. 'I can't even work out my bloody name.'

Then it all came out; not to my friends or my mother, but to him, the complete stranger. I told him everything, about my lost name, and how every day I became more confused, more disillusioned.

'Who do you feel like now?' he asked.

I sobbed and sniffed. 'Just Elena.'

'Well, just Elena.' He smiled softly. 'The right name will come when the time is right.'

He was right, of course. The name, re-identifying myself to others, had become the focus of my discontent. I could control it – unlike the fact Lucas had hounded me from contentment and to a place where everything felt shaky and wrong.

'And there's all of this.' I flung my arm towards the nearest pile of boxes. 'Which I can't face either.'

The stranger brushed my hand. 'Okay. First things first. Today you need something to eat, a toothbrush, toilet roll, a bed, and a teapot.'

I snorted like a pig. Seriously. A pig. 'I don't own a teapot.'

'You need a teapot.' His eyes were hazel, chestnut haloed with green. 'If you sit down and drink a pot, then it de-shits your brain.'

I smiled weakly. 'Is de-shit even a word?'

'It is now.' He hugged me and I soaked up his caring. 'Tomorrow you'll need clean clothes, a towel, the TV or a book. Make a plan and make time to drink tea.'

He smiled and I smiled back.

'Are you a time-management counsellor or something?'

'No. I'm a builder, and I know what it's like to stand on a bare bit of land with the drawings for a six-bedroom house in my hand.' The guy's view flicked from my face to the red dot seeping into my trousers. 'I think you cut yourself on the broken cup. I'll make the drinks while you check it out.'

Five minutes later, he tapped on the bedroom door and asked if I was okay. I opened the door and shrugged off his concern. He glanced at my unmade bed and turned to leave.

'Please don't go. I don't even know your name.'

He held out his hand, and I shook it. 'Alistair.'

Alistair dropped my hand and fidgeted with his fingers. Bruises covered his first swollen finger and another two nails were black.

'Looks painful.' I pointed at the damage. 'What did you do?'

'Erm, I trapped it in a door.' A dapple of red crossed his cheeks. 'I really ought to go.'

'Don't worry. I won't break the rest of your fingers or pinch your phone.'

Alistair laughed, and I dropped my bottom onto the scratchy mattress. He stared at my freshly-painted-for-a-quick-sale wall and I scratched at a tatty nail. My nails hadn't fared well, what with the new biting habit and the unpacking.

'I, erm...' we muttered concurrently.

'The tea's getting cold,' I said.

Alistair handed me a mug and leaned on the wall outside my bedroom, looking uncomfortable.

'Thank you.' I turned my cup handle to palm, handle to palm.

'What do you want to talk about?' Alistair asked.

My view wandered to his feet. His socks were odd, two shades of blue. 'Anything other than broken marriages.'

'Fine by me.'

He didn't wear a wedding ring. There wasn't even a telltale white band or a dint like on my finger. If he had been married, he wasn't anymore, and he hadn't been for a long time.

'You want me to hang around?' he blurted. 'I can help with the unpacking.'

'That would be great,' I replied, clearly shocking the both of us. 'But aren't you meant to be working?'

'I'll pull a sickie.'

Alistair turned off his phone before placing it, along with a Stanley knife, two screwdrivers, and a roll of electrical tape on the wooden hall floor.

He patted his legs. 'Where shall we start?'

'The bed?'

Alistair scratched his head and peered over his shoulder. 'Okay, let's start on the bed.'

I rearranged the bedroom boxes until I found those containing the linen and duvet. Alistair slid his knife along the Sellotape strip, wrenched out the duvet and shook it fluffy. And then, together, Alistair and I made the bed with my new one-hundred percent Egyptian cotton bedding. We took opposite corners and smoothed the sheets and he did the pillowcases while I attended to the very serious matter of scatter cushions.

He nodded at the cushions and said, 'They're as much use as a paper tent in a hailstorm,' and buried me under my throw.

I smiled throughout my escape. I actually smiled.

I liked Alistair; I liked him a lot.

For the next few hours, we emptied boxes and exchanged our potted biographies. I quickly gleaned Alistair was a good person. He moved to the village to be close to his ailing 'Nan' and volunteered for a community construction project, similar to my working pro bono as a solicitor. Further to that, he withheld sniggers and comments when he discovered my fifteen-year-old dressing gown and well-thumbed copy of Fifty Shades of Grey.

Alistair made me feel clean, like a new page, not an old page with crossed out words and mountains of Tippex. I didn't know how, but the logistics were of no consequence.

Checking the time, Alistair sighed and rubbed his neck. 'I need to go.'

A tonne of rocks landed in my gut, yet I smiled thinly. 'Okay, and thank you so much. For helping and being so patient with me this morning.'

'Patience is my middle name. I even get the odd saint asking for tips.' His face twitched. 'And on the subject of saints. You don't have to be one. It's alright to admit you're in a bad place and cry, call him names, throw stuff at the wall...'

'I think I've got enough mess to clear up.'

Although the smashed mug wasn't part of it. Every fragment had gone, from big bits to dust. The only clue to my accident being the swish purple dustpan and brush propped against the bin. Not that I could recall buying said objects.

I leaned against the wall; my arms wrapped around my middle.

'See you, Alistair, and thank you.'

'No, thank you, Elena. It's not often life gives me someone to smile about.'

3

ALISTAIR

I turned in the driver's seat and planted my feet on the drive; a crack slashed the tarmac between my trainers, dark grey between the light. I glared at the house and breathed so hard my belly pressed against my football shirt.

The curtains were closed.

Every curtain, upstairs and down – the living room, bedrooms and the hall. In most places I saw the white lining, but in others the front fabric showed. The curtains had been yanked shut, fast and hard.

For ninety minutes I'd chased the ball around the pitch and my chest hadn't tightened once, not like it did right then. I counted. Five seconds breathing in and ten seconds breathing out. I wanted to be sick. I thought about climbing back in the truck, driving away, and finding a cliff to jump off. But instead, I locked the door and dragged myself up the path. Her car sat crooked on the drive, one wheel crushing the pansies, and the plastic recycling covered the floor next to the bin. There was always a sign, sometimes more than one, but the closed curtains bothered me more than the rubbish thrown in a temper. Because when my wife shut out the world, she turned on me.

Everything coiled up tight, from the muscles in my shoulders to the thoughts in my head. I took another deep breath before I replaced the sounds of distant cars and roosting birds with cold, sterile silence. I kicked off my trainers and dropped my kitbag on the floor. The empty water bottle pinged from the side net and hit the wall.

'It's only me.'

Yes. I marched on, pretending and hoping. Sometimes it worked, though mostly she started on me anyway. Especially when I'd been out and done something for myself.

Twenty minutes earlier, I'd been as happy as a pig in the proverbial, smiling as I knocked the mud off my football boots. We'd won – a miracle considering the other team were at the top of the league and we were clinging on at the bottom – but the happiness had long gone, leaving a breeze block stomach and a brain filled with grit.

I found her sitting at the kitchen table, turning a glass of wine. 'Where the hell have you been?'

I looked down at my shorts, the football socks around my ankles, and the mud smears from a sliding tackle. 'Playing football.'

Obviously.

'You're a fucking liar.'

She was even angrier than usual because I'd lost my phone, and without my phone she couldn't track me. I'd known she hacked into my Apple account and followed my movements for a long time, though it never bothered me because I had nothing to hide.

'I'm not a liar. We played the Miner's Welfare, won three-two. Dave scored the last goal in extra time.'

It was the truth, and she knew it.

She glared at me. 'Dinner's ruined.'

I mooched to the hob and stirred the casserole I'd made the night before. Beef and squash with plenty of black pepper.

I tasted it and then sucked the cold air over my tongue. 'There's nothing wrong with it.'

'So, now you're a chef as well as a bricklayer?'

I might pass as a chef – what with doing most of the cooking. Not that I pointed it out. I glanced at my wife, wondering when our biting non-communication replaced normal conversation. I supposed getting the business going kept me so busy I didn't notice her changing. Or perhaps I did and I ignored it.

After washing my hands, I got two dishes from the cupboard and filled them, though I didn't put them on the table. Steaming-hot food worried me. Steaming-hot food hurt.

'You look like shit, Alistair.' I felt her eyes scouring my face. 'You need to get a professional job. An office job. You need to stop spending so much time outside and you need to think about your appearance.'

I gritted my teeth until the gums ached. The sun had caught my forehead and nose, and it had yet to go properly brown, though I reckoned she was referring to the dark circles under my eyes. 'I need to get some sleep.'

Sometimes I couldn't keep my mouth shut.

'Why exactly don't you sleep? It certainly isn't because we're at it all night.' She rubbed her finger around her glass until it whined. 'When exactly did we last have sex?'

And sometimes I kept my mouth shut. I didn't poke that bear. No pun intended.

'Oh, I forgot. We don't have sex because you're impotent. Thirty-two and impotent.' She laughed and dangled her finger like it was a worm.

Straight for the jugular.

Impotent.

The word rattled around my empty stomach, my empty chest. The stress might be to blame – trial after trial, day and night – not that I wanted to have sex with her. That want went in the bin with the bloody tissues and the broken plates long ago.

'I'm not impotent.'

I stirred my stew until it made a twister of steam. I wished for a genie and one wish.

'Then I suppose it's me. My fault. Everything's my fucking fault.'

I pushed the stew pot to the back of the hob and sneaked the bread knife into the gap between the sink and the washing-up bowl. 'I never said—'

She cut me off with a horrible scream and smashed the wineglass on the table. I got my palm between the shard in her hand and the opposite wrist just in time. She'd never cut her wrists before, but she'd taken tablets and tried to jump into the road so I wouldn't put it past her.

Neither of us breathed. Neither of us moved.

The glass sat between us like a giant snake tooth.

'Please, come with me to the doctor.' My chest heaved into view, out of view. 'Please.'

The plea was a risk. I'd taken her to the doctor before, tricked her into going, but her flawless sane act made me look the crazy one. The cup of boiling black coffee she later threw in my face proved she had the problem. But nobody saw that. They never did. The hospital doctor didn't even ask questions when I turned up a few days later with the damage to my eye.

'It doesn't have to be like this,' I said. 'There's therapy and tablets and stuff.'

She cleared her throat, and the glass drove deeper. I imagined the point and the jagged sides trying to slice me up completely, and it hurt even more.

'I don't need help.'

Her hand dropped and so did my shoulders, my spirit, my view. I couldn't look at her and see what she'd become. I pulled the glass out of my hand and a stream of blood followed. She bounced to her feet, and her chair crashed on the floor.

'Please,' I started, hands in the air.

Face still, she eyeballed my hand. The wet blood crept under my watchstrap. She stepped forward and, not knowing what the hell to expect, I knocked the rest of the broken glass out of her reach.

'Alistair.' Tears poured down her cheeks. 'I've hurt you – I'm so sorry.'

She pressed her face against my chest and wrapped her arms around me, and I hovered my hands until she begged me to hug her. The internet said the anger and guilt was a typical cycle, but it didn't tell me why. There had to be a reason.

'I'm sorry,' she sobbed. 'I'm so sorry. It must be the wine. I promise I'll never...'

Promises, promises, so many promises. I was sick of the promises. I was sick of it all: walking on eggshells, being called a pig to a dog, reining it in week after week. The end of the rope dangled in my face. I wanted to pack my bags and leave, but she wouldn't let me. She'd either hurt herself or she'd finish me somehow. I knew her well. Anyway, men like me didn't walk away. Or tell anybody. Dealing with the broken bones and bloodletting came easier than dealing with the shame.

'I need a bath,' she said, already half out of the kitchen. 'Can you clean up the mess?'

I pulled on the kitchen roll dispenser and it spun around, sprinkling twenty sheets onto the counter. I ripped off a few and pressed them to the cut until the bleeding slowed. The inch-long cut crossed the line which a fortune teller once said was my lifeline; the irony didn't escape me. Luckily, it didn't seem bad, so I'd be able to pass it off as a gardening mishap or something if anybody asked.

I dabbed away the beads of blood which blobbed out. I needed to glue it shut; it would be murder at work, and I didn't do plasters. A stash of butterfly strips and skin glue hid in the rammel drawer behind the perished elastic bands and squashed tealights. The hand would be easy compared to the glue job on my head – or it would have been without the broken finger. It probably needed pinning, but I avoided hospitals as I couldn't stand the questions.

Despairing, I looked around the kitchen. Piles of pots waited by the sink, and the clothes I needed for the morning sat crumpled and dirty in front of the washer. I thought about opening a beer and sitting down; thinking of Elena and how it felt to be happy, ignoring the broken glass and smeared blood. But I didn't have the energy to fight myself if she started again. Her losing her shit frustrated and depressed me, but the fear of me losing mine scared me more. I'd rather be dead than in prison.

I lined up my fix kit and stuck on the kettle. Things might be alright by the morning. Or perhaps they never would.

4

CELIA

Ollie was an unknown quantity. My exciting unknown quantity. He had been since the moment I pinned him with my husky eyes and sent him on the road to insanity, which cost him eight-hundred grand and his marriage. But the problem with having an unknown quantity was that it could never quite be trusted. Especially when the unknown quantity had been away on business with Suzie, his ex-fucking-wife.

I bypassed the hall and went straight to the master suite, what with Ollie still being at work. My feet sunk further into the grey carpet with every step; the white voile at the window caught the breeze and waved me on. His unpacked suitcase waited on the bed, and I wanted to sift through it before he got home.

The zip crossed the teeth like fingertips along a freshly shed snake. I opened the top and smelled him, spices and sea salt, exotic but clean. The suit bag yielded no surprises, just a ludicrously expensive suit with several empty pockets. A sealed bag contained his neatly folded dirty clothes, all of them devoid of foundation or lipstick or perfume. I glanced towards the hall. If Ollie caught me, I would have an incredible story to concoct.

Another incredible story to concoct.

I checked the inner compartments and the out, his wash bag and clothes. I found nothing incriminating: no condoms, women's underwear or smutty notes. Maybe Ollie hadn't screwed around because he had me. Or maybe Ollie had screwed around, and I'd never find out – just like how Suzie, my ex-friend, hadn't known he'd fucked me for months behind her back.

The clock ticked, taunting me, though I stopped re-closing the zip when I spotted the tiny fray in the lining covering the hard outer. I carefully peeled it and wheedled my fingers inside. I skirted the box before I threw caution to the fires of hell and pulled it out. I expected the box to contain a necklace, earrings, or a bracelet. Not an engagement ring. The diamond caught the light, showering my hand with rainbows. The ring was beautiful, platinum and classy and to my expensive taste.

The clock had stopped, the pendulum still.

I listened hard and heard the distant sound of tyres on gravel. Shit. I slipped the ring off my finger and nestled it into its cushion. I closed the box and slid it back into the lining. Ollie would ask in good time.

'Celia.' His voice bounced between the marble counters and the shiny cupboards in the kitchen. 'You upstairs?'

'Yes.'

His shoes landed in the shoe cupboard and the drawer whooshed closed. After a brief fight with the suitcase zip, I undid my jeans and wrestled them off my legs, rubbed my eyes and mussed up my hair. He took the stairs two at a time and my head hit the pillow a moment before he opened the door.

Ollie eyed my white jeans, half inside-out, twisted and abandoned on the carpet. Slowly, deliberately, he undid his cufflinks and placed them on the drawers. He buttoned down his collar and rolled up his sleeves. 'I wasn't expecting you to be here.'

I offered him my cat eyes and a pouty smile. 'I missed you.'

Ollie sat down, his back to me, and his weight tipped the mattress. I got onto my knees, put my arms around him, and kissed the nape of his neck. He tried to shirk away, so I gripped him tighter and grabbed his belt. He offered a few half-hearted complaints, but I carried on, pressing his buttons and pushing him, until he flipped and launched me onto the bed. His body pressed me deep into the feather duvet. His minty breath mingled with mine.

I turned my head, scuffing my lips on his clean-shaven cheek. 'I'm here to make lunch.' I pushed him away, leaving him frustrated. 'I've spent twenty pounds on two pieces of fillet steak. The least you can do is eat it.'

Oh yes, my infallible weapon: treat them mean.

I pan-fried the mushrooms and wilted the spinach – only at the last minute did I put the steak in the pan. He liked it bloody, as did I. With everything resting, I washed my hands and, fingers dripping, scanned the room. Ollie opened a cupboard and passed me the hand towel.

He placed the plates on the table and glanced at his watch. 'I haven't got long. I've got a conference call at two.'

I sat down and cut into my steak. A perfect trickle of pink followed the path of my knife. 'How did the trip go? Did you agree on a price?'

'No. I told him we wanted nine-hundred grand. He refused, so I left the table.'

He towered a slither of meat, a slice of mushroom, and a wrap of spinach onto his fork, carefully and meticulously. I watched him eat, chewing politely.

'Ever heard of the term negotiation?'

'I don't do negotiation, Celia.'

Which was why I acted rather than asked. 'You're too stubborn for your own good.'

Ollie dabbed the corners of his mouth with his cotton napkin. So feral, yet so considered. He folded the napkin once and once again. 'My stubbornness serves me well.'

I was disappointed and cross. Ollie floated his main business many years earlier, but the smaller development belonged largely to him. If he sold, the cash would go straight into the bank. Not that the money provided my sole concern. He established the business with his ex-wife, and I suspected she was the reason for his reluctance. He still cared for her, and I didn't like it because he belonged to me. I didn't do sharing.

'It'd boost your bank account.'

'Don't worry about my bank account. I could quit today and never work again.'

Not that Ollie would give up his job and settle into a privileged life of travel and recreation at thirty-three. He lived to climb the ladder and ambition was an addictive thing, as I very well knew.

'Have you been to the gym this morning?' he asked.

'I'm going this afternoon.'

'I thought you went about ten?'

The perfectly cooked steak felt nice in my mouth. I looked at Ollie, my mind veering to naughtiness.

'Celia?'

'Sorry. Miles away.' I grinned. 'I usually go about ten, but I couldn't be bothered today. Anyway, what's the obsession with my gym habits?'

'You said you prefer exercising in the morning. I think you should go then – when you get the most out of it.'

'Yes, boss.'

'Boss. I like that.' His eyes narrowed. 'Say it again.'

'No. I'll say it tonight.'

'It's football training, and I promised I'd go for a drink after. It'll be too late.'

Ollie looked through the window. At the digital clock on the oven. At the utensils hanging from the magnetic strip on the wall. I needed him back, away from wherever his guilty thoughts were taking him. Crunching the ice from my glass, I rounded the table and sat on his lap, pressing myself against him. I opened my mouth to his and touched his warm tongue with my icy one.

'No, Celia. We can't.'

'Why?'

Ollie growled, so very torn. 'We haven't got time.'

'Make time.'

'I can't.'

I bit him, just short of drawing blood. 'You will.'

The sound of falling cutlery and broken crockery echoed around the room. He threw me on the tabletop and my head landed hard between the icy splashes and a steak knife. It took little persuasion because Ollie, for all of his intellect and certainty, had two weaknesses.

The first one was his guilt.

And the second was me.

5

ELENA

The decision to wear jeans and a pair of well-worn Converse had never taken so long. Nor had the minimal makeup or stay-at-home hair. It really was quite pathetic. Alistair had left his phone at my house, and I'd remembered, from our two-hour life summaries, that he was building an eco-house near a local park. So, what with no longer giving a monkey's what people thought of me, I decided to hunt him down and return it. I parked the Lexus and headed to the only development site in the area. Two vans and a yellow skip came into sight, and I delved into my bag to check for Alistair's phone. Again.

In my head, in my crazy, romantically corrupted head, I'd envisaged the building site as something out of a Diet Coke advert. The scaffolding would be shiny, and a pristine cement mixer would whir away in the corner; and there would be a man taking centre stage, a single bead of sweat running down his bare chest. The reality, however, was very different.

A patchwork of dried mud and life-threatening potholes made up the site, through which ran a snaking hosepipe. The sky-blue Portaloo looked nice enough, though I assumed the interior would be closer to my idea of sanitation hell. I could see two men, one quite young and one in his early forties. They were both fully clothed, thank goodness.

'Hi.'

The younger guy looked up from his pile of bricks. 'Alright love. Are ya lost?'

'Erm, no. I'm looking for Alistair.' I tucked my hair behind my ear and glanced at the wall of scaffolding, from which came a distinctive radio jingle. 'He's a builder working on this site.'

He looked at me like I'd sprouted a horn. 'Nobody called Alistair working here.'

'Oh.'

My stomach dropped. Alistair must have been lying. That's if his name was even Alistair. I hopped from foot to foot, unsure of what to do.

The older guy ambled over and pulled off his tatty gloves. 'I'm Barry. Foreman. Who are you looking for?'

I shook his hand and hoped to God the toilet contained soap and running water. 'I'm looking for somebody called Alistair. He said he worked here.'

He tipped his head, eyes vacant, and then he grinned. 'Oh. You mean Big Al!'

Barry ambled to the house under construction and banged the scaffolding with a metal bar. The sound echoed to the top and Alistair, wearing a hard hat, peered over the edge. His mouth snapped shut when he saw me.

'This woman's looking for you, Al,' Barry shouted.

I could hardly bear to watch Alistair negotiate the two rickety looking platforms and long ladders, though I overcame my nerves because of the view. Of him. Honestly, what had I become? Alistair, smiling and golden from the sun, strode across the yard.

'Nice to meet you again, Elena. Is something wrong with the plan?'

The other men looked at me for an answer, and I looked at Alistair for a clue.

'The drawing I posted. For your extension,' he said, eyes searching, brows high.

The penny dropped. 'No. Everything's fine. But you forgot your phone.'

Alistair took the phone, tossed it high, and caught it again. 'Thanks. I couldn't remember where I had it last. My head's been scrambled for days.' He took off his hard hat and high-vis vest and hung them on the fence. 'Fancy ten minutes in the park? We can talk about your extension while I eat my sandwiches.'

Alistair, a sandwich bag under his arm, marched, yes marched, to the park. Only once we were through the gate and shielded from the road did he drop his pace to one which let me actually breathe.

I had never been to that particular park. Self-seeded buddleias ran amok in the flowerbeds, and dandelions overtook the grass. Yellow and purple and brightness extended as far as the eye could see. And a rusty train track ran through the path, which I assumed belonged to a miniature train which ran no more. Everything about the place looked tired, yet it was beautiful and naturally reborn. Alistair pointed to a bench in an enclave made by the wildness, and we ambled there, one of us balancing on each of the rails.

'How're things?' he asked.

I told him I'd settled in and things were okay. Aside of the combi boiler, which required a degree in coding, and the spiders in the kitchen cupboards. 'I'll find some conkers to scare them away, then I'll be fine.'

The bench was made of new slats slotted between old. I sat down and covered the etching of two initials and a malformed love heart.

Alistair peeled the lid from his dishwasher-scratched lunchbox. 'Want one?'

'Please.' There were four sandwiches: a whole eight slices filled with badly cut orange cheese and Branston pickle. The man ate like a horse; not that I'd ever seen a horse eating a cheese and pickle sandwich. 'I'm surprised I found you. I thought I'd dropped into another galaxy with that lot. Does anybody call you by your real name?'

He laughed, and it made me happy, like a child on Christmas Day happy.

'Nope. They call me Big Al because my name's Alistair, and I'm a big fella.'

I piddled the crust from my bread. 'A big fella... is that right?'

Alistair's mouth twisted into a naughty grin. 'No comment.'

I crammed the crust in my mouth, wanting to stop the flow of words. Inappropriate comments, flirtation, and sexual innuendo – all coming from a woman who previously identified as sensible.

Alistair produced another sandwich. 'You're lucky you caught me on site, actually. I'm only here because I've got an expensive roof skeleton on the way.'

'So, you're not just a builder?'

'No, it's my business. But I spend as much time on site as I can. It gets me out of the house.' He banged the crumbs out of the lunchbox, and they scattered on the path, food for the birds. 'Are you going to eat that sandwich or sit there pecking at it?'

'Would you rather I crammed it in my mouth?'

His eyes sparkled with green and brown and mischief. 'Aye, I would.'

I returned to the sandwich, sans poker face, sans smart-ass return. Anybody would think I worked a carwash not a courtroom.

'I swear,' I sucked a smear of Branston from my finger, 'I enjoyed that more than anything I've eaten in months.'

Alistair sucked a smear of Branston from his finger. 'What are you eating?'

'Hmmm.' I tapped my nose. 'For breakfast, I had smoked salmon and scrambled egg, and for lunch I had goat's cheese on ciabatta.'

'Abandon the grown-up food. When things are hard you should go back to your younger years, when things were easy, and eat something from then. Proper comfort food.'

I scratched the bench until the fresh wood peeped through the aging and dirt. 'Like cheese and pickle sandwiches?'

'Yep.' He rummaged in the cool bag and pulled out a packet. 'And Salt 'n' Shake crisps.'

'Oh my gosh. I can't believe they still make those!'

Alistair shook the bag while I sprinkled the salt from the little blue packet. We took turns with the crisps until they were gone. They'd definitely shrunk the packet – either that or the packet looked small because of Alistair's big hands.

Alistair fidgeted from left to right until he finally leaned back, hands behind his head. 'So, what would you choose – favourite childhood food?'

'Cherry jelly sweets.'

'Good choice. Very good choice.'

A group of shiny pink patches scarred the underside of his arm. I touched them without thinking. 'How did you do this?'

'Erm. I burnt it. Chicken tikka masala.' He dropped his arms and rubbed the scars. The wooden slat beneath my bottom rose and fell when he shifted. 'Fancy a quick walk?'

Conversation closed.

'Absolutely.'

We lapped the park once, and we lapped it again, sometimes following the train track, sometimes leaving it. We laughed, teased each other, and talked about music and cheese and sprained ankles. Company had never been so easy and right. On lap three, we detoured via the ice-cream van, then stayed at the swings until Alistair said he needed to go.

We paused, kicking the woodchip, him catching sneaky glances at my swing-ruffled hair and me catching sneaky glances at the colours the late sun found in his eyes.

I sent a shower of brown wood into the grass. 'Can I see you again?'

I'd gone crazy. There were no two ways about it.

Alistair rubbed his hair, his forehead wrinkled. 'Sorry, I can't. But thanks, I'm flattered. I really am.'

I rocked over my feet and swallowed hard. Of course, he said no. Why would somebody like him want a woman with fine lines and a grey past.

'No problem. Just thought I'd ask.' I smiled weakly and told myself I wore big girl pants and had a responsible job and that meant I wouldn't weep like a Disney princess. Not until I got home. 'Thanks for today. It's been nice.'

I raised my hand and we parted terms, with me taking the flat footpath and him jogging down the steep incline. I peered over my shoulder as he disappeared from sight, then peered again as he reappeared.

'Changed my mind.' Alistair, his cheeks pink, held out his phone. 'Give me your number and I'll call. We can take it from there.'

We agreed to meet in a few days' time.

And I couldn't wait.

6

ALISTAIR

I ran back to the site with my phone safely buttoned in my trousers. The lads must have heard me coming a mile off, what with being a one-man band of dropping boots and jangling pockets. And I was singing. Sacks covered the newly laid bricks, and somebody had closed the lockup and stacked the new timber delivery on the concrete pad in the corner. Aye, I'd been AWOL for hours. Jim had the hosepipe in the cement mixer, giving it a clean down. I rubbed his hair and pointed at a blob of cement.

'You've missed a bit, mate.'

He turned the hosepipe on me, watering my boots. 'Piss off.'

Barry peered up from his toolbox – the one he'd had since college, with more battered corners than straight lines. A couple of weeks earlier, his eldest lad ran up a three-hundred-pound internet bill. He told me all about it, looking angry enough to headbutt a wall. Barry looked ready to headbutt a wall again.

'What's up, Baz?'

He slammed the toolbox lid and snapped down the clip. 'I don't like lying.'

'Huh?'

'Your missus turned up.'

My stomach did seventy miles per hour over a short humpback bridge. This was bad. Her physically hunting me down indicated a bad mental place; a very bad mental place.

'Oh. Did she say what she wanted?'

My attempt at casual sounded too light, too obvious, and my thoughts started to tornado. I wondered if they all knew, talked behind my back. Normal blokes didn't hide under clothes and sunglasses and whiskers, so their workmates didn't realise they looked like a paint by numbers.

'She wanted to know where you were. Something about a problem with a dentist appointment.' Two-handed, he yanked the box off the floor and ambled to his van. I followed and opened the padlock on the back doors. 'I told her you'd gone to Screwfix, but I don't reckon she believed me.'

There was no dentist appointment. The problem was my non-existent phone signal – her way of plotting my every move. I felt my cheek twitch with the sting already there, spreading under my skin. She always used her right hand when I least expected it, when I couldn't stand tall out of her reach.

Barry sat in the boot and changed his filthy boots for filthy trainers. 'What are you playing at, Al? The average man would kill for your missus.'

The average man would kill my missus.

Panic over. Barry saw, but he didn't look too hard, just like everybody else. He believed I got the last shiner playing rugby. He believed I was a big enough man to take the rough and tumble, make the right decisions, manage my business, and keep on paying his wages.

Barry slammed the back doors and stomped to the driver's door. 'See you tomorrow.'

I rubbed a blob of muck from the corner panel; the shiny paint showed no sign of flaking, no rust. 'Aye. And thanks.'

The truck growled the whole way home, hating my brake-to-accelerator driving. I needed to get back and get it over with. I could deal with the things that happened though not the what ifs, which woke me up at three-am and made my heart thump like a last hurrah.

It was Thursday and she'd remembered to put the bin out, which meant she hadn't totally lost the plot. I told myself to ignore the paranoia – she believed I'd gone to buy mallets or a new muck bucket.

'Hello,' I called.

The TV played to an empty room, and no noise came from the kitchen. I shouted her again. Nothing. I went out back and checked the garden. The recliner, complete with cushion, faced the sun, a half-drunk glass of something balanced on the arm. Gin and tonic. Things might be alright, after all – the fact she'd gone home and sat in the sun with a G&T was a good sign. The rat stopped scratching at my insides. I peeled off my socks and dirty T-shirt and put them in the washer with the laundry from the day before; sixty-degrees with a scoop of stain remover and a squirt of detergent.

The bathroom light was off, the extractor fan silent, yet I tapped the door open anyway, just to check. On the tiles, on the cold tiles, I spotted the wrinkly sole of her foot. My hands flew to my head. I pushed open the door and something hard and powdery crushed under my foot.

'What the...'

Her body sprawled across the floor, one arm crooked against the toilet and her face hidden by her scraggy hair. I saw the white ones first, ten or maybe twenty diamond-shaped tablets, and then I noticed the beige tablets scattered from the shower to the bin. I dropped to my knees, in the water and crushed pills and sick, and pulled back her hair.

'What have you done? Jesus, what have you done?'

The white of her eyes peeped from the slit between her lids. 'Where were you...'

'At work. What have you taken?'

I lifted her, and she fell limp in my arms. Her chest heaved and she spat saliva and crumbs of white onto my trousers. Carefully, I propped her against the bath, a towel behind her head, while I searched for the boxes and empty strips. She'd taken paracetamol and the sertraline she'd always refused to take. I scooped her up and hurried to the truck, ignoring her rattling breaths and hysteria.

It was all my fault. She took the tablets because her insecurity couldn't deal with me turning off my phone, so the irrationality ensued. She took the tablets because I dropped my guard and disappeared for a few selfish hours. And I wished she'd just done the usual and punched me in the face.

White light flooded the hospital, making her face ghostly and my torso grey, showing it all. I tried to hold her in front of me, like a human shield, not wanting the stares, not wanting the questions about the bruises on my back or the deep scratches on my chest. The rat stirred in my stomach, all sharp teeth and claws, and I lined up the excuses. Just in case.

After triage, the medics took her straight through to a cubicle. A cardboard-stiff sheet covered the narrow bed, and the rigid curtain didn't want to close. I leaned against the partition wall, my arms folded, and ignored the chair.

The doctor arrived after a few minutes. She shot me a tight-lipped smile and the stone hit with the usual assumption: what have you done?

'Hi. I'm Doctor Ryan. Can you tell me what you've taken?' The doctor lifted Celia's eyelids and shone a light in her eyes.

She said nothing.

'Paracetamol and sertraline.' I pulled the crushed boxes from my pocket and placed them on the trolley, close to the doctor. 'The boxes were full, but there were some on the bathroom floor.'

'How many have you taken?'

'A lot.'

I took a seat and looked away from the blood pressure cuff. Velcro made my teeth ache. The machine whirred and beeped. Blood pressure 118/60. Heart rate fifty-eight. Perfectly normal. The sterile air filled with discomfort as the doctor scribbled her notes. I sat forward and breathed into my steepled hands as the doctor explained about the charcoal drink and the blood tests. My wife stared into nothing, biting her nail. She never bit her nails.

I wet my lips. Hospital air always dumped me in a sandbag.

'I might pop outside for some fresh air.'

I didn't want any fresh air. Leaving before the request simply looked better, less suspicious. They would want to ask her side of the story without me around. The same happened after she 'fell' down the stairs.

I spent the next hour watching the woman I'd failed to honour and protect sipping black gunk and vomiting into a cardboard hat. I watched a nurse draw blood from her vein once and then again, three hours later. I held her cold hand because needles scared her and I didn't want her to cry. The crying was my job, which I later did in a disabled cubicle in the bowels of the hospital.

The sting of the hand gel and the drilling lights had taken me back to the place that my mind kept locked away. I lost my sister in exactly the same way. An overdose. I saw it coming, but I couldn't make it stop, and it still hurt like a coiling snake. Going there again would probably kill me.

The sun shone and the birds sang by the time the discharge papers arrived. The doctor sent her on her way with an appointment letter for another mental health assessment she wouldn't attend, and a request to 'Think about what I've said'. My list of thankyous was short, and no apologies were needed. Unlike the time before, after I told her I was leaving, when I had a sorry for three cars' worth of police officers. I never worked out how she got on that bridge.

I pushed her wheelchair to the truck in silence, my back lashed from sleeping on the plastic chair. The damp air settled on my shoulders and chest, prickling my skin with the cold.

'I didn't know where you'd gone,' she croaked. 'Don't do anything like that again.'

'I won't,' I said, and I meant it.

At the first opportunity, I texted Elena, suggesting a time and place in the middle of nowhere. Then I deleted her number. I needed to tell Elena I couldn't see her again in person.

It was the least I could do.

7

CELIA

I loitered at our bedroom window, shielded by the curtain, watching the dormer bungalow on the corner. The white render, new slate roof and shiny VELUX windows caught the light, making the building sparkle like a mirage; or a whitened tooth recently drilled and topped by a cheap amalgam filling.

I'd never set foot in the bungalow, but I'd toured it online a dozen times. The kitchen-diner shared the floor space of a terraced house, and the master bedroom had French doors overlooking the valley. The newly refurbished property had carried an asking price of five hundred grand. A hybrid Lexus sat on the drive, the colour of gunmetal grey – nondescript and dull, the colour for someone who possessed money not taste.

My new neighbour stepped through her new front door, so I reached for the binoculars for a closer inspection. Casually, she re-tied her hair into an untidy bun. She looked pretty enough, the sort who didn't need makeup, with pale eyes and fair skin. Though her days of going braless were long gone, and her dated jeans said her size twelve frame now hosted size fourteen thighs. I shuddered at the thought. My new neighbour pushed her glasses into her hair and, grinning like an idiot, helped the old woman next door with her wheely bin. My new neighbour seemed the kind sort, which probably made up for her being a fucking mess.

She disappeared inside, so I dragged my tired body to the spare room, where my new bee waited. The new bee, a tree bumblebee, had a white tipped abdomen and a ginger body. He was the second tree bumblebee I'd caught that day, though I crushed the bigger, majestic one under a stone. I rarely kept the females, but I wished I'd kept her; she was pretty and quirky and innocent, and I knew I would have loved her.

For a while, I watched my bee explore and preen and greedily drink the sugared water. I wanted to touch him, stroke the soft hairs on his back, but I couldn't do that until he died. Though I didn't want him to die, not yet, because he was beautiful, enthralling and receptive to my gifts. When he stilled and no longer vied for my attention, I returned to the front of the house.

The woman had disappeared from view. I imagined her all alone inside, hugging her waist, all frayed and unsure, like she did when she spoke with the postman. She needed a good neighbour, a new friend – somebody who could make her feel happy and like she belonged. Luckily for her, I lived close by, and I needed a friend too.

I removed everything from my skinny jeans to my black knickers. Next, I smeared my face with cleansing lotion and wiped away my makeup. I rummaged through the lace and silk and to the back of my underwear drawer, found my only pair of cotton knickers and a tired bra, and the building of a new me began. I covered the depressing underwear with old, stretched jeans and a blue T-shirt with a purple flower on the front. I secured my hair into a sloppy knot, perfected a grin and a giggle, and tried not to burst from excitement.

Passing through the hall, I saw an unremarkable butterfly bounce against the window. Carefully, so as not to damage its delicate cream wings, I caught it in the cup of my hands and carried it upstairs. Using the side of my hand, I pushed open the lid of my bee tank, then posted the butterfly inside. I replaced the lid and then waited. The butterfly fluttered an aimless dance and bounced from one hard place to the next. My perfect bee did not move or fly or clean its dusty antennas; my perfect bee did not notice the tease in his little world.

Which was lucky really.

For them both.

8

ELENA

I sat on a high stool at the island, swung my legs, and sipped a glass of over-priced Cabernet Sauvignon that reminded me of university and house parties and lost pens. I'd started drinking far too early, though I felt the need to celebrate, even on my own. Everything seemed to have changed when I met Alistair. The smiling doll with the scooped-out middle had gone, and in her place stood a happy person who sang along to the radio and laughed at her silly mistakes.

My new clock ticked, telling me to get up and do something positive. Rather than huff or swear or comply, I took it from the wall and removed the batteries. I steered my ship, at least until the nine-to-five re-tethered me. I thought the clock would help, provide some background noise, though it turned out I missed the white noise of company the most; the sound of socks on the carpet, papers shuffling, buttons tapping, and the sound of two people's forks dinking on the plates.

I looked past a tower of boxes. There were unpacked and unsorted things everywhere, so I decided to get off my backside and do something constructive after all; I didn't want to accidentally stumble into an alcohol-imbibed pit of misery.

I had almost dismantled a stack of boxes when a tiny tap came from the front door.

'Hi.'

The visitor looked up from her canvas pumps and smiled. She stood a little over five feet tall, with perfect skin, black hair and pellucid blue eyes – probably of Thai or Malaysian descent. She was the most naturally beautiful woman I'd ever seen.

'Hiya, I'm Celia. I live in the house on the corner.' She held out a brown box with a slightly bashed corner. 'This was on the doorstep.'

'Thank you.'

I took it from her. There was no postal address; just my first name written in uppercase letters in marker pen. I placed it on the stairs for later.

'I'm Elena, by the way. Would you like a drink? I'm drinking wine but the cups and kettle are unpacked. I can make—'

'No, wine is fine,' Celia interrupted. 'Wine at noon. I like you already!'

With that comment, I decided I liked her too. Because wine had become a very good friend of mine, as had chocolate – not that my thighs agreed. Celia followed me to the kitchen, and we chatted over very large glasses of wine. Soon she donned a pair of Marigolds, wiped out cupboards and unpacked my kitchenware, while I intermittently straddled the kitchen sink and fiddled with the broken catch on the top opening window.

'So, are you married, or do you have a boyfriend?' she asked.

I stopped circling the cloth. 'I've just split up with my husband. We'd been married for five years, and it turned out he'd philandered for three of them.'

There had been at least one other affair before her. Yes, the man I married behaved like a hermit crab – though he didn't periodically find a new home for his body, but instead one to put his penis.

'His loss,' she returned.

'Yes.' And his gain, too – a shoulder to cry on – the one who could give him everything. 'Are you married?'

'I am.'

I unloaded my box into the double cupboard under the sink and stood back, hands on my hips. I literally had multi-purpose cleaner, two in one laundry detergent and a bottle of bleach, and the empty cupboard looked vacant and staged – like a pretend cleaning cupboard for a pretend life. I needed to get more stuff and address my work-life balance, so I had time to use it.

She beamed a massive smile, distracting me from the emptiness. 'We're trying for a baby and I'm back to squidgy inside when I think about him. We're like a pair of teenagers again. We even did it on the kitchen table the other day.' She bit her knuckles. 'Sorry, too much information.'

My stomach plummeted. 'What does he do?'

'He started out as a structural engineer, but now he owns his own company.'

'Brilliant. Do you work?'

Celia froze, holding a plate in mid-air. 'I'm an accountant, but I'm currently on leave. My boss made advances on me, and I reported him.'

Shaking my head, I took the plate from her and slotted it into the rack. She said thank you and returned to her wine. An unsavoury man would gravitate to a woman as slight and sweet as Celia – who seemed the exact opposite of me. I might have been stupid with my ex, but I was not renowned for taking prisoners.

'He should be sacked.'

'I know, but everything happened behind closed doors so I can't prove anything. Anyway, let's move on.'

Celia pinged off her rubber glove, and a drop of water hit my face. I tucked my hair behind my ear and pretended not to notice the tightness and stinging. The water was actually Flash.

She folded the second glove and placed it on the counter. 'I better go home and get started on the washing.'

'Gosh, I'm so sorry. You only came to say hello and I've detained you for three hours.'

'It's been a pleasure.' Celia smiled. 'In fact, do you want to come by for dinner in a few days? I'll cook a curry if you like it.'

'That would be lovely, thank you. Oh, what cooking oil do you use?'

Celia's brows pressed tight together. 'Coconut. Is that okay?'

'Yes. I'm fine with anything other than peanuts.'

After Celia left, I washed my face, put the wineglasses in the dishwasher, then returned to the box in the hall. The flaps were stuck down by industrial strength duct tape, and it took the paring knife to split it in two.

Inside was a paper bag filled with horse chestnuts, a notebook, a yellow teapot, and a sealed white envelope; I opened it and unfolded the paper.

> ELENA. I'VE FOUND SOME CONKERS. IT'S WORTH A
> SHOT. MAKE A POT OF TEA AND START ON THE DIARY.
> THINK OF YOUR BIGGIES AND WRITE ONE OF THEM
> ON EACH PAGE.

I could use the diary and make my life into a project – just like Alistair's six-bedroom house. Make a home. Make new friends. Pull myself together.

I could do it. and I would do it.

TAKE ONE DAY AT A TIME. DON'T LOOK FORWARD AND DON'T LOOK BACK. IF YOU NEED ANYTHING DOING, PHONE ONE OF THESE FELLAS AND TELL THEM AL SENT YOU. I'LL SETTLE IT UP. ALISTAIR

P.S WE REALLY NEED TO TALK.

Underneath, he'd written a list of names and phone numbers. Bill the sparky. Ewan the plumber. Geoff the gardener. Tony the 'really good joiner'. The sentiment threw me into a tidal wave of tears. Alistair really was lovely, so kind and considerate, and I couldn't wait to see him again.

9

ALISTAIR

I stopped at the horse field on the way to meet Elena. The grass looked greener than the summer grass should be, as if freshly painted, and the air seemed clean and still. The water in the galvanised trough caught the light and threw it out, making me squint. Three horses grazed in the field – two grey and one chestnut. I clicked my tongue and held out my hand, and the biggest horse, the brown one, clopped casually over. He was a cracking horse, dark and shiny, with a white stripe on his face. I scratched his nose, then slapped his neck. He was solid, in his prime.

'Alright, big fella.'

His ears pointed forward, all attention on me. My sister Marla once said, 'If you want to be listened to, talk to a horse,' and I'd taken notice. It was the last piece of advice she gave me. At her wake, my Aunty Edna said it happened because God gave Marla all the darkness and me all the light. I'd shouldered the blame ever since.

I cursed and rubbed the back of my head. 'Okay, big fella. I'm going to tell Elena I can't see her again because I'm married.'

Married. The word sat like cyanide on my tongue.

'So, I'm going to say this. Hello, Elena. Thanks for coming, but I can't stay. I'm sorry, but I can't see you again.'

The horse blinked and looked at me with a chocolate eye. I leaned on the fence and the wood bent under my weight.

'I really like you, but I've got a wife. She took an overdose because I went to the park with you, and I can't risk her doing something crazy again. I want you to find somebody nice. I want you to be happy. Well, think I can do it?'

The horse jerked his head away, shaking his ears.

'Great. Wish me luck anyway.'

I patted him again before I jogged down the hill, dodging twisty roots and patches of mud, wanting to get it over and done with as kindly as possible. I wore an un-ironed T-shirt and I hadn't shaved, deliberately not making an effort. But it still felt wrong; I didn't hide things from Celia, despite everything.

Elena perched awkwardly on the bottom rail of a fence. Two red circles marked her arms below her white shirt. She'd leaned on something for a while and rolled up the sleeves.

'Hello,' I said. 'I've got something to... are you alright?'

She pressed her puffy eyes with her fingertips, as if to push back the tears, squash away the sadness. 'Shall we walk?'

At which, I aborted the plan.

Elena held out her hand, and I pulled her up. She stumbled into me and I caught her, hugged her, and then I kissed her hair. Elena rested her cheek on my chest, eyes closed, and I wondered what the hell I was doing. She squeezed me tight, did this little 'hmm' and I let her go. We walked, clueless as to where, with me secretly glad my wife had accidentally locked my Apple account and I'd 'accidentally' not noticed. Whoever invented Find My Phone wanted shooting.

The path split into two, one following the river, the other skirting the woods. I chose the woods, the smokescreen. Elena didn't take my hand, and I didn't take hers. It just happened. Her thumb slid on the inside of mine and our fingers wove together; they fit together perfectly.

'Thank you for the box of things. Do conkers really scare spiders away?' she asked.

I kicked a stone along the path. 'Dunno. It's worth a try, but I think it's just an old wives' tale.'

'You don't believe in wives' tales?'

'Not really.' I kicked the stone again and it bumped along in a perfect line. 'I breathed outside a cemetery and didn't die. I sat on a cold step and didn't get piles.'

'Carrots contain vitamin A – which is good for your eyes. Milk contains tryptophan – which helps you sleep. Walking under ladders is stupid. There's no smoke without fire.'

My perfect stone ricocheted into a mess of ferns. I thought about fetching it out, then changed my mind; nettles probably hid in there, nettles or thorns. 'Smouldering makes smoke.'

'Smouldering?' Elena flirted.

'Yes, you know, the bit which comes before you burn the house down.' Like hanging out with another woman when you've got a mentally unstable wife. 'Have you got a fire extinguisher at home?'

I stroked her thumb and her lips twitched. 'I've got two. And a fire blanket.'

'Good.'

We stepped out of the shade and into the sun. I liked the sun, appreciated it. Years of pulling down my hat and pulling up my collar to keep the rain out meant I always would. The sun liked me too. My mother had kindly donated the genes that made my hair blonde and my skin golden from early April through to late

September. I never burned and never got freckles or moles. Elena did. Freckles patterned her arms like a galaxy and the sun had caught her nose. They were sweet, innocent-sweet and totally hot.

Elena stopped, and I froze one step into the quagmire surrounding an old trough with a leaking pipe. I looked at Elena's immaculate canvas trainers.

'Oh dear,' she said.

Avoiding the purple and white flowers, I dragged a stick from the undergrowth and prodded the puddles; they wouldn't come over my boots. 'Are you scared of heights?'

She looked at me, lost. 'No. Why?'

I scooped her up and she shrieked.

'I weigh a tonne. I'll break your bloody back!'

'Don't talk daft.'

The muddy puddle was shallow, yet very slippery. I trod carefully at first, planting one foot before I moved the other. I slid and Elena panicked, putting me off balance. One foot flew out from under me but, rather than fall, I lunged forward, finding the other foot. Then the next. Faster and faster. Elena half-laughed, half-screamed and gripped even tighter.

By the time I reached solid ground, her face pressed against my neck and my heart pounded. I placed her down, and she lifted my hand. Blood oozed from my re-opened cut. I'd forgotten about the cut. Elena pulled a tissue from her pocket. She opened out my fingers and pressed the folded tissue into my palm. I told her not to fuss, but she ignored me.

Her thoughtful blue eyes softened. 'How did you do this?'

A few strands of golden hair played dot-to-dot with her freckles, and I wondered if her mind did the same with the clues.

The black fingernails. The burn under my arm. The graze next to my eye.

'Alistair?'

Reality pushed my chest from the inside out. I wanted to tell the truth. For the first time, I felt like someone wouldn't laugh or make me ashamed.

'Alistair?'

I'd rehearsed the lines while I chopped wood, lay bricks, knocked back a beer. I could have probably recited them pissed-up, spinning 'round in a cement mixer.

I need help.

A couple of moorhens shot across the river and one disappeared, beak-first, under the water. I decided to tell her everything when it popped back up. A bubble popped on the surface. Then another. But no sign of the bird. I couldn't do it. I couldn't tell Elena the extent of my mess. I couldn't tell anyone. They'd think I was a liar because I had put up a front for so long.

'I cut it on a broken glass a few nights ago.' I brushed the hair from her face, erasing the dot-to-dot, and pointed at a bench by the river. One of the back slats had broken and fallen, yet it looked solid enough. 'Fancy a sit down?'

'I suppose so.'

Elena sat, her leg touching mine, in the only place not spotted with bird shit. She peeped under the tissue and I told her not to fret. I didn't like attention or sympathy.

'It must really hurt. I hate the thought of people hurting.' Elena bit her lip until the colour divided. 'I watched my sister hurt for years, but she's much better now. Lives in Australia with her husband and children.'

'What's her name?'

'Lauren.' Elena flattened the tissue, hiding the cut. 'And I miss her like mad.'

I towered my free hand on hers, not knowing what the heck I was doing. 'I miss my sister, too – my sister Marla.'

I told Elena about Marla's depression and the self-harming and her passing away. The words flowed like the river near my feet. Usually, I couldn't talk about Marla – which was probably why, ten years on, I still stood at the foot of the mountain of getting over her. Me and Marla had been close, but I couldn't fight the demons for her and it made me feel helpless and frustrated. And responsible.

But we didn't linger on the past: we talked about hope and happiness and living.

'What do you want from life, Alistair?'

I rested my elbows on my knees, dangled my hands between them. 'Somebody to love. Somebody who loves me back. A family like the one I came from. Mam and dad laughing in the kitchen and a load of kids bickering in the hall. Oh, and I want a dog. What about you?'

'I always wanted to be a hot-shot lawyer. I wanted a big house. Posh car. Exotic holidays. A rich husband and two children. But now...' Elena sighed at the sky and pushed her hair away from her face. 'I want my life to be true. I thought he loved me, but it was all a lie. He wasn't at work or at a conference. And another woman came before her. I want reality – the truth.'

'Elena.' I rubbed my whiskers until it hurt. 'I came here to tell you I can't see you again.'

Our happy train slowed from two hundred to zero miles per hour. Everything inside me felt the wrong weight: my head too light, my stomach like lead. Her face didn't crumple or her eyes flash with spite. She just looked broken.

'I'm married. I tried to tell you at the start.' The river rushed into the rocks where it split and foamed and made angry noises; it looked darker there, almost black. 'My wife's ill, and I wouldn't trust her not to do something stupid if I left. I couldn't live with that on my conscience.'

Elena rubbed an eyelash onto her cheek, but it missed every freckle, didn't make a single bridge.

'Alistair, you shouldn't be here. This,' she swished her hand between us and then hugged her waist, 'isn't right.'

I wiped the eyelash from her cheek, and my hand just stayed there, touching her skin. She turned her face and kissed the place where my fingers met my palm. I wanted to kiss her more than I had anybody, ever. Elena swallowed and wetted her lips. She wanted to kiss me too. I leaned towards her, and it happened, the softest, most perfect kiss. A million words we'd never share spoken within it. She pulled away, guilt in her eyes.

'I'm sorry.' I should have said I made a mistake when I kissed her, but I didn't because it didn't feel that way. 'And please, if you see me, it's best if you ignore me.'

She gazed past me, biting her lip. 'I'll maybe see you around.'

As Elena walked away, I focused on the band of dirt on her colourful shoes. Because seeing her, the rest of her, her brightness and warmth, hurt more than having my fingers trapped in the door for six bastard minutes.

The water flowed by, murky and grey, and the clouds hung over me, murky and grey. Everything seemed so grey, and I was sick of it.

10

ELENA

I didn't curl up and cry for long. That didn't mean I wasn't upset and angry and disappointed, but what with having recently taken a pounding in the emotional stocks, I'd learned that negative energy could be channelled into something else. Like learning German. Or getting ready to go to dinner at my new neighbour's house.

Everything which came out of the boxes and suitcases was clean, yet still, after a day of unpacking, even my hair felt covered by a layer of grime. I needed a shower and makeup and clothes which didn't make me look like a bag-lady. Celia was sweet and beautiful, and I expected her structural engineer husband to be smart and charming and very good-looking. I didn't want my new neighbours to think badly of me, so I hunted down the iron and my favourite blue top – the one which smoothed out my hips.

Celia opened her door, and I held out my offering, a bottle of wine.

'Hiya.' She hugged me like an old friend. 'Come in.'

The warm house smelled of freshness and jasmine. Soft light filtered from a table-top lamp and the sound of Ed Sheeran came from a nearby room. In the hall, beside the doormat, sat two pairs of shoes: a small pair of pumps and a large pair of grey running shoes. I followed her past an open door, through which I could see the dining table. The door beside this was closed. I didn't like closed doors. They reminded me of the life I'd left behind. Hidden tears. Unsettled disputes. Secret conversations.

'Welcome to my kitchen.' Celia smiled. 'My favourite room. My husband extended it so we could make a family room with a table and sofa.'

A noticeboard hung on the wall, on which a postcard jostled for position among supermarket vouchers, a recipe for devil's cake, and a handwritten list of upcoming social events. Pinned to the frame were four letters, cut out of sparkly paper in pastel colours, bearing the word LOVE.

I glanced at the table where Celia and her husband had made love, trying for a baby. I saw the small red sofa where no doubt he sat, talking to her while she cooked. Lucas and I did the same when we were a couple.

Celia crouched down and plucked a few grains of rice from the floor. 'God only knows where my dustpan has gone to.' She took the pan from the hob. 'Let's take this lot to the dining room, then I'll drag him out of his man cave.'

I took a seat and fiddled with the thread hanging from the table runner while I waited. The door opened and Celia walked in, her husband a step behind her, a white cat behind him, and I didn't know whether to laugh or cry.

'Alistair, Elena. Elena, Alistair.' Celia swished her hand between us. 'Elena's moved into number seven.'

I forced a smile. 'Hi.'

Alistair's face turned grey. He looked at me, then back at the door. 'Hi.'

'Sorry, honey. I forgot to tell you we had a guest.' Celia pulled him close and kissed his shoulder through the T-shirt he wore. 'Sit down. Let's eat before the food goes cold.'

Food. Even the sight of it made me want to be sick.

I forced a yawn, politely suggesting that we ended the pantomime performance two long hours later. Alistair was clearly an actor; the person I met before and the surly man at the table were different people – both inhabiting the same body and both as convincing as the other.

And as for me.

Given a pair of yellow dungarees, I'd have passed as Buttons with my fake smiles, sadly watching the beautiful princess and her handsome prince. Celia was the only completely honest person among us, and I felt so sorry for her, so guilty.

I stretched my arms above my head. 'I better go.'

'I suppose it is getting late. Hey, would you mind if I tagged along to your housewarming party?' Celia asked. 'My nights are dismally boring, and I'd love to meet your friends.'

'Erm, no. Of course, you can come. Friday. We're kicking off at about seven-thirty.'

'Oh, thank you. I can't wait.'

Much to my horror, Celia asked Alistair to walk me home. I politely declined the offer, but she insisted, and he'd already crammed his feet into his laced-up trainers.

We crossed the road in silence, with him looking over his shoulder like we were being hounded by MI5.

'I can't believe you didn't tell me you lived across the bloody street,' I snapped.

After rounding the corner, he ushered me to the wall beside my door. 'Sorry.'

'Sorry! First you don't tell me you're married. Then you don't tell me you live a hundred metres away.' I slapped my head. 'I assumed you were delivering the bloody invoice – not running it off your home printer! And to top it off, you lie about your unhappy marriage and trot off to make babies with your wife.'

'We're not trying for a baby. Believe nothing she tells you.' His eyes were grey, the flashes of green and hazel muted by the poor light. 'We can't do this now.'

'We bloody well can.'

He looked around, as furtive as hell. 'I'm sorry. I really am. I tried to tell you, but I couldn't get it out.' His exhalation wobbled the chilly air. 'Elena, please keep away from Celia.'

'Why?'

'Because she's got issues and I don't want her to hurt you.'

'Don't talk wet.' His indications didn't sit right with the speculation. 'What's the matter with her? What do the doctors say?'

If he puffed any harder, he'd blow my house down. 'The doctor said she was fine, but that was because she told him as much. She thinks there's nothing wrong with her.'

'So, let me get this straight.' I held up my hands, flat palms against an invisible wall. 'Celia says she's alright and the medical professionals say she's alright. On what do you base your diagnosis?'

Nothing. He said nothing. The internet had a lot to answer for.

'As lovely as you seem,' I said, 'I no longer take a person's word over the evidence put before me.'

Hotels did not double charge for room service. Phone black spots were non-existent in city locations. A blunt razor did not make the mark on Lucas' neck. If only I'd used my watertight professional judgement instead of my misguided personal judgement back then.

'Please. Trust me on this one. Keep away from her. Keep away from both of us.' He swiped both hands down his face. 'I'm not only asking you to stay away from her because it's awkward.'

I leaned against the wall and the bricks pressed hard and cold onto my scalp. 'No, you don't want me to tell your wife that you held my hand. Made my bed. Bloody kissed me! Well, don't worry – I won't say anything. Forget it ever happened.'

'Elena, please. Celia's not who she seems.'

'Celia's always been lovely. You're the person whose got previous for dishonesty and, forgive me for stating the obvious, but it's in your best interest to keep me away from her so I don't accidentally get you in bother.'

His brows dropped; his expression deflated. 'I won't win this one, will I?'

'No.'

Case closed.

Alistair leaned against the wall; his face tipped to the diamond stars in the crystal-clear sky. He stared into infinity, and I stared at him.

'You need to go home.'

'Aye.' He reached into his pocket, then handed me a paper bag. 'I got you these.'

I peered inside and the smell of cherry sweets hit me. My stomach flipped with happiness before floundering with guilt. 'Thank you.'

The little white cat appeared from nowhere and meowed at his feet. He scooped it up and scratched behind its ears.

Unable to resist, I stroked the cat too. 'I didn't have you down as a cat man.'

'I'm not really. She turned up at a demolition one time and I didn't have the heart to take her to the RSPCA. You know how it is. Anyway, I better go.' Alistair took a few steps away from me, popped down his cat, and stopped to retie the lace snaking around his foot. 'Elena, about Celia, sometimes she...'

He didn't make sense, yet I didn't question him.

'It doesn't matter,' he uttered. 'You wouldn't believe me anyway.'

Laces tied and knotted, Alistair skulked away with his hands in his pockets, back to his home, his wife, his marriage.

I closed my door on the world, yet the world eventually crept in through my open windows. There were two voices, one deep and the other shrill. I couldn't hear the words, though there was no mistaking the anger in Celia and Alistair's argument.

I only hoped that the cause wasn't me.

11

CELIA

The gym was as cold as a fucking morgue.

The air conditioning blew like normal, but the absence of hot bodies dropped the temperature beyond comfortable. Aside from the personal trainer salivating over the tarted-up receptionist, only a dozen people occupied the cavernous gym, me included. The rows of cross trainers and bikes sat waiting, some of them gleaming with cleaning products, and the metal stacks on the weight machines were still. I pounded the treadmill, my heart thumping in time with my feet, staring blankly at my reflection. My jaw tightened while I seethed quietly.

Elena needed to go. No two ways about it.

I wanted her as my friend, but I couldn't have her on the street, day in day out, exchanging if-only-you-could-fuck-me glances with my husband. She completely failed my dinner party test, but so did he, for that matter. The blushing and lack of eye contact gave them away, along with the woolly conversation. They made such a pathetic pair; like a couple of love-struck school kids.

A flickering of cold water hit my neck. I briefly broke stride and looked left. 'Morning, Toby.'

Toby always took the treadmill or weights bench alongside mine, five mornings a week. Everything about him screamed attractive, indecently so. From his dark-hair and blue-eyes, to the way the shorts and vest clung to his ripped body. And yes, I looked, despite him being five-years younger than me.

I glanced around, using the mirrors. A red-faced woman strolled on a nearby treadmill. She had slapped back her sweaty hair, and a small lip of fat bulged over of her trousers.

Toby slapped my ass. 'Fancy her?'

'Er, no. People who look like shit when they exercise should exercise at home.'

He chuckled and set his warm-up pace to meet my run. 'Or perhaps they should all come here. Makes us look even better.'

'Fair point,' I said. 'As always.'

Toby smiled at me, and I smiled back. I enjoyed spending time with Toby, but I had enough men in my life. Alistair looked after me, and Ollie paved my future with gold. To justify the effort, another man needed to bring something new to the equation.

'Hey, I've got a new car,' he said. 'Quattro. Q5.'

The cogs turned, and I wondered how the hell he could afford such a car. He didn't talk like a person from privilege, and he couldn't have a high-powered job given his gym attendance.

'Liar.'

He reached over the side bar and slapped my ass again. I'd be needing arnica at the rate Toby handed out the slaps.

Or he would.

'I'm not a liar.'

I shook my head, incredulous. 'How did you get the money for that?'

'I've got my fingers in many pies, Ceels.'

As had I, but I didn't have a new Audi at my disposal. I wanted an Audi, not a car which screamed middle-England, middle-aged wife – associations which appalled me. Al suggested the VW. I wanted an Audi TT, but he said the boot was too small – just like his salary. Maybe I ought to break my stupid car. Or use it to run somebody over.

'Whatever, Toby.'

I hit stop, grabbed my water bottle, and trotted over to the weights bench with the bright red cover. Toby turned up and began to feed rings onto a long bar. His unexpected affluence had captured my interest. My first thought was drug dealing, which probably meant he knew people.

'Drugs?'

Toby showed me a grin of perfect teeth. 'Do I look like a drug-dealing bad boy?'

I looked him up and down. He looked like a guy who modelled for Men's Fitness, minus the fake tan and airbrushing, and definitely not a drug dealer. I told him it was a shame, what with me needing a bad boy, and pushed on with the front raises. I hated front raises, but they were part of the necessary evil that made me disproportionately strong. I needed to be strong, what with my Alistair being a fucking powerhouse. 'My husband's sleeping with the woman who's moving onto the street, and I need somebody to help me get rid of her.'

The shiny bar hung from Toby's hands, bending under the weights, though he acted like it wasn't there. He was stronger than he looked too. With an Audi and a killer smile.

'Can I trust you?' he asked.

I smiled my sweetest smile, the one I reserved for car mechanics and little old ladies and stupid people.

Can you trust me? Of course you fucking can't.

Toby lived in a yellow brick, circa 2000, small but detached house. A block paved drive sided a neatly trimmed lawn, and a tasteful willow screen hid the bins.

'Who lives here?'

'Me.'

'No parents? No girlfriend?'

'Nope.' He opened the door and pressed lots of numbers on the alarm panel in the hall. 'There's a woman, but we're kinda casual.'

'Oh.'

He slipped off his trainers, and I slipped off mine.

In the hall, a dark cream carpet complimented the walls, which were also cream, aside of that siding the stairs. The deep red of that wall reminded me of Morocco and indulgence, and the canvas prints, originals on first inspection, drew my eye. A contemporary oak bookshelf stood in the corner, complete with a selection of Andy McNab and Dan Brown paperbacks. I'd expected a shared flat, cheap carpets and flatpack furniture. I did not expect Toby to have taste – and expensive taste at that.

Toby ushered me through to the kitchen, all fitted with high-end units, and I took a swivel chair. He pulled the nearby juicer into the centre of the counter and threw in frozen blueberries, a bag of spinach and a couple of bananas. He blitzed the lot and split it between two highball glasses.

He took a drink and cleared his top lip with his tongue. 'What are you fishing for?'

'I want her scaring away before she has the chance to settle.' Elena was vulnerable and wealthy enough to relocate, and she wouldn't stay in a house in which she didn't feel safe. 'The closer she is, the easier it is for her to really get her claws into my husband.'

'I don't deal with violence against the person.'

'Oh, no. I don't want her getting hurt – and she hasn't even moved in properly yet,' I lied. 'But, if say, her house got burgled and her nice new things got pinched or ruined, she'd probably leave. It'll be easy to get in because the catch on her kitchen window is broken.'

'How do you know?'

'Because I saw her trying to fix it.'

I also saw and photographed the registration form for the medical centre, all complete with pre-existing conditions and the note of a severe peanut allergy, and a bill for a twelve-week course with a counsellor.

I sipped my drink and allowed my ramblings to soak in. 'Where do you get your money from, Toby?'

'Many pies. The most lucrative currently being,' he laughed, 'webcam sex.'

My stomach turned with uncourted jealousy. 'That's disgusting. If they're not capable of getting it themselves, they ought to take the fucking hint.'

He swirled his drink, dislodging a bit of spinach from the glass side. 'And you ought to curb your nasty tongue.'

My cheeks burned like Alistair's did after a well-executed slap. I'd not felt so reprimanded since Mr Koh tore me to shreds for putting chewing gum in a girl's hair in primary.

'How much do they pay you?'

'Made about thirty grand last year from that little venture, after tax. Do you want the web address?'

'No.'

Thirty grand meant he had a hefty mortgage on the house and he'd bought the Audi on finance. He wasn't nearly rich enough for me.

I scratched my tongue ferreting a piece of blueberry from my tooth. 'So how the hell can you scare my neighbour away?'

Toby drank some more, slowly, then said he knew people who would do a bit of breaking and entering. 'What about money?'

Money didn't present a problem. I had it stashed in winter boots and coat pockets and under my wardrobe because the thought of going without took me back to stealing from bin liners dumped outside charity shops. Which, in all fairness, was probably the least humiliating thing I did to keep a roof over mine and my mother's heads.

'Five hundred quid?'

'Should keep them happy. And what will you give me as an arrangement fee?'

'Whatever you want.'

Which I would. I wanted temptation out of Alistair's path because I needed his roof over my head and his credit card in my hand. I owned my web of fucking brilliance, and I wouldn't let them destroy it.

I'd hang and bleed the pair of them first.

12

ELENA

I really hadn't thought it through. The housewarming. Celia. And the possibility she would bring Alistair, my immoral fantasy number one.

The doorbell rang, halting my panic. I had a very good lawyer face, and I had every intention of using it. I pulled open the blue door I had wiped and polished with my new cleaning products just hours before.

'Hiya.' I smiled at Celia and severed eye-contact with Alistair after precisely one nanosecond. 'Everybody, say hello to my neighbours – Celia and Alistair.'

Warmed by the familiarity of my friends in my unfamiliar life, I introduced Sophia, James, Conner and Alice, along with a quick synopsis to aid their acquaintance, and then I got to Livia.

She slid off the island stool and held out her hand. 'I'm Livia.'

'Ignore her, she's insane,' Conner joked.

'A crazy person wouldn't earn more than all of this lot.' Livia pointed at me. 'And she's broken the six-figure mark.'

I gave Liv a playful shove, willing her words to cease. 'Can I get the two of you a drink?'

'Wine for me.' Celia strangled Alistair's bare arm in the crook of her elbow. 'And beer for Al. Thanks.'

The kitchen suddenly felt the same size as that in my nan's old caravan, and things were strewn everywhere, disorganised and random. Drinking straws balanced on the kettle. A dandelion tea towel hung from a drawer handle. Ice cubes melted on the grey counter. I needed a wineglass and a pint glass. Where the hell were the glasses? I opened one cupboard and then the next. Plates. Cups. Bloody Marmite. And then I spotted them – lined up on the island where I'd put them earlier, along with a card of silver wine-glass trinkets.

I jangled the trinkets. 'Which one would you like on your glass?'

Celia studied them in turn. 'I'll have the butterfly, please.'

I downed my glass of expensive Pinot, not giving a monkey's about the floral notes or hint of elderflower. I needed the hit. 'That's my favourite too.'

Within a smidgen of time, Celia and my girlfriends were chatting, spread between the corner sofa and the occasional chairs, and Alistair was sitting with James and Conner, happily included in their usual conversations of football, cars, and whether Liverpool would crash down the Premier League. But he didn't speak to me – or Livia, Sophia or Alice, for that matter. Which I thought strange.

Between us, we demolished four bottles of wine, a crate of beer, the chilli and rice, and a party-sized chocolate torte. The trifle, however, which I'd carefully crafted using fruit cocktail, strawberry jelly and tinned custard, remained largely untouched. Alistair had taken the first portion and I'd taken the second, while the others gravitated to the grown-up dessert. What with having the taste for glacier cherries, I decided to risk the label of glutton and get seconds. The custard and jelly sucked the spoon and wouldn't fall into my dish.

'Let me help.' Alistair knocked the dessert into my bowl using his spoon. 'I can say hello properly now.'

I glanced across the room to check Celia hadn't returned from the bathroom. 'And I can say hello properly back.'

His eyes crinkled, and our matching smiles met. In spite of our last meeting – and my concluding he was a shit – I had thought about Alistair a lot. I wondered what music he liked and if he drank coffee. I wondered if the winter made him miserable like it did me. I missed his thoughtful expression and the little creases beside his eyes. I had missed everything about him. Alistair's arm swung and our hands touched. I didn't know if it was accidental or deliberate or both.

'Alistair. Step away from the dessert. Think of your heart,' Celia called from across the room.

I mustered the smile I reserved for people trying to sell windows in the street. 'Don't panic. It's sugar-free jelly and low-fat custard.'

Celia sashayed over and grabbed a clean spoon. With a grin on her face, she dived into my trifle and scooped out my only cherry.

'Sorry, couldn't resist,' she teased, popping it into her mouth. 'What are you two talking about?'

'The weather,' we replied simultaneously.

Celia didn't respond.

I watched them walk away, her hand gripping the back pocket of his jeans. The spoon rattled in my bowl and my insides swirled. I hoped Celia didn't see it, the thing between us, because it was obvious to me and obvious to him and I wouldn't be the woman who broke up their marriage. I breathed hard and took another long drink.

Sophia barrelled past me and grabbed her bag from under the coats. Amidst giggles, she pulled out a tangle of wigs, Lycra and platform boots. 'I cleared out the loft and found the costumes we wore at college. Let's reform ABBA.'

I took my outfit from her hand, a white minidress with golden lapels and a belt, and shook my head. 'There's no way I'm wearing that with these thighs, Soph.'

'Oh, come on. James got so excited when I told him he could dress up as Benny.'

She jabbered on and, before I knew it, James had left the boys to chide me into a transformation too. He lined up the sambuca and Livia plugged in her dreaded karaoke machine.

'No.' I downed another shot. 'We can't anyway – there's no Bjorn.'

Livia kicked off her shoes and held the white catsuit in front of her. 'You have a Bjorn.'

We all changed, and James and Conner moved the table to create a stage in front of the island. With my face burning, I pulled down the skirt which barely covered my arse, and downed two more shots of sambuca. Before the introduction had finished, I was nineteen and happy, every move falling back into place. We danced and we sang, oblivious to our audience, until the music stopped.

The clapping started, Alistair's eyes met mine, then Celia somehow hit the tiled floor. With the help of a bottle of wine and three sambucas, I overcame the inability to walk on ridiculously shod feet and rushed over. The rest became a blur. I took Celia's hand, but her uneven weight unbalanced me when she pulled.

My head crashed into the wall, and a million pinpricks covered my eyes.

Everything went quiet.

I blinked the room back into focus and saw Alistair, deep creases between his brows, asking a hundred silent questions I couldn't answer. He curled his hands around my shoulders and raised me to sitting. Everything seemed overexposed, the colours paled out and the light scorching. Celia was nowhere to be seen.

'Are you alright?'

'I think so.' I pulled off the wig and touched my thumping forehead. 'Where's Celia?'

'Bathroom.'

Alistair plonked me on a chair and James shoved a brandy into my hand. Alistair steadied my hand the moment before the cold glass slipped from my grip. I spotted the wedding band on his finger; the ring looked out of place, scratched and dull against his golden skin.

He looked between the ring and me. 'I haven't got a choice.'

Celia returned from the loo, though she refused a brandy – or any drink for that matter. The fall had knocked her for six and she wanted to go. I hugged her, she thanked me for my hospitality, and they left.

With my glass recharged, I took the seat on which Celia had been sitting all night. Unable to concentrate on the conversation, I followed the grid of tiles until my view landed on something small and silver. My butterfly trinket – the wings turned into metal skeletons and the piles of coloured glass beside my toes.

My butterfly trinket was crushed and broken.

My butterfly trinket was ruined.

13

CELIA

Livid didn't come close. Elena wasn't simply wealthy – she earned a six-figure salary. Further to that, Alistair, my fucking husband, rushed to help her rather than me. The pair of them would have to pay; starting with him.

I filled and switched on our dated silver kettle as soon as we got home. Alistair pottered around, eating a cheese sandwich as he emptied the dishwasher, while I waited, sitting on my usual chair. A shot of steam made for the empty knife magnet when the kettle clicked off. Calmly, I crossed the kitchen, opened the kettle lid, and lunged at Alistair.

A splat of boiling water hit the floor and the rest of it met my husband, along with the kettle. Alistair cried out, froze momentarily, then tore open his shirt. A shower of tiny buttons bounced on the floor. The white sleeve sucked his skin, transparent and steaming, a stark contrast to the lobster pink underneath. Palms together, I hung my hands in front of me and watched as Alistair winced and battled to get his shoulder and arm under the cold tap. His agony made me soar, elated. He blathered on for a minute or two: asking what just happened and what was wrong with me. I didn't warrant his stupid questions with a reply.

I waited until he shut the fuck up. 'What the hell was that?'

'What are you talking about?' Alistair's voice was forced and deep, his words deliberate and slow. Despite his anger, he wouldn't lose control. He never did.

'You and Elena. Are you screwing her?'

'No.'

His eyes ran the length of the wooden blind. Alistair wanted out; he wanted to lay bricks and chop wood like a simpleton. I didn't get it. My husband had a first-class degree and a brain which did numbers like an addict did cocaine, yet he always turned to the life of a fucking simpleton.

'Celia, I can't deal with this anymore. Go and I'll give you half of the house.'

His words rattled my bones, soured my stomach, made my scalp tighten. In the past he'd tried to placate me, and he'd threatened me with the police, but he'd never offered me money to leave. Not that half of the house would suffice. He couldn't kick me out. Not yet. Not until Ollie stepped up to the mark.

'I don't want to be bought out! I want you to love me again. Please Alistair...' I fell to my knees, wobbly shouldered, my salty tears blobbing onto my jeans. 'Please. I'm sorry. I slipped and dropped it.'

'No, you didn't. You threw it at me because you wanted to hurt me.' Alistair pressed his head and glared at the floor like he wanted it obliterated. 'I'm sick of this. Fucking sick of it.'

'Sick of what?'

He glared at me like he wanted me obliterated. 'You.'

It had always been an illness, something out of my control; he had never blamed me before. The kettle cracked as its metal shell cooled and a drop of water fell on the floor.

'How-fucking-dare you! You'd be nothing without me. Nothing.' The voice wasn't my own. 'Without my brains you'd be some shitty builder with a clapped-out van. You wouldn't be successful. You wouldn't be paying twelve people and have the money for trucks and tools. You wouldn't be able to pick and fucking choose your projects.'

Alistair shrugged, totally unshaken by my rant. 'You keep telling yourself that.'

I flew at my husband, teeth bared. My nails dragged down his lip and chin. I wanted him to bleed. He tipped his head, making full height. I could no longer reach his face, so I bit his chest until his flesh parted. Holding him in place with my teeth, I went for his arm, the scalded arm, clawing and scraping. He moved around and pulled away from my mouth and so I bit harder, more brutally, until he pressed my face so tight to his body that I could not breathe. I shot away, gasping and raging, the spittle hot on my cheek.

'Fuck you, Alistair. Fuck you.'

He stormed out of the house, hands in his hair, his scalded arm crisscrossed with scratches. After dropping the blind, I stood in the window and watched him go to the woodstore.

And then I waited for him to return.

Eventually, Alistair crawled into bed and exhaustion forced him to sleep. I slid from the confines of the duvet and crept to the bathroom; there I soaked the largest towel in the bath. I tiptoed down the stairs and half-filled a bucket with water. Only bloody-mindedness got the heavy sodden towel and bucket to the bedroom.

Alistair slept, dead to the world - as vulnerable as a bee following time in the fridge or an Emperor Moth with a wing rubbed to dust. Slowly, I shoved the edge of the towel under the mattress on his side. I crept to the other side, knelt on top of the duvet, and threw the leading edge of the towel over his face. I pinned it down using my knees and hoisted the bucket from the floor. Alistair inhaled the saturated towel and gasped.

'Do not fuck with me, Alistair.' I tipped more water over the towel – wetting him, wetting the pillow, wetting the whole fucking bed he lay in. 'I saw you look at her. You touched her. You helped her off the fucking floor.'

He tried to sit but his weight pinned down one side of the towel and my eight-stone frame the other. He tossed his head from side to side, sucking in the towel, fighting for breath. I slopped more water over his head. I could see the indents of his eye sockets, of his open mouth. He pulled at the towel blindly and frantically before flinging me away.

It was a first. Alistair walked away or restrained me, but he never responded with force. I bounced on the mattress before the rebound saw me land hard on the floor.

He dropped his dripping head into his hands. 'Waterboarding, Celia! You're crazy.'

'I'm not crazy and I'm not going anywhere.' I shook, filled with adrenaline and chilled by my wet clothes. 'Fuck me over and you'll both suffer. You don't know who you're messing with.'

Alistair didn't have a clue what I was capable of. Though he'd have an idea if he knew about John.

John came on the scene during my first year at university, before Alistair. He thought he was my boyfriend, but I considered him and his aging cock a necessary evil. Poor John. Not that I killed him – the hypoglycaemia did that. I simply administered the fatal insulin shot, ate his Haribo's and twiddled my hair rather than call for an ambulance. Still, he needed to go. I wanted the fourteen grand stashed in his house and I wanted Alistair, and I knew John wouldn't grant me the privilege of either.

Watching John die was strangely therapeutic, cathartic almost, and it confirmed I could do anything, given the incentive. Anything at all.

A lesson which Alistair might come to learn.

Unless he got in line.

14

The house felt like a prison so I threw on a T-shirt, crammed my feet into my trainers and marched to the garage. My garage. I hit the switch and the fluorescent tube, after a couple of flashes, pinged into life. I paced the dusty floor, leaving a track, counting my breaths.

I was a martyr.

No two ways about it.

Growling like a bear, I booted the stack of newspapers by the door. Next, I emptied the drawer containing a dozen paintbrushes and swept the boxes of screws and fittings from the workbench. Brass and copper twinkled everywhere; I'd never find the right screw again. A spinning paintbrush, dotted with white, stopped and pointed at the metal racking – at my 1990s CD player. I switched it on and the CD scraped as it spun into life.

Rage Against the Machine.

Not the greatest of calm down choices, but at least it drowned out the whooshing in my ears. The whooshing scared me. My anger scared me. The fact I'd lobbed her like a shotput scared me.

Celia's behaviour had changed too. Before Elena, after Celia's acts of crazy, she'd pretend nothing happened, and I'd get days, sometimes weeks, to get back to baseline. But post-Elena, the battles had rolled into one and hounded me to the edge. Not a good place to be.

I reached on top of the locker, took down a football, and kicked it against the roller shutter door. Kick, rattle. Kick, rattle. The football flew back, and I dropped it to my feet. I needed to get rid of my wet boxer shorts and T-shirt and get in the spare bed with the memory foam mattress that didn't remember. Though only for one night. If I tried to sleep on my own for longer, she would sneak into my bed.

She was bizarre. Screaming at me one day and crying, saying sorry the next. Smacking me with a cricket bat at night and threatening to kill herself if I left her the next morning. Her moods exhausted me, but I couldn't leave and risk her doing something bad. Which she probably would, given her history. Offering to pay her off was the most stupid thing I'd said in years. Her leaving me for the other bloke would be the only way we'd get out unscathed – I only hoped the other bloke wasn't wishful thinking.

After flicking off the CD player, I headed to the side door.

What the...

I pushed the handle down harder and rammed the door.

Shit.

I'd left the key in the outer lock. Perhaps it clicked over when I'd slammed the door. Or perhaps the key clicked over when somebody turned it.

I dropped on the weights bench and rested my elbows on my knees. Goose-bumps covered my skin, and my breath hung in the air. I turned on the small fan heater and coughed away the dust that puffed out. The smell of dust reminded me of old things, days past, times before my life became a battle.

After pacing some more, I blew on my hands, rubbed them together, and scanned my concrete cell for things to make into a bed. A rolled-up tarpaulin hung from the roof joists and another newspaper tower stood in the corner. That was it.

The night would be an uncomfortable one.

I woke up gasping, dreaming a body bag surrounded me. I clawed the tarpaulin off my face and sat up. The creases from the plastic lined my arms and my head pounded. I wanted to be sick. A tap-tap got my attention, and I turned to the open side door, which swung in the breeze, confirming what I'd suspected. She'd locked me in. I covered my face and swore.

Another day in paradise.

After persuading my stiff legs to take me back to the house, I fed the cat, showered, drank a bucket of coffee and ate four Weetabix. It was a nice morning – the sky a pre-hazy shade of blue and the light bright. The fresh air would hopefully make me feel better.

I jogged to the end of the lane flanking our street and vaulted the gate. Long grass criss-crossed the footpath, so I watched my step until the style. I peered up and saw Elena's familiar figure, doing some crazy power walk up the hill.

I needed to hide.

Crouching by the wall, I made for the bushes, but as I reached a hollowed-out hawthorn the grass crunched close by. Elena looked right at me, one hand on her hip and the other holding a stick. I stood up, well and truly had.

'Morning,' I said, trying not to sound like a teenage boy caught with porn.

'Alistair, what the hell are you doing?'

I shrugged and nodded; my mind turned to mush.

Elena crossed one trainer over the other. The white lace tapped the stiff leather. 'Are you okay?'

'Aye, just tired out. Slept on the garage floor last night.'

Elena smiled shyly and tucked her hair behind her ears. 'Aren't you meant to go in the doghouse when you've done something bad?'

I scratched the hem of my worn T-shirt, then picked one of the lint balls made by the hours in the washer. 'I didn't do anything bad.'

'Whatever.'

Elena smirked and stared at her shoes; one balanced on a ridge, the other in a furrow. The green bushes shifted, and I stared hard at them. A load of leaves fell from the trees. The hairs on the back of my neck crawled. An empty field lay on the left, and bushes and the odd silver birch grew on the right. I scanned the hedgerow. The brambles and waist-height nettles offered so many hiding places. I dropped my backside onto the bottom step of the stile, shattered by it all.

'It's a bird, Alistair. Will you calm down? You're making me nervous.'

'Sorry, I feel like we're being watched.'

Elena tipped her head. 'That's because we are.'

I followed her line of sight to the brown cow with the twitching ears. My stomach stopped lurching, though my pulse still drummed at over a hundred.

'For goodness' sake. We're in the middle of a field and we're not doing anything wrong,' she said.

'What are you thinking?'

Her cheeks changed from strawberry to plum. 'I can't tell you, but it involves your very nicely toned and very nicely tanned legs.'

I glanced down. All I saw were scarred knees and the bit of dried grass stuck to a hair on my calf. 'And I'm thinking I want to kiss you.'

Mascara stuck a few of her lashes together. Her irises sparkled, as blue as ever, though her eyes looked heavier and more confused. A second cow appeared at the wall, and a third. The brown cow shoved the black and white one, and the black and white one mooed.

'So, we are doing something wrong,' she said.

'Aye, we are.'

A stick cracked and the bushes rustled again. I listened hard, but all I heard was a magpie squawking, probably halfway through pecking a songbird to death. I hated magpies.

Elena hugged her waist nervously. 'Is it a bird?'

'No. Too big and too low.'

It moved again. I touched my lips to quieten Elena, stomped down a few nettles and followed the sound further and further into the scrub. A bramble branch flicked out and scratched my ear, and a face shot forward.

'Bloody hell.' I nearly had a coronary. It was a close call whether my wife or the stress would kill me first. 'Just a horse in the next field.'

'Did you think it was Celia?'

'I don't know.' I strode out, wiping the blood from my ear, full of false confidence. 'Actually, no. She's got a meeting with the union and a PT session at the gym.'

Elena gazed past me to the drystone wall. Things seemed awkward, really awkward, like we both had something to say, but we didn't know how. I rolled a few stones in the dirt.

'Elena, about Celia. You really need to keep away from her. She's...'

'Alistair, please don't tell me what to do.'

'I'm not – I just don't want anything bad to happen.' I took a deep breath and rubbed the back of my neck. 'Can I tell you something?'

She walked around me and began a foot-march up the hill. 'I don't want to hear it.'

Shrinking by the second, I blocked her path and pulled up my sleeve. My shoulders narrowed and my arms shrank, as thin as beans. 'Celia did this last night.' The cold water limited the damage, so only a pink swelling and a half-full blister remained. 'She threw a kettle of boiling water at me 'cos I helped you off the floor.'

'Have you any idea how crazy that sounds?'

'I know. She said she got dizzy and tripped, but I know she did it on purpose.'

I caught Elena's hand, wanting her to side with me, and squinted at the sky. It was alive with dandelion seeds, flying in the breeze, taking off, looking for somewhere new.

'Celia didn't look well when she left, and accidents happen. She had no reason to lie.'

My insides turned to stone. Elena didn't believe me. Of course she didn't. Nobody would believe my tiny wife punched, scratched, and spat on me – her six-foot-three husband, the one who played defence in football, who had a hundred-kilos on his bench bar. Nobody would believe I ripped the helpline number off the back of a toilet door either.

'What were you thinking last night, touching my hand?'

I picked a dandelion seed out of her hair. 'I didn't think. That's the problem. I see you and nothing else.'

The cows stopped jostling at the wall, all their eyes on us. Waiting to see what would happen now I'd crossed another line. She said nothing, and sometimes saying nothing says it all. I plonked down on the floor, totally done. For years, my head had said no, but my body pushed on anyway. But not anymore. In Elena, I saw my dream. Somebody to love and someone who could love me back. Except my dream waited behind razor wire and landmines.

Elena knelt in front of me, her hands on my knees, and she hesitated, herding her words. 'This stops now, okay? It's not fair to anybody.'

Elena pressed her lips to mine, eyes closed, in a soft, final kiss. Then she left.

I plucked a blade of grass from the ground, split it vertically, and threw both halves down. One became lost in the thatch, and the other rested on the top, refusing to hide. I picked it back up and wrapped it around my finger. The flesh turned pink in the gaps between the leaf, and my fingertip turned white. I unwound the leaf, and the flesh went back to normal.

Normal.

Everything would return to normal once the pressure was off.

Not that I recognised normal any longer.

15

CELIA

The taxi driver blathered about the weather and the football, though Al hardly said a word. He looked tense and edgy, tired out. The campaign of pretend night terrors was really taking effect – so many days of hard work followed by nights of disrupted sleep. Al needed to be managed like a dangerous animal: kept permanently broken, never at full strength.

Alistair's terrible mood greyed the atmosphere in the car. We were on the way to my ex-colleague's birthday party and he hated coming to my events. He hated the lies, and he hated the pretending, whereas I loved nothing more than to see him squirm. Maybe his annoyance was because I'd forced him to accompany me; or maybe he'd annoyed himself for falling for Elena when he should have known fucking better.

We arrived at Lenny and Marie's house as the sun dropped in the sky. Marie opened the door, and I greeted her with a bottle of wine, a bunch of flowers, and a hug. She hugged and kissed Al too. I pressed my teeth together. I didn't like people touching things which belonged to me, and Alistair knew it. And there I thought he learned the lesson the time a woman dragged him onto a dancefloor, and I later woke him up using his cricket bat. He could get ready.

Lenny greeted us in the lounge and reacquainted us with the other guests. We'd met everybody before. Pete and Jane – my ex-colleagues. Barry and Laura – the neighbours. Tom and Zoe – a couple they'd met through their kid's school. Lenny herded the men into the conservatory, and, after a few beers, Alistair seemed like he'd make it through dinner without belly flopping into a depression. I excused myself from the ladies and headed over to Al. I touched his arm and he shuddered like hypothermia had just kicked in.

'Alistair, honey. I need some fresh air. Can you come with me?'

He wouldn't reject me in front of other people; he'd made that mistake before.

We took a few steps away from the menfolk and I said, under my breath, 'Hold my hand'. Pissed off, he grabbed it a bit too hard. Jane noticed and looked away. I weaved my fingers through his and towed him out to the garden.

Flowers grew everywhere, so bright and heavenly smelling, each calling to me more than the last. I slowed by an azalea, heavy with delicate flowers – its white petals splayed to reveal the pink, vulnerable insides. I couldn't resist the urge to touch a few. Or pluck their stamens and toss them on the floor.

Eventually, I stopped in front of the summerhouse, out of range of the outside lights, and sat on the swinging seat. I patted the cushion, liberating the smell of dust and summer, and he sat down, saying nothing.

'You look hot tonight, Al. Those jeans show off your ass, and your hair has grown. I like it longer.' I stroked his almost grabbable hair. 'But I'm not sure about your face. You're not far off a beard.'

'Tough, I'm keeping it.'

At one time, I thought he grew the beard when he suffered the 'accidents' which caused the cuts and bruises he wanted to hide from the world. I later realised the beard also hid the bruises from himself.

'Celia, dinner will be on the table in ten minutes. What are we doing out here?'

The seat offered a perfect view of the koi pond, in which an expectant mass of silver, orange and white had gathered. I picked a few spilled food pellets from the deck and threw them into the water. The fish scrambled, slithering over each other, forcing the lesser fish down.

'I need some fresh air.' I pushed through my heels and set the chair in motion. 'I've been thinking about Elena today. I probably overreacted the other night when I accused you of sleeping with her, but do you like her?'

'She seems alright. Why?'

'I reckon she fancies you. Not that I blame her.' I placed my glass of wine on the decking, and he braced the shifting seat with his legs. 'I'm scared of losing you, Al. My thoughts turn dark, and I'm scared of what I might do.'

I'd already tried a few things. One time, I'd sat in the bath and waited for him to get home, upon which I'd made a few little cuts on my thighs and squeezed them until they bled a lot. Another time, I had a large gin, crunched a paracetamol and covered the kitchen table in lots of coloured tablets. Then came the event on the bridge, which made for an interesting night.

A moth careered into the outside light, and the brightness flickered with grey. Over and over it threw its body at the glass, wings bashing, risking it all for a fake moon.

'Are you ill?' he asked.

Laughter squeezed out of the conservatory, through the open windows and the door forced wide by a planter. Everybody looked in, rolling with the conversation, and nobody looked out.

'No, Al. I'm absolutely fine.' The outside light clicked off and the darkness closed in, though my eyes adjusted and changed him from black to grey. 'I don't really have mental health issues. I just let you think I have.'

He made a caveman sound then said, 'What? Why?'

'Because you'd always stand by me while you thought it wasn't my fault.'

I jumped up, and the seat twisted and wobbled in its frame. He braced it with his legs again and leaned back in the chair, hands in his pockets.

'Let me tell you a story.' My view dropped to the decking, to where the pale moth rested, realising the deceit of the lost light. I stretched out my foot, my painted toes curled, ready to stamp on the thing.

'Leave it,' he snapped.

I pulled back my foot and crossed it over the other. I'd kill it later. 'There once lived a beautiful princess who met a handsome peasant and fell madly in love. They married in haste, in a whirlwind of lust. Then one day, the peasant took his new bride to meet his family. She watched him play fight with his nephews and draw stickmen with his niece and hug his mother and banter with his father. And the princess realised he would never be truly happy until he had a family of his own.'

Alistair remembered that holiday. We shared a four-foot bed for five nights, listening to the hot water tank in his old bedroom. He smiled a lot back then and he held my hand; and he loved me properly.

'Which presented the princess with a massive problem,' I continued. 'Because she wouldn't give the peasant a family. Not ever.'

'But you said–'

'I remember what the princess said.' I rolled my eyes. 'That she wanted a quick wedding on a tropical beach and a houseful of children and a dog. However, not only did the princess hate dogs, but she'd also had an elective hysterectomy because her mother died of cancer and her risk factors were high.' The moth tiptoed closer to me and my foot twitched. 'So, the princess lied because she wanted the peasant desperately, and she didn't want him to abandon her for somebody else.'

'You know I'm not like that. You didn't have to lie and scheme. Just because you couldn't carry a child...'

'Couldn't and wouldn't carry a child. The princess despised children, so she made up a story because she knew her peasant was a good man, a compassionate man, who wouldn't abandon her if he suspected she was ill, a threat to herself. Love had made her a crazy person – prepared to do anything to keep him.'

'And what about the rest of it?' He peered around me at the house. All he saw were the backs of the heads belonging to people not noticing us. 'The punching, biting, scalding me with the kettle. I don't believe you hurt me to make me stay.'

I flicked my hair over my shoulders and uncrossed my leg. The sweet little princess had gone.

'No. I hurt myself to make you stay. I hurt you because I enjoy it.' I smiled, closed-lipped and spiteful. 'I get off on the control, making people dance for me. And by the way, you're a fucking superhero. You put up with hell because you're shit-scared of me topping myself.'

Alistair got to his feet and stood over me; he grew taller and bigger and more male. He seemed different when I looked up at him, all strong lines and toughness, yet I could still break him. Mentally.

'I need you,' I said. 'It's your house, and I eat your food and drink your wine. You pay my credit card when I buy clothes I can't afford. You cook, clean, do the garden and sort the bills. What's the chances of me finding another man who is good enough to do everything or rich enough to pay somebody else to do it? And anyway, fucking with you is so much fun.'

'But the overdose,' he said. 'You took a bloody overdose.'

'The overdose never happened. I took two paracetamol and split the rest between the toilet and the floor. Then I stuck my fingers down my throat to make myself sick.' I smiled and folded my arms. 'The doctor knew, my bloods and observations said as much, but she pitied me anyway. Poor little me. A cry for help after a nasty fight. I am so good at this game.'

My husband's jaw tightened. He was livid. A bastard would have called my bluff, knocked me about or left me to my demons years back. But Al wasn't capable of that, and I knew it.

'Guess what, Celia. The game's over. I'm going to the solicitor's first thing.'

And for that, he got a glass of red wine thrown at his crotch.

'Bloody hell.' He pulled his jeans away from his boxers.

I drained the remaining five millilitres of wine, inadequate as it was. 'Sometimes, Alistair, you can be really fucking stupid.'

He grabbed my arm and leant right over me. 'No, Celia. You're the stupid one if you think I'm gonna keep dancing like a bear to stop you topping yourself.'

'Do as I say or me topping myself will be the least of your worries.'

The air between us filled with molecules and murkiness and biting insects. He jammed his hands into his pockets and stared at me. I blinked. He didn't. I'd really pissed him off.

'You have no idea how much I admire you,' I eventually cooed. 'Your patience and resolve. Your ability to implode.'

'Have you finished?'

He dismissed me, totally, wouldn't even bite.

My sandal slapped on the deck, and I grinned as I studied the crush of fluff and wing which I'd made. 'I've barely fucking started.'

The house felt hotter than I remembered it. And messier. Things for the party cluttered the kitchen counter. A blueberry cheesecake sitting in a flan dish, the M&S cardboard box next to it. Two bunches of flowers, still in the cellophane, slowly wilting in the heat. A carton containing hundreds of sachets of Sweetex.

'Marie,' Alistair said, face like he'd gate-crashed a funeral, 'please can I have my coat?'

'Is everything okay?'

'Yes,' he said to Marie.

'Celia?' Marie asked.

My pretend friend glanced away from my bloodshot, tear-filled eyes. Playing back the night my mother died always upset me; hence why I did it when I ambled up the path ten steps behind Alistair.

'Marie, do you have a cloth or a towel?' I lifted his shirt to show Marie the stain on his jeans. 'Oh, gosh, Alistair. I'm so sorry. It's worse than I thought.'

He shoved my hand away, stepping up quite nicely. 'Just leave it, will you.'

Jane appeared in the door. 'What's happened?'

'Alistair sat in the seat then pushed me, so I spilled my drink.'

'Why did you push her, Alistair?' Jane barked.

Al looked at the wall and breathed so deeply his stomach pushed out his shirt. 'I didn't. That's not what happened.'

'It was my fault, Jane,' I sobbed, siding up to him. 'Marie, do you have some clothes Alistair could borrow?'

'Yes, of course.'

Al sighed, despairing. Lenny's thirty-two-inch trousers would be too small for him. He'd never get them over his thighs, let alone fasten them, and he'd look ridiculous, even more ridiculous than he did soaked in something resembling pink piss.

'I don't need to borrow anything. I'll be fine. But thanks anyway,' he said to Marie.

Though I went on and on. Twittering about borrowing some clothes. Trying to dab at his crotch. Pushing him into losing his temper. I so wanted him to flip and shout or throw something at the wall.

'Celia.' He grabbed my wrist. 'I'm fine. Stop fussing.'

By then, everybody had crammed into the kitchen, investigating the ruckus.

'Why did you push her?' Pete asked.

'Pete,' Al said, his hands up in surrender; 'I didn't push her, and I don't want any trouble.'

Lenny looked between us, and the women fiddled with their prosecco glasses. I drank prosecco with them. Red wine with the woman next door. Sherry with Myra at number six. Yes, I was a fucking chameleon.

Pete scoffed and leaned against the doorframe. 'Yeah. It's different when you're up against a fella.'

'What's that meant to mean?'

'I saw the bruises, Alistair,' Jane said. 'After Celia "fell" down the stairs.'

'I did fall down the stairs. Alistair, I haven't said anything, I promise.'

'For the record,' Al calmly said, 'Celia did fall down the stairs. I didn't touch her.' He could have told them I fell deliberately to stop him attending a meeting with an attractive woman, but they wouldn't have believed him. 'I'm going home.'

My tears had dried up by the time we reached the end of the drive. I wrapped my arms around myself, for the sake of any observers, and faced the road.

'You walked into that one,' I said. 'What would you get for beating your wife?'

I hadn't just begun that particular scheme: I'd started sowing the seeds long ago. Just in case.

'I've never laid a finger on you.'

'It doesn't matter. The truth equates to the most believable version of events. I hit you. You hit me. I know which version I'd believe.' My body swelled with strength and determination. 'I will connive and fight. I will do whatever it takes to keep you and my perfect little world. You won't leave me, Alistair. I won't let you.'

'I'll do as I please, Celia. You don't own me.'

Au contraire, Alistair.

Au fucking contraire.

16

ELENA

I lifted my head from the pillow, dragged from the comfort of sleep. Everything seemed too pronounced, too loud and too bright; from the rustling sheets to the light kicked out by the bedside clock. Something clattered in the kitchen sink, and a chair scraped along the floor. There was definitely somebody in my house.

I pulled the duvet over my head and tried to quieten my breaths. I didn't know what to do. Nothing nearby would serve as a weapon, and I'd left my phone in the kitchen. I couldn't even flee through the French doors because the keys were in the hall. I needed to hide. The white flash of a torch sweeping the hall spurred me on. The bed covers scrunched, my feet thumped on the carpet, and the boxes under the bed tussled loudly when I squeezed between them. Or so it seemed.

A pair of skinny ankles and Nike trainers came into view. The feet came closer, and the smell of damp fabric and soggy socks crept up my nose. I held my breath. The wearer stilled, either thinking or listening intently. And then a second figure came into view, a much heftier figure, and his blue pristine trainers joined the line.

'I'll check upstairs,' a male voice said, and the blue trainers turned to leave.

I wondered if I should make a run for it, what with only the small one being close by but, just as I persuaded my terror-stricken body to move, heavy footsteps sounded on the staircase and the larger figure reappeared.

'I don't like this. This house doesn't feel empty. Check the bedrooms.'

The large man came into my ground floor room, filling the air with crisp aftershave and my head with panic. The duvet swished a few inches above my head. Hinges creaked and the hangers in my wardrobe rattled.

'Nobody in here,' the other guy called. 'But somethin' isn't right.'

'I know.' The sound of hands rubbing scratchy stubble accompanied his words. 'Keep your eyes open and get what you want.'

Cupboards and drawers opened with hope and slammed with disappointment. I'd told Lucas to shove his expensive jewellery and left my Mac at the office. The Lexus would be a decent haul, but the average thief couldn't ring a car. And anyway, they'd have more chance of finding a Rembrandt than the car keys – as I'd discovered earlier that day.

'I thought the place woz dripping with Apple shit,' the skinny guy said.

'At least you've got the money for the job. Empty the wardrobe and pull the stuff out from under the beds.'

The larger man pulled the blanket box from in front of my face and my throat tightened like I'd been sick. He told me to get out.

'Please don't hurt me.' I scrambled out from under the bed, sobbing like a toddler. 'Take whatever you want. There's money in the kitchen drawer and a laptop upstairs.'

'Shut up,' the small one snapped. 'Get in the hall and get on ya knees.' His eyes were wild from adrenaline or drugs. 'Now what?'

The big guy touched his head. 'I'm thinking.'

The skinny man stalked over and grabbed my face so hard my teeth dug into my cheeks. Then he released me and rocketed to his feet. Help had arrived, but it wasn't the police. Just Alistair, brandishing a cricket bat. The skinny man delved inside his jacket, and I heard the click of a knife. Alistair raised the bat and eyed the flick-knife like he would a fishfinger. The man waved the blade around, spitting curses and making threats, while the big man froze, assessing.

'Get up and call the police, Elena,' Alistair said.

I rushed past the men within a millimetre of the wall. I dared not look away from the trio.

A tentative silence filled the hall.

Without warning, the gum-chewing, knife-wielding skinny one ran towards Alistair. With two swings of the bat, Alistair knocked the knife from his hand and dropped him to the floor. The big man grabbed the knife handle, and I screamed. Alistair raised the bat and, thwack, the knife flew, ricocheted off the wall and landed on the rug. Clutching his hand, the big guy ran off. The skinny guy quickly followed. The utensil pot from the windowsill smashed on the ground before the window slammed.

Alistair followed them, then called me in. 'They've gone, Elena.'

He looked at me with soft eyes and a weak smile. I thanked him and he pulled me onto his chest. He kissed my head and growled, frustrated.

'Alistair, I...'

'Don't. Don't say it.'

I shook my head, smearing his T-shirt with my tears. Our feelings for each other still existed, stronger still. It felt like we'd existed before we had even met, understood each other, wanted each other in every way. The significance of things weighed heavily.

'Elena, you need to sell up and leave. Use this as an excuse. We can't live on the same street. We really can't.'

'I can't start over again. Not right now.'

I didn't want to run away from another self-perpetuated mess. I didn't have the energy, and I couldn't stand the thought of our paths never crossing again. I squeezed my eyes closed.

A shrill ring came from Alistair's pocket. My heart raced like the smoke alarm had sounded or an airbag was about to explode. He groaned and answered the phone. I heard Celia's voice and jumped away from him, guilty and grounded.

'What!' he said, sounding shocked.

More hurried words followed.

'Aye, okay. I'll bring her back when things are sorted here.'

Alistair ended the call and told me that Celia had invited me to stay at theirs for the night, what with the upset and my dubious house security. I thanked him but said I'd find a hotel instead.

Chewing his lip, he checked his watch. 'It's nearly eleven – you'll struggle to get a hotel. Anyway, it'll seem odd if you turn down her offer without a good reason.'

He was right, absolutely. There was no logical reason I wouldn't pack my nightclothes, walk across the street, and sleep in the spare room belonging to the neighbour who'd become my friend. Aside from the secret attraction between me and her husband.

'Okay,' I said. 'I'm not sure I've really got a choice.'

While we waited for the police, he talked through his thoughts and fiddled with the lock on the window through which the burglars got in. I ended the speculation and told him about the broken handle I hadn't yet got repaired.

He tried to click the floppy handle mechanism into place. 'I'll secure it tonight and fix it tomorrow.'

Bang, bang.

I opened the door to a uniformed police officer who looked bored and resigned. He trotted through the formalities, gave me a crime reference number, and left soon after.

'They might catch them,' Alistair said hopefully.

I shook my head. My old neighbour provided the police with CCTV footage and a tipoff, and they still didn't catch the person who burgled him. 'Two white men. One tall and muscular and one short and skinny. Both wearing gloves. There's no chance.'

'Aye, I suppose not. Come on, pack a few things. She'll be on my back in a minute.'

Celia pounced on Alistair the moment we entered the house. She blurted her relief at getting him home unhurt and, following a terse exchange of about four words, he went to the kitchen and Celia showed me to the guestroom. She twittered on about Alistair spotting the torchlight in my house and her being glad; who knew what could have happened if he'd not gone to my aid. She fussed over me then. Drew the curtains and pointed out the folded towels on the chair. I thanked her, thanked her again, then reminded her of the time and the fact we should all get some sleep.

I lay in the cloud-soft bed on the silk-covered pillow, unable to settle, staring at the pretty lightshade with the glass beads snagged by a tangle of metal arms. Celia was my friend, and I'd rewarded her kindness by lusting after her husband. Their situation mirrored that of my failed marriage: him turned by boredom and me blissfully unaware. The realisation scorched me with guilt and regret.

Eventually, I started to doze, though a buzzing sound cut it short. The buzzing started again, so I reluctantly left my warm cocoon. My ears led me to the window where, behind the curtain, next to a small indoor garden, stood a down-turned pint glass with a bumblebee trapped underneath. Somebody must have caught the bee and forgotten to put it outside, so I released it onto the windowsill. Its initial steps were stiff and intrepid, so I touched it gently and urged it to fly away. Which it did, into the unknown of the night.

I set it free.

A stiff breeze rustled the curtain, and I shivered.

Yet it wasn't even cold.

17

ALISTAIR

I switched on every ceiling light and lamp and glared at the stuff on the bed: her purple fleecy throw and her purple fluffy cushions, and the lace nighty she'd laid out like some twisted booby prize. I hated everything about the bed, though I still needed to keep my mouth shut and lie in it. My throat tightened at the smell of body lotion, face cream, and the perfume the closed window trapped inside. I flung it open, desperate to breathe.

On tired legs, I trudged back to the bed, and sat down with my battered hands in my lap and my battered thoughts in my head. What a mess. The feelings between Elena and me. The fact I'd spent years tiptoeing around a wife who had manipulated me into believing she was mentally ill. In reality, I was up to my neck in it. I couldn't even tell Elena the full story – she'd either suspect me of lying or confront Celia, and I'd get it even more.

Bang.

My jaw moved in the socket, making my teeth crash. I didn't even hear her coming – Celia, the stealth bomber, and newly revealed megalo-fucking-maniac. I shot to my feet and met her murderous, manic expression. Celia shoved me in the chest, but I was the fortress, and her the golf ball.

'You came into this house smelling of her,' she spat.

'She cried, and I hugged her. That's all.'

'That's all!' Celia threw a shoe at my face.

I held up my arm and the shoe landed on the bed, its dirty sole on the white silk of her nightie. 'For God's sake, Celia. Leave Elena out of your games.'

I immediately regretted mentioning Elena, because I'd handed my wife a hefty stick to beat me with.

'Let's make something clear, Alistair. You can't tell somebody like me what to do.'

Stomping around the room, she switched off the big light and slammed the window.

I breathed hard and rubbed my face. 'And what exactly is somebody like you?'

She showed me her perfect whitened smile, the bill for which had appeared on my credit card. 'I had private tutors and a pony, and my father owns a multimillion-pound company. I'm better than you, Al.'

I wore the same pair of battered Nike trainers for school, football, and parties. Dad worked up to foreman at the boatyard and Mum worked as a dinner lady. Yet it didn't make me worse – it made me a grafter.

Celia folded her blanket in half, then quarters, and placed it on my side of the bed. 'Now, Elena. Do you want her?'

'No,' I lied, and crossed my arms.

'Fine. Make love to me and prove it.'

'No.'

Grinning like Satan, she fluffed up two cushions and arranged them on the blanket. 'Here's the deal. You satisfy me or she gets a pillow over her face while she sleeps. I might even sexually assault her after I've suffocated her, so you get the blame.'

Celia often made crazy threats when she felt desperate, though they only involved her or me. Deep down, I didn't think Celia would hurt Elena because she liked her. She seemed a different person, a person on the right side of the bipolar coin after spending time with her.

'You wouldn't dare.'

'Just fucking try me.' She twisted her hair into a rope, then slid her hand down it, looking for hairs ready to fall. 'Remember Abbie Gunner from uni?'

Abbie and Celia were friends. If I remembered rightly, she briefly had a massive crush on me. 'What about her?'

Celia held a long black hair in front of her, then wrapped the end around her finger, watching me as she did. 'She asked you out, remember? Then the poor girl got salmonella – it kind of happens when you eat ham painted with raw chicken juice. Ended up so ill her kidneys packed up. The poor, poor thing.'

My mouth dropped. 'You poisoned her!'

'No, silly. The ham poisoned her.' Around and around the hair went, twisted into a lasso. Celia's eyes shone brighter than the northern lights. 'Let's get a few things straight, honey. You do not look at Elena, you do not think about Elena, and when I say dance like a bear, you dance like a fucking bear. Gary didn't dance and remember what happened to him.'

Gary. Her old boss. The sun shined out his arse until he passed her up for a promotion, then sexually harassed her; he asked for nude photos and groped her against a wall when she said no. Apparently.

My stomach turned into a gizzard, over and over, filled with stones. 'You made it all up?'

She didn't simply throw the story out there. No. She cried and cried, and I saw the line of finger mark bruises along her hip.

'Would I.' The laugh came right from her poisoned core. 'Seriously, Al, the things you come up with. You're insane.' She stroked her bottom lip. 'But you're also very hot and I'm very horny. So, either you fuck me or I'll fuck with you. Well?'

'Do I actually have a choice?'

'No. But you'll feel better if you tell yourself otherwise.'

The zip on her skirt snagged on the hem. She pulled it apart, no doubt ruining it. I saw her belly. It used to be soft and perfect, along with the rest of her, but her obsessive diet and hours at the gym had stripped her of every ounce of body fat and turned her into something tough and hard to the touch. I told her I didn't like it when the counting calories and obsessing over carbs started. Because the control scared me, reminded me of my sister – though, looking back, my upset made her even worse.

Celia peeled off her vest and slid down the skirt, dragging it out like a tattooist lecturing how much the tattoo would hurt instead of getting on with it. I tried to pretend we were other people, but I couldn't. Too much had happened, too many insults, too much hurt.

She wrapped my T-shirt around her fist and kissed me. I cringed when her tongue touched mine, and I almost shoved her away when her nails scratched my chest. I dropped my hands and looked at the ceiling. The shadows hung in every corner, creeping in, making everything darker and gloomier.

'I can't do it.'

She shoved her hand inside my boxers and found me soft. 'Jesus, Al. You're an embarrassment.'

I closed my eyes, willing it to happen. But the harder I tried, the worse it got. I couldn't get it up, not even close. I swallowed down the ball in my throat; I wanted to cry.

'You're meant to be in the prime of your life. Imagine what your friends would say if they found out the best you offered your wife was that.' She kicked off her knickers, sat on her blanket and cushion throne, and opened her legs. 'Get on your knees and stay there 'til I tell you I'm done.'

'What?' I said, shaking my head.

This couldn't be happening.

'You went for option two, my love.' Celia smirked. 'Which means I get to fuck with you.'

'No.' I looked her over, the bucket of cyanide on my bed. 'You can't make me do something like that. It isn't right.'

'Life isn't right, Al. None of it fucking is. And I swear, your life and her life will get a hell of a lot worse if you don't do as you're told.' Celia leaned back, propped on her elbows. 'Now, get on your knees.'

After, she threw her bra on the chair and climbed into bed, and I knelt there, feeling filthy and humiliated, not having the energy to move. I stared at my useless hands. She couldn't make me consent to anything physically, but I would trade my mental consent if she withheld her threat. I wouldn't risk her hurting Elena to get at me and she knew it.

Yes, I was screwed. Well and truly.

18

CELIA

After plying my newly sworn enemy with coffee, croissants and beautiful smiles, I got rid of her and made my way to Toby's for the debrief following the unforeseen events of the previous night. I rang the bell and waited, kicking the step, my blood boiling, my insides hurting with the loss of the precious bee I'd carefully separated from its flowers. And all because of her – fucking Elena – and she didn't know how close I'd come to strangling her for it.

Toby answered the door with a tight jaw and a knotted brow. I glanced at his bandaged hand and put two and two together.

'What the hell were you doing in her house?' I asked him.

'Ceels.' He looked over my shoulder. 'Come in.'

I kicked off my shoes, and he ushered me into a tastefully furnished sitting room. A huge, curved television took up the corner and framed photographs sat everywhere – mostly of a dark-haired girl, a dark-haired man, and an affectionate-looking woman. My view rested on a large professional photograph, printed on canvas, hanging above the fireplace. I drew closer to the print. Like Toby, his mum looked kind and smiley, and his dad shared his twinkly eyes.

'Your dad looks like you.'

Toby put his arm around me; I shirked away, though he pulled me back.

'We're very alike. Laugh at the same things. Both like chilling at the golf course. I suppose he's my best mate. What's your dad like?'

Toby's arm rested heavy around my shoulders, holding me close. 'He...'

'He what?'

Like usual, Toby barrelled on, irrespective of my mood or the subject. And, like usual, it made me want to offer him something.

'He wasn't a good father.' My legs drained of substance, and I dropped on the sofa. Toby followed suit. 'He either worked or made my life hell. Yelled at me when I didn't get full marks. Shut me away in a guestroom if I said something out of turn.'

'Sounds like you're better off without him.'

Toby scratched the arm of the sofa and the silence fell, thick and viscous.

I pointed at the canvas hanging on the wall. 'I take it the girl's your sister?'

'Yes. Chloe. I don't see her much now – she lives in America. Have you got brothers or sisters?'

The epiglottis lodged in my throat. 'I had a twin brother. Osman. He died the week after we were sixteen. Slipped and banged his head. Fell in our swimming pool and drowned. I pulled him out of the water, but I couldn't save him.'

'At least you tried.'

'Eventually – I let him suffer a bit first. I thought he'd swim up and clutch his head for a while. I didn't think he'd die.'

'Jesus, Ceels. You killed him!?'

'No, I didn't kill him. The water did.'

Toby visually mined the air between us, burrowing for the cracks in my story which weren't there. My brother did fall in the pool and drown, and I did wait until his limbs splayed like a starfish before I undid the white sandals with the forget-me-not trim and jumped in. I didn't tell Toby that I was glad Osman died because I loved him, and he betrayed me – didn't stand up for me – when I needed him most.

I didn't tell Toby that my anger and resentment had a nasty habit of owning me.

'I don't get you, Ceels. I really don't get you. All I know is we shouldn't have met in the first place, and I should run right now. Far and fast.'

'Then why aren't you?'

'We all have our reasons.' He flopped back in his chair and ceded to the call of the window, the distance. His eyelids became half-closed shutters with a fringe of dark lashes for which women paid money and had glued to their faces. 'Strange they called your brother Osman and you Celia.'

'My name's really Sarajania. Celia's what my mother always called me.' I pulled a scatter cushion onto my knee and wheedled the soft velour strands between my fingers. 'My mother and I did some administrative fiddling when we came into the country – things were easier then – and I adopted her maiden name too.'

What the hell was I saying, telling him my name and about my necessary name-shifting? Maybe I verged on a catharsis. Or a breakdown.

The Star Wars theme tune called out and, with a scowl, Toby quietened his ringing iPhone. He received more calls than The Samaritans.

'Anyway. What about you – what's your real name?'

He smiled a weak smile. 'Mam and Dad call me Tobias, but I call myself Toby cos it makes me sound less like a gangster!'

'You're funny.' I laughed. 'So, back to why I came. What happened the other night?'

'Oh, ah. The other bloke bailed, and I couldn't trust that little druggy not to do something stupid like set her house on fire. I thought she wouldn't be there – and it nearly went totally pear-shaped when the big bloke turned up.'

'I didn't think she would be there,' I lied. 'The big bloke is my husband. See why I'm scared of him?'

Toby's fleeting expression was just what I wanted to see.

'Never knew you were.'

For effect, I chewed my lip. 'I don't broadcast it, Toby. I'm ashamed, and he'd go spare if he found out I'd told people.'

'Does he hit you?' he asked.

I looked at my hands, choosing silence. The omission was as good as a lie; and anyway, a convincing story about Al hitting me might not be instantly creatable. Unless I mentally put another man's face in place of Al's. Such as my old landlord, who liked slapping. Or Calvin, the only other guy I dated at university, who got handy after a drink. I stopped my deliberation there, because I had to.

'If he's that scary, you wouldn't be here, Ceels.'

'He doesn't know. He's at work,' I uttered. 'Did the police catch the other guy?'

The amusement reached Toby's eyes, and he chuckled. 'Course they didn't! They don't follow up on house jobs unless somebody gets hurt. They dish out a crime number and they're done.' Toby held up his bandaged hand. 'Anyway, I'm injured now and it's your fault. The least you could do is make me a brew and a batch of muffins so I can do some comfort eating. I can't do much at the gym and I'm at a major occupational disadvantage – what with my right hand being very important in my night job.'

'I can make you a drink, but I don't bake.' I dropped my view to the illuminated phone on the arm of the sofa. 'Are you answering that?'

'Nah, I need to tell you how to make my muffins.'

I trundled into his kitchen and set my eyes on his kettle. He switched on an iPad and presented it, displaying a recipe. And then I made bloody cakes, quietly and compliantly, without explanation or motive.

The next twenty minutes were filled with a comprehensive description of the events of the night before, instruction and criticism regarding my lack of baking skills, and two abrupt phone conversations.

I was sitting opposite him, nibbling on a hot blueberry muffin, chatting like we did, when the knock came from the door.

'Shit,' Toby said; 'I forgot about him. You need to disappear.'

I looked at the doors which opened onto the decking and considered the shoes in front of the glass-paned door at which the visitor knocked. Toby cut short my deliberation and told me to go upstairs until the visitor left.

The house faced south, and the late morning sun turned Toby's bedroom into a sheltered cove on a Malaysian island. It also smelled of him, in all of his alluring masculine glory. I perched on the slept-in bed and strained my ears, though I couldn't make out a single word coming from downstairs, only serious tones and a lack of pleasantries.

Exactly nine minutes later, Toby sprinted the stairs and burst into the room. He threw something on the chair and knocked me flat out on the bed. I scrambled onto my elbows and tried to sit, but he shoved me back down and tickled my ribs with his uninjured hand.

'Stop it. Stop it,' I said between giggles, trying to be serious.

His weight landed on me, pressing me into the mattress, and his lips touched mine. I shoved his chest and protested, but not for long. I breathed him in. I wanted him. But he wasn't in the plan. Managing Alistair and Ollie was hard enough, so I pushed him away.

'Toby, I'm married.'

It was a ridiculous reason, but the only one I could muster.

I eyeballed the chair. 'I thought you weren't a drug dealer.'

'I'm not. It's GHB, and I had it taken from somebody peddling it as a date rape drug. Not happening on my patch. And before you ask, I wouldn't put drugs in my body if you paid me.'

Toby prised my wandering hand from his delectable posterior and pinned it above my head. If Ollie had done such a thing, my insides would be squirming with anxiety, but Toby didn't make me anxious at all.

'Kiss me,' he said.

'Why?'

He swallowed and glanced at my mouth. 'Kiss me because you want to.'

It had been years since Alistair and I had kissed like the world didn't matter. Ollie and I had never kissed like that, and we never would. Yet with Toby... Perhaps it was because the baking, hugs and organised crime made him a contradiction. I liked contradictions. We made life interesting. I didn't understand, though I didn't want it to stop. But eventually, he growled, kissed my nose and left me wanting.

'Seems you forgot about the married thing, Ceels.'

He slapped my leg and laughed, and his plodding on the stairs disguised the sound of me stealing two vials of GHB.

Toby smiled at me from the bottom of the stairs. 'Wanna stay for tea?'

'I can't.' I gripped the banister like it would stop me spinning away into my insanity. 'Al will be home soon, and I haven't got the dinner on.'

'About this fella of yours.' He untied the laces on my trainers and handed them over like they weighed four hundred pounds and were fit to explode. 'Does he knock you about?'

I slid my feet into my shoes and dropped to a crouch. I focused on the laces, my newly undone laces, and the fingers that were stumbling over a bow. 'I don't want to talk about him.'

Toby crouched too, moved my hands and fastened my snaking laces into two sets of perfect droopy rabbit ears. 'If he hurts you, I can help, Ceels.'

My knees cracked when I stood. I was fucking falling apart. 'I'm fine, Toby. Really.'

He pulled down the handle but hesitated to open the door. 'Then I'll see you at the gym tomorrow, usual time?'

'I'll save you a treadmill. And thanks.'

19

ALISTAIR

I loitered at my mate's eight-foot metal gates, kicking my feet, wondering whether to press the buzzer or disappear to a pub where I'd be anonymous. Watching the midweek match at my wingman's house bordered on religion. I'd made it there through poverty and flooding and, perhaps stupidly, after he had the sickness bug from hell. For the first time ever though, I had second thoughts. I didn't want him to see through me, and I didn't want him to know. I was so ashamed of myself I couldn't look in the mirror to clean my teeth.

What Celia did, what she made me do, was sexual activity without consent. A crime. I'd looked it up, then cleared my internet history. Theoretically, I'd consented, but only because of the coercion, the threat. Regardless, I'd let her make me a victim.

A victim.

When I lived back home, someone sexually assaulted my mum's friend's daughter at a party. I saw her at Mum's Avon nights, and I remembered thinking she used to be colourful and then she became grey. Though I didn't get it, the grey thing, until Celia forced me to perform oral sex on her.

Grey is hollow. Grey comes after violation.

I put my finger on the bell, then stopped, thinking. Maybe it wasn't obvious, because the only person who'd noticed I'd turned to papier mâché inside and alloyed steel outside was Celia. Though she noticed everything. Like the extra hole in my belt, and the way I'd started rubbing my face like I wanted it gone.

I put my hand in my pocket, already lining up the excuses why I couldn't stay. The electric's out. She's got a flat tyre. The excuses used to stick on my tongue, but they started coming easily when going out became a choice of getting permission or getting hell. I started walking into a lot of doors at around the same time. I turned to leave, though two steps along the gravel the intercom beeped.

'Oy, Big Man,' Andre shouted. 'You're late. Get your arse through my gates before I get the guy in the lookout tower to shoot you.'

I laughed, properly laughed, then promised myself I wouldn't start finding monsters where there were none.

I zipped down my hoody. 'Alright, Andre.'

The floor-to-vaulted-ceiling windows in the hallway overlooked unlit fields, but it was as bright and uncluttered inside as ever. A runway of polished wood sat before me, and the glass bannisters made the space endless. Whereas Celia filled our house to make it feel like my prison, Andre had an interior designer turn his house into my escape. My lungs opened and my hand stopped throbbing under the pressure.

'Will you stop calling me that,' he said.

'Nope.' He might have abandoned his first name and reinvented himself at university, but I'd been calling him Andre for fifteen years and I couldn't break the habit. 'You know I don't like change.'

I plonked my bag on the island and pulled out four beers, a bag of peanuts and a bottle of twenty-five-year-old Oban. The baby-pink bag had 'Life is for shopping and prosecco' printed on the side. She'd cleaned out the kitchen cupboards and the rest of the carrier bags were gone. I could have dug out a rucksack, but after argument number four of five, I didn't have the energy.

He noted everything as usual, but kept his gob shut. He slid an open bottle of beer along the counter and nodded at my hand. 'What have you done now?'

I hid the black nails in my pocket with the fluff, sand, and bits from my washer, probably adding an infection to the problem of a messy break and a nail which wouldn't stick down or fall off.

'Trapped it.'

A phone rang, and I touched my pocket. It wasn't mine, thank goodness.

'Evening, Penny,' he said, rolling a piece of label into a ball.

His assistant, Penny, phoned him every time we met. Andre listened, peeling the label from his beer bottle, and then he interrupted her. Rearrange this. Reallocate that. Resources. Finance. Acronym after acronym. The bullshit bingo lasted a few minutes before he ended the call.

'What's up?' I asked.

'My senior procurement manager has some family crisis, so Penny and I need to get a train to London tomorrow in his place.'

'Are you still sleeping with her?'

His paper ball bounced off the fruit bowl and hit him in the face, and the shock made him choke until the beer came down his nose. 'Who?'

'Penny.'

'I've never had sex with Penny.' He grabbed a sheet of kitchen roll and wiped his face. 'I never will either.'

Andre pulled a sheet of kitchen roll from his shiny chrome dispenser; it continued to turn, though every time a sheet dropped it got caught back up again.

'I assumed she was the clever blonde woman who finished your marriage.'

'You assumed wrong.' Andre stopped the circling dispenser and tightly re-rolled the tissue. He tore the crumpled corner off the last sheet, making the roll perfect, and screwed the damaged piece into a tight ball. 'And can we not talk about my failed marriage and the woman who nearly finished me?'

'Aye.'

Sticking to the safe subjects of sport, work, and politics suited me just fine.

'What's with the taxi?' He turned his bottle until it grated on the granite. 'West Ham aren't usually worthy of a session on a school night.'

I sighed and downed beer number one. 'I need a drink.'

I'd needed a drink since I saw Elena limping on the street. Risking life and limb, I mooched over and asked her what she'd done. Apparently, she cut her foot on a broken glass in my spare room – which explained the bloody face cloth I found on my pillow, along with a note which said, 'You did this.' I told Elena Celia had done it purposely, and she really needed to keep away from her, to which she dismissed me as crazy. Again. And she wasn't far wrong. A sane person would have left the woman I'd stupidly married years back.

'You remembered to order that pizza?' I asked.

'Yes. With extra anchovies,' he joked. 'Just how you like it.'

With my mood flipping from black to yellow, I flopped on a chair and chuckled. I had three hours of freedom. Three whole hours without having to walk on eggshells or watch my back. I felt my permanent scowl lessen.

'Cheers.'

I stared at the bottle, pretending not to notice him studying me. I scratched my neck and shuffled in the chair. I swallowed. The beer didn't taste right. Nothing had since that night. I'd brushed my tongue and swilled with Listerine until my mouth stung and I got sores to add to the ulcers on my tongue and on the inside of my lip. Not that it stopped me eating the salt and vinegar crisps Jed handed out on site. No. I gritted my teeth and pretended, as usual.

'What?' I said, not able to stand it any longer.

'You been hitting the weights big time?'

I'd been hitting everything. The weights. The punchbag. I'd ignored the JCB and turned an outhouse into a pile of rubble with a sledgehammer that day.

'Why?'

He plucked four whole peanuts from the bowl and tossed them into his mouth. 'Just asking. You look bigger than when I saw you last.'

Which came as no surprise. If I wasn't running, I was training, moving aggregates, minus machine, or eating. I'd be the size of a mountain if I didn't rein it in – or I'd bag myself arthritis or a coronary. Feeling hot, I slung my hoodie over the back of the chair. It slid on the floor, so I picked it up and did it again. I might be beaten by a woman, but I wouldn't be beaten by a jumper.

'Stuff alright with the business?'

'Yeah.' My phone buzzed in my pocket. I checked the caller, put the phone face down on the counter, and took a long swig of my drink. I needed the hit before I spoke to her. So much for having three hours of freedom. 'And I've got a big job coming up if I can pull it out of the bag.'

I told him about the project I'd been working on for weeks. Stage one was to renovate a massive farmhouse. Stage two, to convert three barns into holiday cottages. And stage three, to build an indoor swimming pool. The job would keep my men in work for months.

'You need to borrow any money – get some capital behind you?'

'No. But thanks.'

'Sounds like a big investment.'

I shrugged. The speculation and money I'd already invested caused lots of arguments, but I had a decent head on my shoulders, and I wouldn't put the house at risk.

He shoved the peanuts in front of me. 'Eat some nuts to stop me eating them all. We can't all eat five thousand calories a day and not get a belly.'

A few peanuts later, I shoved the shiny bowl away. 'You'll have to sub me some chocolate instead, buddy. I've got a mouthful of ulcers, so the salt isn't doing me any favours.'

I peeled down my lip and showed him the bastard which doubled in size every time I bit it.

'Christ.'

I'd put my foot in it, letting on about the ulcers. I got ulcers after Marla died. I got ulcers when I realised a bloke had been pinching off me and I had to get the police involved. I got ulcers when the building industry crashed and I thought I might need to lay people off.

'Sure you don't need help, Al?'

I shook my head and turned my attention to the window on which a remote-controlled blind hid the glass, the outside, the space to run. The sun hadn't even set yet, not fully.

My phone buzzed, and I glared at it, wanting it gone. I opened the Oban before I swiped.

'Celia. What's up?'

'Why haven't you been answering your phone?' she asked. 'I couldn't remember what time you said you'd be home.'

The whisky burned like fire, but it warmed my belly and I liked it.

'The kick-off's at eight. Ninety minutes plus half time. I'll be in at half ten.'

I repeated, word for word, what I'd told her twice already. A cupboard opened and closed and then a bar of Galaxy and a Yorkie landed in front of me. I gave Andre the thumbs up and reached for the Yorkie.

'Celia, can't this wait?'

'Whatever. Just don't be late,' she snapped, and ended the call.

Circling his thumbs, Andre talked about the sort of stuff that filled a space, meaning nothing. My mum called it 'nattering' and it bothered me; me and Andre didn't do nattering. I leaned back and stretched out my legs, adopting a couldn't-give-a-shit pose, putting some distance between us. He asked me if I fancied buying the new Mitsubishi Animal and what I thought about the hosepipe ban, and I asked him if he thought the British summer was inclement and how his knitting was coming along. He swore at me, as usual, though my laughter stopped when my phone started again.

In some kind of trance, I watched it buzz along the counter then drop on the floor. It stopped ringing when it fell into a satisfying collection of parts: case, screen and battery. I ignored it, raised my bottle and said, 'It had a good life'. Right then, I wanted it broken, and I certainly wasn't scrambling around on my knees in front of him. I'd take the hit when I got home. Literally, most likely.

Andre scratched his chest, just below the collar of his shirt. 'Al, are you alright? I've got three spare bedrooms and the grannie flat over the garage if you need it.'

'I'm fine. What makes you think I need to leave home?'

Lips down-turned, he showed me his palms. Though I carried on anyway, over-reacting and over-defensive. I'd told Barry to keep his 'bastard nose out' when he suggested I ought to use the digger before I gave myself a hernia, and now I was giving my best mate crap too.

'Al, for fuck's sake. Calm down. This isn't like you. I don't know whether you're stressed or what. Even Celia said—'

'Celia said what?'

Realising drinking whisky from the bottle really didn't look good, I shot to my feet and got two tumblers. I poured for us both. He sipped and rolled the whisky around his mouth while he chose his words.

'She said she's worried about you.'

I unwrapped the Yorkie and snapped it in half, scattering crumbs in his shiny posh kitchen. 'She's not worried about me. She's worried I'll ruin her plans and kick her out before the other bloke gives her a bed to lie in.'

Andre stopped sweeping my mess into a neat little pile. 'What bloke?'

I shrugged. 'I don't know. But my money's on him being the reason she has a bath in the afternoons when I know she's showered at the gym. And why she guards her phone with her life.'

Andre's face turned the same colour as someone with a freshly broken arm. My admission shocked him as much as it shocked me.

'You think she's having an affair?'

'I know she is.'

He sipped his whisky and regrouped the pile of ruined chocolate. 'Is that why you're losing your temper over nothing and drinking every night?'

'I don't lose my temper over nothing and I have one beer.' A tickertape of thoughts pinged through my head. 'When did she tell you this?'

'Today. She came to the office. Told me you were having problems and asked me to lend you some money for your new project.' With the beer in one hand and the whisky in the other, he took turns drinking each, undecided. 'I promised to talk to you.' He put the bottle down, choosing the whisky. 'So, I am. And I'm telling you, I know a good divorce solicitor.'

I steepled my fingers against my nose and curtained my eyes. He knew. He'd seen what I worked morning, noon and night to hide, and I wanted to hug him and cry.

'She's a beautiful woman, but she rubs you up the wrong way,' he went on. 'And you drinking and losing your temper. Look at the size of you, Al. If things got out of hand, you could end up hurting her accidentally and find yourself in deep shit.'

'What?' My chair tipped over and the sound it made bounced from wall to wall. 'Do you actually think I'd lay a finger on her? Have you ever known me to lose my temper?'

'No.' He pointed at the bottle I choked with my hand. 'But I've never seen you drink whisky from the bottle either.'

My earthy world shook in his sterile one. She got everywhere. In my face and in the shadows, turning everything and everybody against me, and my anger rose like the bubbles in my Peroni. He was right. I'd never lost my temper before, but I'd never sworn at my foreman either. Or kicked my car because I'd got a flat. Or threatened a dog because it went for my cat. If things got out of hand, it wouldn't take much.

I wondered who I should be more scared of – her or me?

'Come on, Big Man,' he said. 'The game's about to kick off.'

I rubbed my face and screwed my eyes shut.

The game had kicked off already.

20

CELIA

I gazed through the French doors leading onto the balcony. A nearby rowan tree rustled in the breeze and a band of clouds made for a new patch of blue. I waited alone in Ollie's bed while he attended a conference call. The feather pillow gave behind my neck and the silk sheets stroked my skin.

The luxury took me to the past. To my childhood home, my opulent upbringing, to the silver spoons and subservient housemaids - to where I belonged. Not the shameful place where I sold my hair and swallowed my landlord. Not the mediocre place provided by a husband with limited affluence and limited ambition. I wanted the magazine house and the forecourt car. I wanted the beauty treatments and the private healthcare. I wanted to travel the world, first class and five-star. I wanted to live my life before I rotted like my mother. Which was where Ollie came in, despite his reluctance.

Hearing the footfall on the stairs, I fluffed my hair and adjusted the sheet so he could see enough. Ollie sat on the bed. The mattress tipped and rolled me towards him. He looked amenable, so I decided to take my chance.

'Ollie, I've been thinking.' I touched his face and kissed his jaw. Ollie flinched. He would have sex with me willingly, but the affection sat like a snail on a razor blade. 'I can't keep doing this.

Please let me leave him and come here. Not straight away, obviously. I'll move out. Then we can get together a few months later after the dust has settled.'

'No.' He jerked his face clear of my hand. 'He'll know you cheated, and I don't want to be caught up in that shit.'

'But I want to be with you. I'm sick of snatching hours and sneaking around.'

Ollie sighed. 'Leave it, will you? Don't mention it again.'

'Why?' Complying with his every whim was testing my patience. Aside from Alistair, I'd had a lifetime of it. 'What if I say enough is enough?'

Ollie sprang away and marched to the wooden cabinet across the bedroom. I scrambled up the bed, heart hammering in my chest. Unlike my mild-mannered husband, Ollie had a volatile temper and a dark streak, and he scared me. He held something in his hand.

'No. Please don't.'

Ollie grabbed my wrist and dragged me towards him as my fingers and toes scrambled for purchase on the loose sheets. He flipped me onto my stomach and pinned me by the shoulders, using his knees.

'I told you to leave it.'

'I'm sorry. Please don't.'

I threw my head from side-to-side, but I couldn't stop him cramming a ball of screwed up fabric into my mouth. He dragged me, thrashing, to the bottom of the bed and tied my wrists to the ironwork with a belt. Crying, I fought aimlessly and then I didn't. I froze and I flopped: a survival instinct, a kind of dissociation that I learned aged sixteen. When Ollie had finished with me, I gripped the cold metal so I didn't fall when he undid the belt.

'I don't like being disobeyed, Celia.' Ollie towered over me. 'Don't make me do anything like that again.'

I waited until I heard the last of his heavy footsteps on the stairs before I moved. I dropped my phone, then I dropped it again, though I eventually managed to take photos of my face, my red wrists and the finger-marks on my thighs. The belt he used to bind my wrists laid coiled on the carpet like a snake. I ran the soft leather between my fingers, touched the metal buckle cast into his initials, and put the belt in my bag. I didn't know why. Burning inside, with the evidence of what he'd done on my skin, I wiped my tears and got dressed.

It would never happen again.

I lay on Toby's sofa, nestled between the plush fabric and his cuddle, and stroked the hairs on his arm. I shouldn't have gone there, not to him, because he softened me, and I already felt broken after what Ollie did to me. My life was a mess. Elena was determined to stay put and Alistair was tempted to stray. Ollie wouldn't commit and Toby was a fly-by-night liability. To top it off, getting another job with a gross misconduct dismissal behind me would be nigh on impossible. I'd have accused my boss of sexually assaulting me elsewhere if I'd noticed the CCTV camera. Which brought me back to Ollie. After the events of the day, I absolutely needed a Plan B, because Ollie might not be my get out. Ollie had crossed a line, and I feared he might cross it again, repeatedly – which was not a reality I could endure.

Toby slipped his hand down the front of my trousers; I grabbed his wrist and pulled his hand away.

'Sorry. I'm really sore.'

He wriggled and turned me to face him. 'Does he hurt you sexually?'

'Sometimes.'

It wasn't a lie. I just declined to add that my lover caused the harm and not my husband.

'Ceels, I don't understand. Why not leave him and the other woman to it? Make a clean break.'

'He won't let me go. Even if he did, he'd make sure I left with nothing. I own nothing. I've never paid for anything. It's his house, in his name. Even my car belongs to him. I can't face destitution, Toby. I really can't.'

'Leave him and live with me.'

I nearly choked. 'I can't. It's not just about the money. It's about him. He'll never let me leave and he'll kill me if I try.'

'Then kill him first.'

Killing Alistair had never realistically crossed my mind, but it would certainly solve my problems. I had no intention of hurting Elena, though with her on the scene I had genuine concerns he might call my bluff and divorce me. Divorce meant half of the house. End of. If he was dead, I would get the unmortgaged house, his pension, his life insurance and the business. There would be no grief, no battle in the divorce courts, and nobody to tell of my little misdemeanours.

'Ceels. I can't stand the thought of him hurting you.'

I didn't look up from the creases on Toby's T-shirt. Captain America. Three circles, all inside each other. 'We all get hurt. It's part of life.'

And if Alistair didn't get back in line, I would hurt him too.

More than I ever had before.

21

ALISTAIR

I squinted against the spotlight of sunshine that came through the gap in the curtains. The pillow next to mine carried the dint from Celia's head, yet there was no sign of her. Which struck me as odd because she never got up first. I slung my arm over my eyes, found some heavenly cold sheet, and let my mind wander to Elena. She smiled all the time, even that first day when she cried, like she felt guilty for being sad. And as for the sight of her in that ABBA dress. I grinned. Aye, it turned out Elena made me the opposite of impotent.

I swung my legs out of bed and rubbed my gritty eyes. My body felt leaden, aged by five years in as many weeks, and I had an important meeting scheduled with a team of architects. I really needed the cotton wool out of my brain.

The wardrobe door squeaked on its hinges and the hangers clattered as I pulled out my short-sleeved white shirt. I slung it over my back, fed my arms into the sleeves and fastened the first button.

What the...

The second button was gone. And the third. Every button missing. I noticed a small white button in the bottom of the wardrobe. I shoved a pair of Celia's high-heeled shoes to the side and saw lots of buttons – white and blue, big and small, some with four holes, not two. I scooped them up and swore. Every button from every shirt, cut off and tossed in the cupboard bottom. I had forty-five minutes to shower, eat, and drive to the meeting. I could do without having to search through the buttons and make good a shirt.

She had punished me again.

Under pressure, it took forever to thread the needle, and I stabbed my finger over and over as I sewed. As I battled to tie the last impossibly small knot, a spot of blood soaked through the white fabric, from the reverse to the front. I licked my finger and tried to rub it off, but it didn't go, didn't even fade.

The blood and the rushing made my heart beat ten to the dozen, agitating my insides, making my hands feel shaky. Then I discovered the flat battery in my laptop. Again. I hid my face behind my hands and swore over and over. The little things – like running my computer to dead – sometimes got to me more than the physical stuff. I wished she'd hurry up and leave me for him before I snapped.

After breakfast, I put on my shoes and made for the car. Elena's curtains were open and her car was parked on the drive. I wanted to talk to her and warn her about Celia. Celia had clearly noticed something between us at the housewarming – hence the scalding, the waterboarding, and cutting the buttons off my shirts. I jogged down her path and knocked on the door.

Elena didn't answer.

22

CELIA

I drove onto the road, saw Alistair walking through Elena's gate, and quickly shot down the side street until his truck came past and disappeared out of sight. Alistair had gone from not daring to look at another woman to knocking on Elena's door in broad daylight. He was fucking stupid. If Alistair thought he could pick up with Elena and kick me out, he had another think coming.

What with having a busy day (for me), I didn't hang around. The first stop was to visit the garage, his domain. I pressed the switch inside the doorway and the antiquated strip light flickered into action. To my delight, the garage looked ransacked; Alistair really didn't like the waterboarding. I searched carefully, touching everything with my fingertips, not wanting to upset anything. Eventually, I refined my hunt to the metal lockers on the far wall. The first door groaned open and a bottle of slug pellets caught my attention. I didn't actually have a use for them, though I tipped a palmful into the pocket of my hooded sweater anyway. Eventually, beneath a mass of brightly coloured rags and a few dozen paint-spotted paintbrushes, I found a wound length of rope.

The rope spat out a cloud of dusty fibres when I tied it around my wrist and tightened it with my teeth. Grabbing the lengths in the other hand, I sawed until my wrist reddened and scored. I then repeated the process on the other side. Pleased with my efforts, I returned the rope to its home and went back to the house. After taking photos of the rope-burns, I sprinted up the stairs and changed into a flared skirt and a white vest trimmed with pretty lace. I slipped on a cardigan to hide my wrists, applied a sweep of lip gloss and a flash of mascara, and pinned my hair with a clip adorned with a white flower.

My heart raced in delight as I left the house and dialled Alistair's number. I needed to keep Elena and Alistair apart until I left him for my lover. Ollie sometimes upset me, but I was only shaken and not perturbed. I wanted the privilege and security he could provide, and I would get them. Eventually.

I stopped by our front wall and dialled Alistair's number. In the cracks, patches of lichen clung between the moss and loose mortar. The air smelled organic and alive.

'Hi honey, only me.'

'Celia.' Given the scratchy sound, I knew Alistair had placed his hand over the phone speaker. 'I need to take this call. See you in there.'

'What a lovely day! And better still, I'm going shopping later and taking Elena.' I paused to muster his anxiety. 'We're going for coffee before we hit the clothes shops – if she can be bothered. Her arms looked a little raw yesterday. Have you touched her arms at any point, honey?'

The silence sat between us, crackling and uncomfortable. I crushed a dozen tiny red clover mites and wiped the wall with the war paint made by their death.

'What have you done to her?'

'Nothing,' I said.

Physically.

Though I don't think the bleach I put in her body lotion the night of the party was helping. She really shouldn't have gained the attention of my husband. Or stored her emergency anaphylaxis medication in an unlocked bathroom cabinet. Or left her spare house keys on display in the hall. I'd always enjoyed collecting things. Pencil rubbers, misplaced money, other women's partners, life-saving medical treatment...

I giggled and bounced my flip-flop against my heel. 'Alistair, I'd like you to make the most of the outdoors. I know you like sport and it would be dreadful if your actions got you incarcerated.'

'What the hell is that supposed to mean?'

'Put behind bars. Locked up. It doesn't make me happy when you look at other women, and it definitely doesn't fill me with joy when you sneak to their fucking houses.'

I neither paused for thought nor deliberation. 'I only delivered a parcel they dropped at our house.'

'And I'm Princess Diana reincarnated. Enjoy your freedom, Alistair. You never know when you're going to lose it.'

I ended the phone call and left him to suffer.

I strolled down the bridal path though my cloudy thoughts were elsewhere. It had all been so simple: retain Alistair until Ollie would have me. But then Elena turned up, catching Alistair's eye, then Ollie pissed me off big time. Toby jogged to my side, caught my hand and strode ahead, taking me with him.

'Excuse me, love.' The voice came from behind me; from a parking attendant wearing green clothes and a stupid peeked hat. 'You parked so close to the next car they won't be able to get in.'

I took two determined strides to the man, towing Toby behind me. 'I parked inside the lines – all four tyres. The other driver is not within the lines, so it's not my problem.'

His jaw dropped, face suddenly glowing. 'I'd like you to move the car. Please.'

'You're a carpark attendant,' I snapped, jabbing my finger, 'and I won't be dictated to by somebody like you.'

I turned, though Toby twisted me back.

'Sorry about her,' he said to the carpark guy. 'I'll move it. Give me the keys.'

Toby's hand shot out, a severe expression on his face. I did what he said and watched, half amazed by myself, half in awe of him, as he trotted back along the path, talking to the attendant like an old friend.

After he moved the car, Toby jogged back, uncurled my fingers and made me hold his hand. I had no idea why I didn't let rip like I would at anybody else.

'You shouldn't talk to people like that. He's only doing his job. Show a bit of respect,' Toby said.

'I give respect where it's due. He's a fucking carpark attendant.'

'He's a person, just like me and you. Tip for you, Ceels, what with you being socially inept and me being a social dreamboat – if you wanna get on in life, don't treat people like shit.' He pulled me close and kissed my face a hundred times. 'Come on, smile with me, Ceels.'

I shoved him off, smothering a grin. 'I actually hate you sometimes, Toby.'

'Yeah, I know. But you love me too much to keep it up.' He zipped down his hoody and wafted his T-shirt, and I noticed the perfectly sized traps peeking out at the neck. 'Nice day.'

The sky was clear and blue, and the gentle breeze did nothing to dampen the warm sun. Such a perfect day.

'Hmmm. It is.'

'Though I suppose it's always warm in Singapore. Why exactly did you come to miserable Britain?' Toby asked.

Before Toby came along, I kept the real version of me shielded, preferring to morph and adapt to whoever, because it was easier and kinder. Yet I wanted to give him a part of me; a really bad part, I supposed, just to see.

I undid the last button on my cardigan and let it fall open. 'There was a man. In his late forties, maybe, and my father wanted to buy his company. They were aligned with my father's biggest competitor, and he wanted them gone. Simple as. My father was ruthless. Hard as a fucking marble. Anyway, the man always refused to trade. Then he said he'd sell in exchange for me, so my father told him he could have me when I came of age.'

Toby's complexion greyed. 'You had sex with him?'

'No. He had sex with me. I just laid there, crying. I saved my breath after the first few times. The more upset I got the worse it became.' I paused for breath. 'I didn't have a choice. I knew my father would do worse if I disgraced him. It lasted for six months – until my mother brought me here.'

Toby ferreted a stone from the grass edging the path and kicked it down the middle.

'We actually fled to Britain,' I said. 'With two bags and fake passports. I was in serious shit. Because the rapist bastard got very drunk and smashed his skull on the marble sink – and I saw it happen.'

'Did he die?'

'Yes.'

I didn't actually kill him; he choked to death. I simply facilitated the fall and rolled the unconscious man onto his back when the vomiting started.

'Good.' Toby kicked the stone, chased it, then kicked it again. 'If you want to talk about it, you know where I am. If you don't want to talk about it, I'm happy to put your story and my story in a big hole and leave them there.'

'Thanks.' I stopped him in his tracks and placed my hands on his rock-hard abs. A lesser person would have paid for his services; however, I wasn't a lesser person, so I could have Toby for free. 'But I don't need a counsellor. I've got a better job for you.'

He held my hips, grinning with mischief, swaying his way closer. 'Which is?'

I bit his neck and then kissed it better. 'Guess?'

Toby tossed me over a dilapidated wall and pushed me onto the dry, bouncy grass. His bent arms fell on either side of my face, isolating me from the difficult outside world, trapping me in his easy one. The thoughts ping-ponged around my brain. I wondered if Toby should have a place in my long-term plan because I really liked him, and Ollie's recent behaviour had proved him to be a world-class twat; not that I would abandon the world-class twat without a more practical option.

'Toby. Do you plan on getting a proper job? Do you actually have any qualifications? Because what you do now won't last forever.'

'Ceels, stop worrying.' He kissed my nose. 'I got a D in GCSE English and an A in PE. The world is my oyster. Anyway, why would I want a proper job?'

My wondering stopped. I couldn't have a future with somebody who made a living from stripping on the internet in between meddling in drugs and petty crime. As with Alistair, if the shit hit the fan with Toby, destitution might arrive at our door within a year. Unlike Alistair, the shit with Toby might also involve prison or broken kneecaps. Ollie, on the other hand, need never work again, and his canny nature meant his accounts stayed transparent and his hands stayed clean.

'You need a stable income.'

'I've got plenty of income.'

Somehow, I'd squashed the grass beside my face and made the vibrant green mottled and ruined.

'But so much of it's illegal.'

He kissed my neck three times. 'What do you care? Will you leave him for me?'

'No. He'll never let me leave, and anyway, you're not my type.'

'What, lacking a sensible profession?' he teased.

I hitched my legs around his and met his trusting blue eyes. 'No, single.'

Toby gazed at nothing. 'I'm not quite single. I kind of undersold the casual thing. Her name's Laura.'

My insides turned to rock on lava. I wasn't happy. Women had a tendency to fuck up my plans. My mother died and left me up to my neck in it, Ollie's wife hindered me for years, then Elena caught the eye of my well-trained husband. I dug my elbows in the ground and squirmed from under him. I picked up a small stone with a sharp nose and squeezed it until it stung.

'I hardly see her, Ceels. She's at uni doing some psychology degree. No, it's criminology.' Toby sighed and sat up, too. He unpeeled my fingers and threw the stone into the long grass. 'It's not like you ever told me we can make a go of it.'

'Criminology! Does she not see the irony in studying that and dating you?'

Toby licked his finger and wiped the spot of blood off my hand. 'I only dabble in crime these days – and anyway, as far as she's concerned, I'm Prince Charming.'

'So, you're a liar.'

'We're all liars, Ceels.' Toby kissed me as his hand roamed up my skirt. 'Divorce him.'

He slid my knickers down my thighs, and I kicked the shoes off my feet. I felt the soft grass between my toes. 'I can't. He'll never let me go.'

He opened my legs with his knees and unfastened his jeans. 'Then I'll kill him.'

I hooked my feet over his calves and raised to meet him. 'You can't kill him.'

'I can. I'll poison him.'

The endorphins crashed in like a hit, and I rocked my head, intoxicated. 'It'll show in the post-mortem.'

'Then I'll think of something else.'

'I'm quite... Oh, shit.' I stopped to catch my breath. 'Capable of thinking of a way to kill him myself.'

'Yeah, I can see that.' Toby moved, taking me somewhere new. 'Though you don't worry me.'

I couldn't think through the colours and the feelings and the fact we were making love while plotting a murder. I buried my face into Toby's neck and tasted the molecules which made him. He said my name and pulled me from the clouds.

'He hurts you, so he needs to go.'

Alistair's demise was a magnetic prospect which would guarantee his silence and line my pockets. With him dead, Ollie and his monetary benefits would be an option and not a necessity.

Yes.

Alistair's death would give me the choice that bastard after bastard had taken from me. If push came to shove, I could get rid of Ollie too.

It would be the perfect plan.

Toby kissed me and touched me and called me beautiful, and I came so hard I thought I'd never stop my neurones from swimming, never regain the strength in my legs. His body dropped onto mine and I pulled him closer, wanting the weight of his gravity.

'I want you in my life,' he whispered.

And I wanted him too.

In the short-term, I wanted them all: Alistair and Ollie and Toby. But the long-term bought with it conflicted thoughts and indecision. I liked Elena, but she liked my husband and he liked her back. Not only did it insult me, but it could totally screw up my plans. I needed Alistair until the time came to get rid of him.

Regardless, I would get whatever I decided should be mine.

Because I was the catcher, the keeper of things that I wanted.

And I was also the destroyer of people who took them away.

23

ELENA

Through the door glass, I saw the distorted outline of Celia's petite frame. I took a deep breath, and my sore arms itched again, as if to remind me of the restless night I'd spent uncomfortable in bed. I couldn't understand it, I really couldn't, because I'd never suffered from skin problems before.

'Good afternoon,' Celia said, slipping off her sandals.

'Hi, Celia. Fancy a cuppa before we go? I've made a pot.'

Celia nodded and smiled, and I smiled back at her. Her smiley character was contagious, which made me forget about it all, the mess, if only momentarily.

I placed two mugs on the table and took the seat opposite. A small brown stain marred the pale tabletop and it wouldn't come off, regardless of how hard I rubbed. The swish of my shirt set off the itching again, so I pressed on my sleeve and tried to make it stop without scratching.

'You're a creature of habit.' Celia nodded at my red and white mug, the one a paralegal bought me after we shared a joke about my excessive tea drinking. 'You used the same cups last time.'

I curled my hand around it, covering the 'Keep Calm and Carry On Brewing' slogan, and told her I always used it and nothing seemed to taste right from the others. Apparently, Celia didn't have a favourite mug or gin glass, though she did have a favourite knife with a perfectly sized handle and a sharp blade, which she kept top slot in the knife block, always to hand.

Silence.

Celia held the tea in her mouth for a moment before she swallowed. 'You make good tea – nearly as good as Alistair. Though you must be the only two people in Britain who bother with a teapot.'

I touched my cheek and hoped my face wouldn't flare like a sparkler. Absent-mindedly, I ran my hand up my forearm. Through the thin fabric, I felt the cracking, and when the fabric ended, I felt the damaged skin peeking out.

'Have you got eczema?'

I held out my arm and peered at it, hovering my hand. 'No, but my skin's sore and crawling. It's driving me mad.'

'It looks dry. Try some moisturiser.'

'I have. I've put loads on.' Yet it still got worse by the day. Drier and more red, new inflammation on the old. I paused, thinking. 'Perhaps it's the lotion?'

'Not if it's your usual brand. Put on some more. Your skin definitely looks dry.'

Without warning, she touched a raw place with her fingertips and I froze, breath baited, waiting for the accidental stab of a nail. 'We'll pop to the pharmacy in town and get you some hydrocortisone cream. I need to buy a pregnancy test anyway.'

A pregnancy test. As much as I tried to hide it, I sensed the hollow behind my eyes. At the thought of them, their intimacy, the unwelcome and immoral bitterness soured the milk in my drink. I couldn't stand to drink it, so I pushed it away.

'Have you finished?' I asked. 'Maybe we should go before it gets too late.'

We avoided the Costa and decided upon a coffee shop-come-deli off the high street. The small coffee shop always buzzed with the energy of people happy to be out, and I liked it there. I liked the mismatched wooden furniture and the mismatched people, and the cakes and local dairy products.

I froze, foot in the air, a few steps into the café, and dropped to my haunches. On the floor rested a red ladybird with black spots. I didn't want it getting squashed, so I picked it up. Celia spotted a free table, pointed it out, then headed to the counter. The ladybird was still crawling on my hands when she returned with the coffee.

'I like beetles,' I said. 'They're kind of cool. Somebody once told me that cockroaches would survive a nuclear war.'

Celia warmed her hands on her skinny latte, despite it being a hot day, sticky out of the shadows of the buildings. 'I like insects.'

'Honeybees? Butterflies? Don't tell me you like wasps?'

'Bumblebees are my favourite, actually.' Celia blew over the froth sitting on the top of her drink, making the bubbles fold and burst. 'Did you know that, contrary to popular belief, they don't die after they sting. They have a smooth sting so they can use it over and over – but they don't because it's not in their nature.'

I mined my brain for what I knew about bees, all tucked away behind employment law and the recipe for the perfect cherry flapjack. 'Or they don't sting because they're male, so can't. Only the females can sting – the queens and workers.'

'Are you sure?'

The ladybird crawled onto the menu and I picked up my mug. 'I'm positive.'

'Oh.'

Celia and I finished one coffee and started another, chatting like old friends. She stirred her drink as I twittered on about my new trainers. The man in the running shop fitted them to my foot shape and gait, yet they turned out to have the comfort rating of wooden clogs and they gave me a bad knee.

'Rory the new milkman has a bad knee,' Celia said.

'I hope he's as good as my old milkman. He even stopped delivering when I went on holiday... very lucky, considering I never remembered to cancel.'

'I'll keep an eye out whenever you go away, Elena. I'll take the milk from your doorstep if you forget.'

'Oh, I will forget. I always do. Clean knickers. Hairdryer. Antihistamines. It's as much as my out-of-work brain can take.'

Celia glanced around the room, then refocused on my arm. The area where I'd applied the hydrocortisone already looked less angry, the steroid cream working miracles.

'Hey, changing the subject, how long is it since you met a man you liked?' Celia asked. 'A man you want to kiss.'

I touched my face to hide my glowing cheeks and the lip I bit tightly. Celia knew, which didn't make sense, because she wasn't angry with me and I doubted Alistair would have told her.

'How did you know?'

A loud crash came from behind and a shower of white porcelain skittered past my flip-flop. I wriggled my toes, waiting for a cut, for a stabbing pain, though nothing came.

Celia peered at me from over her mug. 'Know what?'

'Excuse me.' I turned in the direction of the woman's voice. She waved a long-handled sweeping brush. 'Is it okay if I sweep around your feet?'

Which she did, quickly.

'Oh, come on, Elena,' Celia continued. 'You split with the ex ages ago and I don't have you down as the dating app sort of person. Anyway, Alistair's got this friend. He's lovely. Good-looking, smart and rich. He got divorced recently and I think you'd get on.'

I breathed out my relief quietly and carefully, like a coached witness on the stand. 'No, I'm really not ready.'

The doorbell chimed and the door protested, clinging to its frame before it shot open. In what seemed like an accumulation of conspiracy, Lucas walked in wearing trendy blue jeans and a casual shirt, with my replacement hanging on his arm. Oh, my gosh.

'You alright?' Celia asked.

I looked at my hands, wrung them together. 'Over there. My ex, Lucas, just came in. With her.'

Lucas and I exchanged a meek smile, and he carried on walking. I plopped an ugly lump of brown sugar into my coffee and stirred it like a madwoman. I always gravitated to sugar when I felt bad. The sound of people dropped to a buzz, and the scraping of my chair announced my standing.

'Excuse me, I need some air. Can you watch my bag?'

I wanted to vomit, and I wanted to cry. Seeing him and her together didn't hurt so much – unlike the gentle touch of his hand, low on her swollen stomach, while they waited at the counter. The shrapnel in my womb slowly carved its way out. Unlike Lucas, I hadn't escaped from our mess unscathed.

After a few deep breaths and a screw of my eyes, I touched a bright new leaf on the tree. A metal cage protected the immature trunk, though it did nothing to protect the vulnerable leaves which lived to grow. Life went on. I inhaled their waxy scent and went back inside.

'Okay?' Celia asked.

'Yes, I'm fine.' I filled my mouth with sickly sweet coffee.

Celia turned my napkin, studying the ladybird. 'What happened between you?'

'Basically, Lucas was a serial cheat – not that I ever proved or did anything about it. Then I met this guy, professionally. We got on really well, became friends, met for coffee and lunch sometimes. Then I caught Lucas with the woman over there, turned to the guy and ended up in his bed. Turned out he was married too.' My stomach churned the milk and sugar into stodge. 'But it got much worse. Because I fell pregnant. Ironically, Lucas and I had been trying for a year, and I conceived a baby with the guy after that one time. He wanted me to keep the baby and outed his wife – turned up at my house with a ring and everything.'

'What kind of ring?'

My insides froze at the thought of it, like they did that day. 'An engagement ring. Anyway, I told him no because I wanted to fix my marriage. Lucas demanded I have an abortion, so I did – then I ended up with an infection which damaged my fallopian tubes.'

'Oh, Elena...'

I pressed my fingertips on my hot coffee cup, wanting to feel something tangible, something real, something not a wound from my past.

'I underwent a procedure to unblock my tubes, but still nothing happened, so I started the fertility treatment. Tablets, hormone injections, and eventually IVF, which failed. The baby became the be all and end all for me, something to alleviate the hurt and the guilt. My obsession ruined what we'd rebuilt and drove him into her arms. It looks like she's pregnant now, and I'm pleased for him.'

'Elena, I'm gutted for you, I really am, but you need to take heed of the lesson and move on.'

'What lesson?'

Discreetly, I glanced to where the two of them hid in a booth made from reclaimed wood and old velvet.

'That screwing another woman's husband always ends in tears.'

I squirmed, worried by Celia's sudden hardness. 'I wouldn't have slept with him if I'd known he had a wife.'

'Hey,' she chirped, almost bipolar. 'Come on. Alistair's friend. Lucas moved on and so should you. What do you think about tonight? The four of us.'

'I'm not ready and he probably won't be interested in me anyway.'

'You are and he'll love you. I'll take that as a yes!'

Celia passed me, swinging her bag like I'd made her the happiest person in the world. I forced my leaden body to stand and shoved my chair under the table. I lifted my napkin and found the ladybird gone; the cute little thing had flown away. And then I saw it across the table. Squashed into a disk of red and black, the edges oozing with yellow green.

And it made me want to cry.

24

ALISTAIR

My best mate lifted his sunglasses then rubbed his face. New lines sat beside his eye, like a wince that wouldn't leave him. We'd played the worst day of cricket ever, forty-two runs all out, yet everyone except him laughed about it. He dropped his glasses when he noticed me looking, and I returned my view to the road.

'Cheer up, Andre. It's only a game, and that coffee and walnut cake made up for the thrashing.'

He stared across the bonnet, at the tarmac. 'I don't eat cake.'

Talk about having a kid in the car. He'd be walking home if he started talking about YouTubers or throwing tantrums over slow Wi-Fi. Denise, my big sister, said that's what kids did these days.

I sniggered and he glared. 'Come on, what's up? You can't be this miserable over a game of cricket.'

'I've got a lot on my plate.' Head down, he scratched the edge of one perfectly cut, perfectly clean nail with the other. 'You know how it is. We all have our shit to deal with.'

I nodded. He didn't know the half of mine.

The drive sat empty, Celia's car gone, which lifted my mood until I remembered why. Celia and Elena, out together. The discomfort bit like an infected rat, though I could do nothing about it. He accepted my offer of a quick drink and followed me into the house, eyes on his phone, scowling at his emails. I stuck on the kettle.

A few minutes later, I sat down and placed the drinks on a couple of coasters. Beneath mine sat a small stack of photos. Intrigued, I wiggled them out. Then a fist, without physical existence, hit me so hard I nearly fell off the chair.

I leafed through the photos. The first showed a woman's wrist circled with rope welts and the next a breast with a bite mark on it. The images became increasingly disturbing. Bruised flesh. Celia's face, her mouth filled by a gag, tear tracks on her cheeks. An explicit picture of between her legs. Behind the photos was a photocopy of some handwritten text.

> 14th May
> I can't take much more. I am so afraid of my husband, but I have no escape. He says if I leave, he will find me and kill me. If I go to the police, he will deny everything. I am so scared.

> 14th June
> He did it again. The gag. He knows I hate it. I feel suffocated, I cannot breathe. I want to curl up and die.

Her words from that morning hit me like a house brick. 'Enjoy your freedom. You never know when you're going to lose it.' The brick battered me to dust. Celia had assimilated fake evidence of her alleged domestic abuse and fabricated a diary detailing the whole fictitious story. If I displeased her, she'd go to the police and have me put behind bars.

My hands shook.

Being with Celia was like following a drunk driver. Brake lights flashing, weaving all over, herding me into a ditch. And, yeah, I braced myself for the airbag.

'What's going on, Al?'

'I'm over a barrel and up to my neck in shit.'

I handed him the photo of the rope marks and his face turned ashen with the shock.

'I'm nothing to do with this.' I dropped my heavy head into my hands. 'What the hell shall I do?'

The kitchen door opened, and Celia and Elena walked in. In a panic, I took the photo from Andre and threw them all on the high freezer.

'Hiya, Alistair. Hiya, Ollie,' Celia said. 'Elena, this is Ollie – well, his name's actually Andre, but only Al calls him that. Ollie, this is Elena our new neighbour. I've told her all about you today. What do you say about dinner tonight? Just the four of us.'

I nearly threw up.

'Ollie?' Celia asked.

I expected him to refuse, but he willingly agreed. I glared at Celia, not that anybody else saw it, and she returned a self-satisfied smile. And there I thought things couldn't get any worse.

25

CELIA

The dining table bustled with spent activity. Dropped crumbs from the crusty bread. A serving dish sprinkled with tiny, shed flowers from the stem broccoli. The water jug which contained too little liquid to drown a fly.

The mood had settled from awkward and expectant to pleasant and sated. Between considered forkfuls of Waitrose goat's cheese salad, followed by beef Wellington, we had chatted and laughed and sipped wine. Alistair didn't have much to say, though Ollie expertly carried the conversation with humour, wit, and current affairs.

I knew Ollie would rise to the challenge; him showing an interest in Elena would, in his man's little mind, prove his innocence where being the other man was concerned. Ollie flirted and flattered and performed, and I almost admired his flawless act. Yet I admired my web of fucking brilliance more. I'd got all three of them dancing like puppets and they didn't even realise it.

'So then, Elena,' Ollie said, charming as an antique teapot. 'Do you work?'

With the tip of her finger, she gathered a few crumbs from the tablecloth and rubbed them onto her side plate. 'Cut the act, Ollie. We both know I'm only here because of you.'

Bang.

An upstairs door slammed shut, and I nearly had a heart attack. The only doors open in the house should have been those I had opened, and those upstairs should have been closed, firmly fucking closed.

Smirking, Ollie rested his dessert fork on the plate. 'Not strictly true.'

I turned my glass on the slate coaster until the grating sound bored into my teeth. 'Am I missing something? Have you already met?'

'Many times,' Ollie returned.

'Through work,' Elena said.

Alistair's fork stopped mid-air. The cheesecake fell and splattered on his plate like a jumper splats on the ground. 'Do you work for him, Elena?'

His casual tone was forced and so transparent. He so wanted their relationship to be professional. But not as much as I did.

'No. She works against me, Big Man,' Ollie said.

Elena hitched her sleeves, looking flustered. 'I've only worked against you twice – though two battles and two victories aren't bad going.'

'You won once. The second case ended with an out-of-court settlement.'

'You realised you were in the wrong, so you ceded. I won.'

'I ceded because I don't like people trying to do me over publicly. And it doesn't come more public than in the stand.'

'I never tried to do you over publicly, Ollie.' Elena stared Ollie down. I hadn't thought she had it in her to stand up in court until then. 'I simply did it, and I'll do it again next time you dismiss somebody out of turn.'

'Ah, so much fighting talk.' He undid the buttons on his shirt and rolled the sleeves up to the elbows. 'You won't do it again.'

'Two cases. Two victories.'

'The details are a technicality.' Ollie leaned back in his chair, features flat, muscles pressing onto his shirt. 'I still want you on permanent staff.'

She grinned, totally unphased by his arrogance, his power. 'In your dreams, Ollie. In your bloody dreams.'

'So, Elena.' I severed the look passing between them. 'Why are you here because of Ollie? I'm at a total loss.'

'He emailed me the details of my bungalow on the day it came up for sale. Said it was perfect for me. And he was right.'

Grinning, Ollie returned his attention to his plate. He cut through the cheesecake topping using the side of his fork, though stopped precisely where it met the biscuit base. He turned the fork to horizontal and sliced the fluffy topping clean off. 'I'm always right.'

'Great size. Great location,' she continued, dismissing him with a disappointed mother shake of the head. 'Not a thing to do.'

Alistair peered up from his empty glass. His eyes were vague and his movements unsure. Not that it came as a surprise. I'd not seen him drink wine since I dragged him to a Christmas meal several jobs earlier, and he'd knocked it back like there was no tomorrow. 'How did he know you were looking for somewhere to live?'

'Because...' Ollie said.

Elena silenced him with a stare, and he refocused on his dessert: the dessert he typically wouldn't entertain – the dessert he dissected and savoured like it was the most perfect thing he'd tasted, ever.

'He knew Lucas and I were separating.'

Alistair topped up our glasses and the added volume turned the dregs from fruity and pale to thick and red. Like blood. Yes, blood. Which was ironic really, because mine was fucking boiling.

For the next hour, Ollie's subtle flirtation with Elena stomped on. He hardly looked at me, he barely noticed my presence next to hers, and each time I touched his foot with mine he moved away. Ollie was good, the second-best charlatan in the room, yet the thought did not fill me with comfort.

Alistair placed his napkin on the table, untidily folded. 'Excuse me.'

'I'll visit the bathroom too,' Ollie said. 'Am I alright to use the one upstairs?'

'Yeah,' Alistair replied. 'Knock yourself out.'

I gathered the dinner plates, clinking them loudly. 'Would you like a coffee, Elena?'

'Yes. Thanks.'

I waited in the kitchen until I heard the upstairs bathroom door open, then sprinted up the stairs, calling something about 'my spare rubber gloves'. I found Ollie on the landing; his hands rammed in his trouser pockets.

'What the hell are you up to?' Ollie snapped. 'Trying to set me up with Elena?'

'It wasn't my idea.' I showed him my best miserable expression and tried to touch his face. 'She asked if Alistair had any single friends and he suggested you. What could I say? If I said no, he'd be suspicious and then you'd be pissed with me for letting the cat out of the bag.'

'Yes. I would. And what are you playing at with those photos?'

'I thought taking photos of what he did to me would scare him – stop him hurting me.'

Ollie looked past me and to the pictures hanging on the wall. I'd chosen each one myself. Alistair and me when we got married in the Seychelles; a wedding without a congregation on account of my 'heartbreak' at not having my mother around. A photo of my beautiful mum before she got ill. A photograph I'd taken of a stormy sky and waves crashing against the rocks. The frames used to be straight and square, though the slamming of doors and the throwing of objects had left them crooked.

'Him? Al did that stuff to you? He looked innocent to me.'

'He doesn't want you to know what he's like. You aren't the only person in the world who likes it rough.' I pulled down his zipper and wrapped my hand around him. 'I've had enough, Ollie. I want us to be together properly.'

'We can't.' Ollie sighed and tried to pull away from me. 'This is a mess. A fucking mess. It needs to stop.'

His words turned my stomach into a coiling python. It could not stop: it would not stop until I'd bled my husband dry, stashed his money somewhere safe, and become the permanent, with-legal-rights resident of Ollie's queen-sized bed.

'I won't let you dump me, Ollie. I'll tell him if I have to.'

I regretted my threatening tone immediately; roleplay and coercion were always better than threat.

The tension started at Ollie's hands and finished at his muscular stomach. 'I sacked somebody today. I sacked him because he spoke to a competitor about something which got him a few personal perks but cost me money. His name's Duncan. Nice bloke. Three young boys. Married to Paula, a classroom assistant. He's forty-six, so he'll struggle to get another job so they'll probably lose everything. You see, Duncan didn't open his mouth because he is inherently disloyal – he wanted to improve his little world. But I don't allow people to better themselves at my expense. I annihilate them before they have the chance to damage me. Do you understand what I'm saying, Celia?'

'Of course.' I would need to be very smart, cover my tracks, and Ollie would have to come willingly without realising it. 'We stay a secret.' I stood on tiptoes and kissed his neck. 'Do you want Elena?'

Ollie gripped my hips so tightly I felt his bones on mine. 'I'll go back to her house if the opportunity arises. It'll look good if nothing else.'

'Go back to her house but don't have sex with her. Please.'

'We won't have sex. Not a chance.'

He wasn't lying. I licked the pretend pre-cum off my thumb and Ollie's jaw tightened; banging me until I cried lurked at the forefront of his mind. I shot him my best fuck me eyes and scurried to the bathroom to get the rubber gloves.

Elena stretched and glanced at the clock. 'Crickey. Is that the time? I better go.'

'I'll walk you around, Onion.' Ollie got to his feet. 'You've been drinking. Somebody needs to make sure you don't accost any teenagers.'

'Erm, I'm fine, thanks.' She fidgeted with her hair. 'And my name isn't bloody Onion.'

First the flirting and then a fucking nickname.

I swallowed hard then pointed at the box of DVDs sitting in the corner, the ones I'd promised to lend her. 'Don't forget those. Can you manage it on your own?'

'I'll carry it,' Ollie offered. 'Honestly, it's no trouble.'

Elena, babbling and nervous, asked if she could visit the loo before she went. Ollie left the room to put on his shoes and, not wanting a confrontation with Alistair while they were still around, I scooped the dirty glasses from the table and scurried to the kitchen. Shit. Ollie stood in there, leaning against the table, with the photos in his hand.

'What are you doing?'

Ignoring me, he studied the prints, one by one. He paused at the one of me, legs akimbo on his bed, then stopped at the one showing my mouth crammed with fabric. Ollie wasn't stupid. He recognised his black sheets and the improvised gag. Elena peered around the door, and he casually returned the photos to the freezer top.

'Thanks for tonight, Celia.'

I hugged her. 'It's my pleasure. Now, don't let Oliver lead you astray.'

26

ELENA

Bloody hell. I was one drink away from swaying and slurring my words again. Doing something stupid was probably inevitable. I only hoped I wouldn't drop the confessional bombshell that I'd fallen madly and fathomlessly for Ollie's best friend.

'Would you like me to make you a coffee?' Ollie asked.

'Oh, erm. I'll do it, but thankyou anyway. Would you like one?'

Ollie smiled. He had a nice smile and nice grey-blue eyes. Not that they always looked nice. Off-guard they were bluer and twinkly, but with his guard up, they were cold enough to freeze sand.

'Please. Black. No sugar.'

I stared at my glass kettle while Ollie pressed the air beside me. I concentrated on the light changing from blue to orange as the water got hotter. The bubbles grew bigger, more riotous, and the heat from his body reached mine. Ollie's fresh aftershave touched my nose. The light turned red, and the switch flicked.

'I like your kettle,' Ollie said.

'Thanks.'

A heaped spoon of coffee into his mug. Half a dozen coffee granules on the counter. A heaped spoon of coffee into my mug. Half a dozen coffee granules on the floor. Not good at all.

'You shouldn't be here,' I said. 'You could be a murderer for all I know.'

'I'm totally trustworthy – and it never crossed your mind before.'

'We were never alone in my house before.'

'Phone Al for a reference. We've been best mates since we were twelve. He knows me better than my ex-wife.'

'That won't be necessary.' I filled the mugs, stirring and contemplating as I went. 'Why doesn't Alistair call you Ollie?'

'He says it's because he'd called me Andre for too long to stop.'

'Why did you change your name?'

'I didn't. Oliver's my middle name. I never liked Andre, so I stopped using it when I went to uni.'

'Oh.' Some coffee granules bobbed to the surface. The water wasn't hot enough to dissolve them, though my determined, exuberant stirring would. 'So, what's the strangest chat-up line you've ever received?'

He rubbed his chin, feigning contemplation. 'Hmmm. "You could be a murderer for all I know!" What's the strangest chat-up line you ever received?'

'"I like your kettle!"'

Not that it was true. On the first attempt, Ollie said my leather satchel made me look like a 'fox on pheromones', and on the second he asked me if I could be tempted by a clotted cream scone. Which worked, obviously.

He nodded at my sofa. 'Mind if I sit down?'

'I suppose not. Considering you haven't got a history of homicide.'

'She fell for it.' Ollie did an evil chuckle and wiggled his fingers like a creep. 'I can't believe she fell for it!'

I quickly decided I still liked this version of Ollie. In work, he was absolutely vile. I'd met some arrogant dickheads in my time, but he easily topped the tree. Away from work, the different Ollie emerged. He made me laugh and he didn't take himself seriously at all. He referred to himself as a dictator, told me about his obsession with antibacterial cleaner, and admitted he used caffeine shampoo because he was, 'Shit scared of his hair falling out'.

'So,' I started, feeling inquisitive and brave, 'why did you tell me about this house? To get back into my knickers?'

'No, but if you're offering...' I play punched his leg and he rubbed it theatrically. 'I wanted to help. I felt guilty, Onion. If it wasn't for me, you'd have still been with him, got a couple of kids. I wanted you to have a good place to get your life back together.'

I tapped Ollie's hand. 'Thank you. I'm touched. And there I thought you were an arrogant, domineering git.'

'I am.' Ollie's face changed, light to dark. 'Hey, Al seemed a bit off tonight. Has Celia mentioned a fallout or anything?'

'No. He didn't seem much different from the last time I visited their house. Perhaps he's shy.'

Ollie pulled the cushion from behind him and bashed it back into shape. I noticed an orange stain in the corner, but I ignored it, said nothing. It must have happened at the party.

'He's not shy.' He crammed the cushion between his body and the sofa, then shuffled on the seat to get comfy. 'You could drop that big Irish goon in the middle of a war zone and he'd come out with a carload of new mates. They've fallen out about something. Come on, tell me. Has she maxed out his credit card or is she seeing somebody else?'

I laughed. 'She doesn't seem the type to do either.'

'Go on, tell me, Onion. Or do I have to torture it out of you?'

Ollie started to tickle me, ribs and tummy. I was close to wetting myself, and if I lost a drop, he'd send Tena Lady to my office on a weekly basis. Ollie loved winding me up more than he loved making money. He admitted it once when he phoned me up drunk. Hence, why he sent a stripper to work on my birthday; hence, why he called me Onion – multi-layered and with the ability to make a grown man cry, apparently.

'Who does he reckon she's screwing around with?' he asked.

He tickled on and I laughed hard, despite his insane inquisition pushing me to the shame of incontinence. Oh, bugger it. I tickled him back. Well, I tried, but I couldn't get past his arms or stone-hard stomach to find his ribs. He took my hands in turn and pinned them onto the sofa behind my head.

The thread of the conversation suddenly struck me as odd. 'Why are you so interested in what Celia does and what Alistair thinks?'

'I'm not. I'm joking.' His cushion flopped over the arm and fell on the floor. 'I reckon their marriage is bombproof.'

Nausea passed in a wave. 'I hear them argue quite a lot...'

'Means nothing. They've always argued. Celia is totally obsessed with Al. She crowds him and he likes his peace. It's a recipe for blazing rows.'

'Alistair always seems mild-mannered to me.'

'He is, but she pulls his strings big time.' His cheek twitched and a laughter line beside his mouth deepened. 'Anyway, back to you. I quite fancy pulling your strings again.'

I glanced at my hands. Ollie's fingers were between mine, our palms pressed together. Unlike Alistair's, his hands didn't shield mine completely. Alistair's hands were big, the pads of skin on his palms and fingertips thick and strong. Maybe I hadn't drawn a line under the Alistair thing after all.

'We wouldn't work, and I don't want a relationship,' I said.

'What about a one-night stand?'

Shaking my head, I laughed playfully. Though rather than push him away, I pulled him closer. I wanted to be wanted, to be held, to forget the total mess which was my life. Ollie kissed me on the lips, so softly I hardly felt it, and it brought back every wonderful moment and every painful consequence.

'For the record, Elena, I don't want a relationship either. I've got enough on my plate.'

'Oh.'

Though a little kiss wouldn't do any harm.

27

CELIA

Ollie's kitchen was twenty-one degrees, according to the thermostat on the wall. Not that it felt it. Crystals of ice filled my body, and the air between us seemed charged and uncertain.

I'd messed up.

I did not mean for Ollie to see the photos, so my tactics needed to evolve, and coercion would be accompanied by threat. That said, threatening everybody could work. Alistair would get back in line to stop me incriminating him, and Ollie would play nice because he knew if I blabbed to Alistair, he'd lose us both. I just needed to make sure Alistair and Elena didn't get it together until Ollie would commit to me.

'Why did you take the pictures?' he asked.

I looked away from the lying thermostat and shrugged, chewing my lip. 'I suppose I got off on it.'

'What, knowing what we did or thinking you could fuck me over?'

I smiled and took Ollie's privilege-smoothed hand. 'I had no intention of fucking you over, Ollie.'

His face twitched with affection, and his eyes darted to the door. 'Okay, I believe you. Let's go upstairs.'

I climbed the stairs, stroking the white oak handrail with my fingers, with Ollie one step behind me. He tipped my chin and kissed me before pulling me towards a guestroom.

'Go in there and take off your clothes.'

I had never set foot in his enormous guest-room. The queen-sized bed, quilted and sheeted in white, looked marooned, no nightstands beside it, and no wardrobe on a facing wall. Just a red chaise longue, which I touched.

'What do you want?' he asked.

I circled my finger on the red velvet, which held the pattern like a target. 'I want sex. With you.'

He smirked with that smug, self-satisfied smile of his, so I took my fingers from the comforting fabric and moved them to the buttons of my top. Ollie liked to watch and so I made a show out of removing my clothes, touching myself as a went, wanting to get back in his favour. Still fully clothed, Ollie looked me up and down like I was an object for his enjoyment. He usually folded my clothes and piled them neatly, but he left them on the chaise where I threw them. My vest lay trapped in a crumpled ball beside a bra strap, and my pretty red knickers slid on the floor.

I smiled. 'What are you waiting for?'

'I don't want you, Celia. I'm not interested. Now, can you stop throwing yourself at me like this. It's not fair.'

'What!'

Ollie, looking even smugger than usual, pointed towards the corner of the room. I followed his line of sight and saw a small black object.

A fucking video camera.

'You can get your clothes on now. I've got what I need. Well done.'

Well done.

The words mirrored those said by the exploitative bastard who stole my virginity on my sixteenth birthday, as if my tolerance had been a choice, something of which to be proud. I used the same words when the exploitative bastard drew his last breath.

I slammed my hands into Ollie's chest and he stepped away, his jaw slack. 'Delete it now. Delete that fucking film. I don't want you to have a film of me.'

He folded his arms and grew meaner and more intimidating. 'Tough.'

I didn't foresee the anger, but it came. Orange-red and spewing, burning a path through everything I had wanted. I wanted to kill Ollie. I wanted to torture him and then kill him. Watch him cough and vomit, see his eyes bulge in their sockets.

'You've nobody to blame but yourself. I wouldn't have made the film if you hadn't cooked up a scheme to drop me in the shit with my best mate.'

I grabbed a candle holder and slung it at him. It smacked his shoulder and ricocheted into the wall. 'None of this would have happened if you hadn't stuck your cock in your best mate's wife.'

Ollie's fists balled, the tendons taut and the veins proud. 'Yes, you're right, and it's time I stopped.'

Something emanated from him then, something callous and resentful. Something had changed.

'Did you fuck Elena last night?'

'No.'

'Did you touch her? Kiss her?'

He glared at me. 'Yes, and you can't complain because you set the whole thing up.'

I snagged my foot in my knickers and scraped the back of my thigh when I yanked them up.

'I wanted you to flirt with her. Put on a show in front of Alistair. Not fucking seduce her. How dare you! How dare you disrespect me like that? Finding out you already knew her was bad enough, but then you have the audacity to...'

I pulled on my top, leaving off the bra. My body felt sullied, marred by his actions and broken promises, and I wanted it hidden. And as for that fucking bitch, she had caught the eye of my husband and my lover. Talk about adding insult to injury.

'Is there anything you want to tell me? About you and her?' I fastened my buttons. One, two, three.

'There is no me and her.'

'What about before?'

Ollie plonked on the chaise, crumpling my jeans. 'It doesn't matter.'

'Yes, it does.'

'Fine, we had a thing years ago. I split with Suzie, but she wouldn't leave that cheating husband of hers.'

I sat down before I fell. 'You were screwing Elena at the same time as me?'

'Elena and I weren't like that. We had coffee and chatted on the phone. We only slept together once.'

I wrapped my arms around myself and tucked in my hands, holding myself together, bracing myself for the inevitable realisation. 'Bullshit.'

'It's the truth.'

Sadness and despondency filled his tone, though definitely not regret.

'You were in love with her?'

Ollie focused on a spot on the wall, an invisible spot.

I asked him again, accused him again, but he said nothing. 'Answer me, for fuck's sake. Answer me.'

He gave me silence, probably not wanting to say the wrong thing, but his lack of response said everything. He was in love with Elena while he courted me.

It fell into place, piece by painful piece. 'You were the man who made her pregnant!'

Ollie growled and scrubbed his face. 'Yes.'

I bounced to my feet; my legs reinforced with steel. I would not fall. Nothing could break through my rage. I wrenched the rest of my clothes from under him.

'So, you orchestrated the whole fucking thing. You put her on our street so you could keep her close and go for round two.'

Ollie shook his head defiantly. 'No – not that it would ever happen. She made that very clear after I left Suzie, when she still carried my child. I told Elena about the house to help her get back on her feet.'

'But you wanted her. I don't understand what's so brilliant about her.'

His eyes ran the length of the room. 'Elena's a ray of sunshine. She smiles and you can't help being happy when you're with her.' His view returned to me. 'And she's honest. The kind of woman I want to marry and grow old with.'

'And I'm not?'

He laughed. 'You didn't actually...?'

'Yes, I did. I only catered to your every fucking whim because I thought you left Suzie for me and you'd commit eventually.' Disgust covered me over like cobwebs, suffocating me with my own fucking web. 'And the engagement ring, the one hidden in your suitcase?'

Ollie's face turned, and I saw every shade. Shock. Fury. Wrath. 'Did you put it on?'

I stared at him blankly.

'I said, did you put it on?'

He stood between me and the door. His hands would fit around my throat and my eyes would bulge. I could read his mind.

'Yes.'

'You had no right, no fucking right to put that ring on your finger.' Ollie grew in height and size and superiority. 'It wasn't for you.'

None of it was. Not his divorce, the ring, or his future. My vest strap dropped and tapped my arm. I shoved it back onto my shoulder and covered my collarbone with my hand. 'You used me. You fucking used me.'

'No, Celia. You used me. I never wanted this mess – I just wanted you to fuck up and fuck off. My only joy comes from seeing you hurt.' He showed me his palms. 'I won't give him up. You're not worth it.'

My clothes felt all wrong. Snagged and turned. My top tight under one arm, my jeans twisted behind a knee. 'Then I'll tell him to spite you.'

'And now we get to the inevitable.' His eyes narrowed. 'All this time I've been carrying on with you – putting up with your shit – because I suspected the first time I said no, you'd say you'd tell Al. But I don't care now I know he realises you're a lying, deceitful bitch. I'll tell him you tried to lure me into your twisted shit, but I turned you down. And when if it comes to it, I'll get the Oscar and you'll end up with nothing.'

'He won't believe you.'

'He will. I'm a better liar than you, Celia. You don't know the half of it.' Ollie squared up his shoulders, asserted himself. 'Make sure you lock the door. And put the spare key you stole from my office through the letterbox – you don't need it anymore.'

I fixed my stare on the doorway long after Ollie had passed through it. He'd lied to me. Deceived me. Insulted me. Planted her in my world and treated me like a fool. He had fucked up big time and he would pay.

They all would.

I did to others as others had done to me.

And I had been humiliated and trapped. I would humiliate Elena and trap Alistair – because he could keep me whether he liked it or not. And as for Ollie, fucking Ollie, he'd wish he were dead by the time I'd finished with him.

28

ELENA

I sat back in my chair and patted my overly full stomach, while Celia, her wineglass in one hand, picked at the scraps of chow mein. I'd eaten too much, far too much for a pair of skinny jeans. They were an impulsive purchase from earlier that day – those and a set of tea towels embroidered with butterflies.

'You make great Chinese food, Elena.'

I fished out and ate a bean sprout, risking explosion. 'I either learned or did without. I can't risk the groundnut oil in a takeaway.'

'You have a peanut allergy?' she asked.

'Yes, a rather severe one, actually.'

'That's not so good.' With her brows pressed together, she twirled a noodle around her fork until the end tucked in neatly. 'Noodles remind me of the night I ate Chinese, then foolishly rode the Waltzers at the fair. Regurgitated noodles everywhere – I looked like Davey bloody Jones.' She hung her fingers from her jaw, like fake tentacles, then made a monster noise. 'I thought I'd never eat Chinese again. But no, a day later and I was back at the trough.'

She never failed to make me chuckle. Once we'd exhausted the subject of vomit, we veered onto gynaecological examinations and getting caught short on walks in the countryside. We laughed until the tears stung my eyes and the get-to-the-toilet-before-you-pee-on-your-chair alarm sounded in my head. I excused myself and went to the bathroom.

Celia was refilling my glass when I returned, which I found odd, as I was certain I left it almost full. Momentarily, I remembered a talk they gave us at college about not leaving drinks unattended; though they also talked about not sleeping in the showers or climbing in tumble dryers, which were stupid things – along with the theory that I needed to cling to my drink in my own home.

I retook my seat then shuffled to get comfy.

'I'm not sure about this bottle.' Celia rolled her wine around her mouth. 'It tastes cheap.'

It did taste a little odd, almost bitter. Like effervescent paracetamol minus the saccharine.

'Do you think it's alright?' I asked.

Celia took a big swig. 'Yes. Not much can go wrong with a sealed bottle of wine.' She turned the bottle and checked the label, black with a swirl of silver writing. 'It's Italian, and I've never had a decent Italian red. Al must have bought it.'

The glass creaked when I slid it along the table. 'I think I'll give it a miss.'

Celia pushed it back, looking offended. 'It contains alcohol and it probably cost us eight quid. Please drink it.'

As a teenager, I'd drunk snakebite and alcopops by the pint. 'Go on then. I suppose I've drunk worse.'

By the time I'd emptied my glass, the bottom of the wine bottle randomly confused me. I'd never really noticed the convex bit before. Celia told me they used the bottom as a method of measurement in the olden days, but I couldn't work out how to use it without spilling the contents. I tipped the bottle, and a spot of red landed on the white tabletop. It looked like blood. Transfixed, Celia ran her finger through the drip. She looked weird, though to be fair, everything did. I felt so drunk. The walls moved and moved again, along with my chair.

'I swear there's a conspiracy,' I slurred.

Celia pulled her eyes from the wine on the table. 'Pardon, honey?'

'A conspiracy. Me. Drunk. Again.'

'It's no conspiracy, Elena. You reap what you sow. As you very well know.'

My stomach tightened, forcing the acid up my throat.

'What did you say?' Celia asked.

I couldn't remember saying anything, but the thickness and muddling in my brain meant I wasn't certain. My thoughts swam like custard in a pan of gravy.

'If that's what you want,' she said, her lips out of sync with the words.

I didn't understand. But her gentle hands helped me stand, and I didn't protest.

Celia touched my face, saying, 'Okay, okay. I will.'

Her gentle hand led me through the hall and to my bedroom, where a bed of clouds waited. They floated me through my white wispy thoughts and supported me from my head to my feet. Celia's legs fell on both sides of me, and her lips fell on mine. I tried to tell her to stop, but the instructions from my brain came in a different language to what my muscles understood. No words came. My jaw felt heavy, my tongue lazy and thick.

'You suggested this, Elena. Don't you forget that.'

I didn't understand. I didn't understand.

Celia kissed me while I laid there, silent, trapped in my non-responsive body. She did things to me, physical things, sexual things. Then she told me she'd made a mistake, and I'd blackmailed her into doing it, and I needed to disappear before I ruined her and Alistair and ruined myself in the process.

She left then, her feet half in her shoes and her clothes creased. I picked a long black hair from my pillow, the only evidence of what had just happened, and I threw it, revolted. Yet it clung on, it simply wouldn't go, along with the taste of her lip balm, and the smell of her skin. I started to cry. Really cry. Because I knew, suspended in the unreality of disbelief and hurting, that I'd probably ruined everything already.

Some things simply couldn't be undone.

29

ALISTAIR

The dream, like a lot of them, involved my mousy-haired neighbour and me. Except this time, we were at the seaside, on a boat, and an octopus threw us a tub of vanilla ice cream and two spoons. We laughed and kissed, and she brushed the sand off my shoulders, where it had stuck to the sun lotion. Then the intimate taste of a woman replaced that of vanilla.

What the…

Consciousness arrived with a sonic boom. I opened my eyes and came face-to-face with my wife, grinning like the devil incarnate. Her fingers filled my mouth. I pushed her away.

Celia scrambled to her knees, fluffed up her pillows, and rearranged the pile. 'Come on. We haven't had sex for months.'

I wiped my mouth and stared at my lipstick-smeared hand in disbelief. She didn't wear lipstick. 'Celia, what the hell are you up to?'

Flick. The real Celia returned, and I swore she cackled. A hundred years earlier, she'd have been tied to a dunking stool. She clambered off the bed and stood over me, looking down at me, then she pulled her hair into a thick rope.

'Okay, I'll just say it. Me and Elena got it on tonight. I loved every second and so did she. And if I think you've so much as looked at her, I'll fall into her bed again and punish you with every last detail. Are we reading from the same page, honey?'

Celia twisted the rope of hair tighter and tighter until it wound back on itself and made a knot. She let go, but the knot did not fall.

'No, we're not,' I said. 'You're not right in the head. You need help and I'm offering it for the last time.'

The duvet puffed when she sat, and the mattress bottomed out on the bedframe. 'Fine.'

Her turnaround stopped my breath, stunned me, had me scanning the room for something – a trap, a sniper, I really didn't know. Celia didn't deny her condition or swear, and her hands stayed gripped in her lap, not pummelling me.

'I'll help you, but we're through. I can't live like this anymore. I want a divorce,' I told her.

I expected the words to stick in my throat and I expected her to respond with hellfire. But it never happened. We looked at each other, forced together but a world apart. The clock chimed in the hall; twelve bongs, all separated by silence. Calm replaced escalation. Or resignation. And I dared to hope I might finally escape without backlash. Celia hugged her knees. She looked tiny and broken, like my words had thrashed the demon out of her.

'I don't know how things got this bad, Celia, and I'm sorry if any of it's because of me.'

I promised to love and protect her, and I'd failed at both. I'd tried, I really had, but my love had gone up like a hedgehog in a bonfire and I couldn't stop her hurting the pair of us.

'Do you really want a divorce?'

'Yes,' I said.

Her shoulders slumped the same as mine. Celia hid her face and her body began to shake. I apologised for upsetting her, and said I'd help financially and find her somewhere to live. Through her sobs, she asked if anything would change my mind. I said no and left her there.

The bathroom mirror showed my dark puffy eyes and grey skin. I was scrubbed and mangled and at the end of my rope. I'd had enough. If she ran to the police, I'd deal with it – the photos were nothing to do with me and she'd fabricated the diary, so it would be her word against mine. I reckoned if I offered her enough money, she'd leave without a fuss anyway.

I tracked the cracks on the ceiling as I took a piss. One led to another, like a journey, and then crash, a new crack appeared. The bathroom door bounced off the wall, and the force of it launched the shampoo bottles and razor into the bath. A line of cold crossed my back, followed by a splurge of hot. I spun around, reaching behind me, and watched in disbelief as she slashed my stomach too.

'How dare you cast me aside like a piece of fucking rubbish?' she screeched, slicing the air.

I jumped out of her way just in time. She lunged forward and slipped on the blood. I grabbed her wrist, and she struggled and fought with her teeth, nails and fists. I'd never seen her so angry, so vicious. She came at me again, teeth bared like a Pitbull, and I shoved her against the wall. The air whooshed from her lungs and the Stanley knife hit the floor.

And I lost my shit.

Celia clawed at my hand, trying to get it off her throat. She stared at my fist, drawn back, hard as a brick, ready to smash into her face. It burned white-hot inside me, filling my chest and arms. I wanted to hurt her, make her suffer, like she had me.

Celia froze, her eyes dark slits. 'Go on then, Alistair. Fucking hit me.'

The years of anger and frustration stretched me like rubber, and I couldn't hold it back. The smashing sound bounced from glass to tiles. Celia screamed and dropped to her knees, and flakes of paint and crumbled plaster covered her over like sugar sprinkles on a poisoned cake. I stepped away, my hands on my head, my heart banging; trying to ignore the adrenaline and the testosterone, and every fibre in my biology which told me to fight. And, yeah, I'd fight it with every ounce of strength I had.

I wouldn't hit her. I'd smash the house up first.

Celia reached for the knife. It skated and turned. I went to kick it away, but she got there first. I leapt on her, knocking her on her back, and a jolt of pain shot through my arm. It shot again, deeper still, when I pinned her arms above her head. She bit my chest and smacked her heels into my calves, bucking like a horse. I dropped my weight to restrain her.

Eventually, she stopped still.

I sat back on my haunches and pulled the knife from the top of my arm. I retracted the blade and tossed it behind the toilet.

Celia gasped for air. 'You will pay for dumping me, Alistair. I swear you will fucking pay.'

She wrapped her arms around her stomach and chest. The last of the knot in her hair unravelled and fell. A scale of grey paint landed on her leg.

'I think I've paid quite enough.' I glared at her. 'Now, pack some things and get out of my house.'

My boxer shorts felt wet, front and back. I counted three cuts on my stomach; two of them were big cat scratches, but one gaped, spewing blood onto my boxers. I grabbed the hand towel, pressed it against my stomach, and craned my neck to see my back. The incision was even worse, deep and about eight inches long. The blood poured. Wincing, I pressed the edges together and pushed down hard.

I'd never asked for help before. I'd dealt with everything myself: the cuts, bruises, broken ribs, and shame. Because I could – and because I wasn't man enough to admit I let my wife hurt me. But I was bleeding a lot and my swollen hand throbbed like a pulse. I needed help. I needed to get to A&E and then I needed to talk to somebody.

I couldn't fix the mess on my own and I no longer wanted to.

30

ELENA

The feather pillow was a brick next to my bones. Hungover didn't come close. My head banged, my eyes heaved in their sockets, and my stomach churned as if on the backend of a sickness bug. I remembered eating and throwing up, but the hours in between were blank with the occasional minute of visual. Falling in the hall. Celia peering up at me. Celia telling me she'd made a mistake and I needed to move away. I pulled the duvet up to my chin and blew out hard. I needed to apologise to Celia and promise her I wouldn't tell a soul.

We could pretend it never happened.

I hoped.

The twenty steps to Celia's front door were an endurance test, and the apprehension made me think of high zip wires and a full bladder. I knocked on the door, then I knocked on it again. The key scratched around the lock, the door finally opened, and my heart sank. Alistair. The last person I wanted to see. He rammed his hands in his pocket and raised an eyebrow.

'Alistair. Your car isn't here.' I peered over my shoulder, confirming what I thought I knew. 'I assumed you were at work. Is Celia in?'

'No.'

'Okay.' I crossed one foot over the other, and the flip-flop tapped on the ground. 'I'll come back later.'

His eyes softened, but not his scowl. 'She won't be here later. She's not coming back.'

Celia must have told Alistair about us. I'd heard them arguing from my inelegant vantage point in front of the toilet in the early hours. What if they fought, and he'd gone too far?

He started to close the door, though I barrelled inside.

'I hear you arguing and smashing things up in the garage, so I know you've got a nasty temper. Have you done something to her?'

Alistair denied both his temper and the suggestion that he'd hurt her, but his blanched face told me different. Something was wrong, very wrong; I sensed it in the stillness of him, in his posture, the way he held himself too upright and too tight. Lucas did the same on the defensive, as did many of the people I encountered in court. He blinked, and I noticed the nervous flick of his eyes. In the direction of the floor.

At the large canvas bag on the floor.

In which Celia's body would fit.

A high-pitched buzzing filled my ears, like that from rock concerts or chronic anxiety. I leaned away and grabbed the door frame behind me. My thumb touched smooth oak and my fingers rough brick. I wanted to run, run and run, though my legs wouldn't move.

'Oh, my god.' My eyes stung, wide open and dry. 'Oh, my god.'

Alistair's line of sight followed mine. His lips turned at the corners, then his face crumpled into a wince. He might have cursed. The zip snagged, such was his impatience, his rush to open it, and he trapped his skin. He might have cursed again.

Though eventually it came open, upon which he tossed sports equipment against the radiator and on the floor.

'Cricket bat. Pads. Gloves. Helmet. Balls.'

I curled my toes, gripping my flip-flops, ready to run. A spot of blood beaded on his finger.

'Now, please. You need to go, Elena. Just go and stay away.'

'Absolutely,' I said to him. 'I will.'

31

ALISTAIR

The kitchen didn't feel like it usually did in the morning.

Something felt wrong.

I searched the floor for anything like glass or bleach and checked the knobs on the gas hob. I opened the fridge. The milk smelled alright though I tipped it away anyway, then I threw the cheese, butter, and everything from the fridge in the bin. I emptied the bread bin and the freezer too. Just in case.

I braced my arms against the table, careful not to stretch the stitched skin on my stomach and back, and looked around. A ten-kilo weight sat on my chest. Then I realised. My cat, Fluffy, wasn't at my feet, meowing like she'd not eaten in a year. I called her name, opened the back door and called her again, though still she didn't come. With my phone to my ear, I stuck my head in the dining room. Her favourite chair sat empty. She wasn't on the landing where the hot-water pipes passed under the floor either. Barry answered the phone.

'Morning, Al. What's up?'

'Mate, I won't be in for the next few days.' I peered under the stairs and saw the empty cat basket. 'I've got a few things to deal with.' I didn't mention the twenty-eight stitches running across my back or the dozen in my arm or the Steri-strips holding my stomach together. 'Call me if you have any problems.'

'Sure. Is everything alright?'

'Aye, it's fine. See you in a day or two, Baz.'

Yet again, I held back the truth. I still wanted to be the guy who laughed and joked about his random accidents. I didn't want the judgement or pity. Which was the reason I left the victim support leaflet at the hospital and why I didn't tell Elena what really happened the night Celia left.

I wriggled my un-socked feet into my favourite trainers and ambled out into the garden, calling the cat's name as I went. I opened the garage door, though she didn't come out creating, and I pressed my hands to the summer house window and checked in there too. It was then I noticed a little ball of fur between the rhododendron and the side of the shed.

I reached out and curled my hand around her. The wound on my back stretched and threatened to tear. Fluffy's shallow breaths hardly moved her body, and her glazed eyes stared back at me. Dried vomit covered her white fur. I ran to the house and grabbed the car keys. Then I spotted the almost finished bowl of food on the floor. Blue-green specks dotted the brown of the meat.

'What the… Slug pellets. Bloody slug pellets.'

I put my cat in her basket and sprinted to the car.

32

ELENA

The bed sheets waved from the washing line, beckoning me outside. Earlier in the day they'd looked fresh and bright, though the dropping sun left them sad and sorry. I needed to get them in. Glad of the fading light, I gingerly walked across the decking and down the steps to the lawn.

As I dropped the first peg into the basket, I heard a heavy spade slice through the ground. I sneaked back into the house, tiptoed upstairs, and stuck my head through the dormer window. My hands flew to my mouth. Alistair was in his garden, digging a very big hole between the garage and the summerhouse.

Ten minutes later, he went to the house, then returned carrying something across his arms: something large, wrapped in a purple throw. He placed the wrapped object into the hole and slowly shovelled the soil back in. I watched him wince, screw up his eyes, and take deep breaths that he blew out through his mouth. Everything spoke of regret. After backfilling the hole, he patted the surface and plodded back to the house.

He had killed Celia.

He'd killed her and buried her in the garden.

Unable to trust my jelly legs, I sat on the stairs and phoned 999.

During the next few hours, the street turned into a scene from a TV drama. Two police cars arrived and one took Alistair away, whilst the forensics team erected a tent and floodlights in the garden. Reality brought with it a grim feeling which sat in my bones. Celia's eyes would be vacant and staring, and her beautiful skin would be waxy and cold. I could not see her body being lugged across the lawn in a body bag, so I forced down a glass of water and climbed into bed.

I needed to have a clear head by morning; the police would be around with questions, and I might have been the last person to have seen her alive. My chest screwed up tight and my eyes filled with tears.

Poor Celia.

What had he done?

The next day, I pulled back the living room curtains to discover a distinct absence of police vehicles or cordoning. The street had reverted to a scene of suburban tranquillity, and it turned out I'd been horribly mistaken. According to my neighbour, the police unearthed the very suspicious parcel, though it only contained a well-worn cat bed and a poisoned cat. I felt terrible, and I needed to say sorry.

Alistair looked absolutely dreadful when he answered the door; his eyes were bloodshot, and he moved like clingfilm wrapped his torso. He smiled weakly, opened the door and stepped back inside, so offering me an informal invitation to enter.

Celia had obviously gone. The curtains hung unevenly, one tucked behind the radiator, and the smell of fresh minerals and outside air replaced that of jasmine and body lotion.

'Alistair. I'm so sorry for phoning the police. For everything.'

He shrugged and placed two steaming cups of coffee on the table. 'It gave me the chance to tell the police some stuff. Not that I want to press charges.'

'Charges for what?'

Alistair creaked to his feet and shuffled to the counter, where he opened the small window, adding it to the big ones already open and straining their hinges. He returned to me and placed his hands on the table, weighing things up.

'Elena, I want to tell you something. I tried to tell you before, but I felt too ashamed.' Alistair pressed his finger on a grain of spilled salt, then set his hazel eyes on me. 'Our marriage has been abusive for a long time.'

His admission knocked me sideways. 'You can get help for the anger or whatever makes you—'

Alistair raised his T-shirt, and my words stopped.

He didn't abuse Celia. She abused him.

The worst cut extended for about seven inches, held together with crusty blood and white adhesive strips. Shallower cuts surrounded it, haphazard and scattered in a frenzy. Alistair turned around, and I almost vomited the dry toast, acid, and regret from my body. The cut on his back was worse, much worse, long and deep enough to be sutured with proper stitches.

'She did that?'

'Yes, after she came back from your house. Though I suppose it's a blessing in disguise, because she can't pretend it was an accident or self-defence. She can't lie her way out of this one.'

The coffee burned my tongue and throat when I swallowed it down. I placed the mug on the table and asked Alistair what happened and how on earth things got so bad.

'Celia woke me up and we argued. I told her I wanted a divorce, so she sliced me across the back when I turned away. Went for my stomach when I turned around.'

I almost felt it, the pain of it, the shock, and the tears came despite my wanting to be strong. Alistair handed me a sheet of kitchen roll so I could wipe my eyes and blow my nose.

'I've got something to tell you, too.' I looked skyward. 'Something happened when Celia came to my house.'

'I know. She told me.'

Alistair reached out and took my hand. I opened my fingers and his fingers dropped between mine like we'd done it a thousand times.

'I didn't even want to. I promise. She said I told her to do it, then threatened to ruin me if I didn't keep away from you. Though I don't know exactly what happened because I was so ridiculously drunk. It feels like a dream.'

'I'm not sure you were drunk.' He lumbered to the kitchen drawer and threw a small plastic vial onto the table. 'I found this in her gym bag. My guess is it's a date rape drug.'

'What the...'

Everything moved, turned and tipped upside down, and I squeezed Alistair's hand so I didn't fly away.

'I reckon she drugged and sexually assaulted you. Tried to make you think you instigated it all, so you'd be so embarrassed you'd leave. Then she threatened to sleep with you if I so much as looked at you. She was crazy that night, like Jekyll and Hyde. Something's happened and made her snap. You should go to the police – perhaps they can do a blood test to prove it.'

'The drugs will be out of my system by now.' I pinched the bridge of my nose. 'I can't go through questioning and examinations anyway.'

My brain turned to alphabet spaghetti. She forced herself on me and hurt Alistair, seriously and repeatedly, over a long period of time. I didn't realise such things happened to people like us – we were simply too normal, too unassuming, and lacking in vulnerability. Or so I'd naively thought.

'Why, Alistair?' I asked. 'Why did you let her?'

He looked away, tracked a house sparrow flying past the window. 'She used to hurt herself if I upset her – and I thought she was sick. I couldn't do anything because I knew nobody would believe me before she did this. She blackmailed me too.'

Alistair fetched something from the top of the freezer. He tossed a small pile of home-printed photos on the table. I recognised Celia's skin on a photo of a sore wrist and another of a bruised thigh. I cringed at the intimate shots, tried not to see.

'Holy shit.'

'Yeah, she's sleeping with somebody else, but she still told me they'd get me locked up if I stepped out of line.'

'So that's why you've been avoiding me. Alistair, you can't let her get away with doing those things. Especially hurting you like that.'

Lip between his teeth, Alistair stared at the wall.

'Alistair.'

He shook his head. 'I can't have her charged, Elena. I can't face the questions from the police, the solicitors, and I can't face the looks from the people I know. I feel bad enough without everybody knowing, judging, talking behind my back – saying what I should have done when they don't have a clue.'

I squeezed his hand and stroked the knuckles free of gauze and surgical tape. My heart reached out to him. I once worked with a woman who sometimes showed up with bruised skin and bandaged wrists; everyone said she should leave him, that she shouldn't tolerate such things, but nobody really understood. Relationships were never black and white.

'Let them talk, Alistair. Anyway, people will respect you for not retaliating. Like I do. Celia will be the one they think bad of.'

He touched my cheek, then brushed his lips against mine. It tickled and I smiled.

'I'm married until the divorce comes through,' I said.

'So am I.'

'I don't like infidelity.'

Alistair groaned. 'I'll divorce her when she comes out from under her stone, and anyway, there'll be no infidelity until I've been to the clinic. She's been unfaithful and I don't know who with.'

I shuddered inside. 'What if she's lurking around?'

'She isn't,' he said, certainly. 'Celia withdrew two thousand pounds from our current account about an hour ago, at a bank two hundred miles away. They phoned me for the security check.'

'Oh.'

I pulled him as close as I dare. We held each other for a long, long time. Until the practicalities tore us apart. Alistair needed to pack her things, and I had somewhere to be.

'I better go.' I kissed him once. 'I'll see you soon.'

'That you will,' he said. 'If fate is kind.'

33

CELIA

I drove for many miles. In the back of the car was a suitcase crammed with my things. I'd taken nothing extravagant – just essential clothes, a few toiletries, and an envelope containing five thousand pounds. Stupidly, I'd forgotten my expensive engagement ring and passport; though I had remembered to feed Alistair's cat a pouch of salmon cat food, seasoned with a good dose of slug pellets.

Eventually, I stopped in a carpark outside a faceless hotel on the commuter belt. A scruffy bush sat on one side of the entrance and a shiny smoking shelter sat on the other. The place reeked of road fumes and dust. For a while, I sat there, gripping the steering wheel, rendered catatonic by exhaustion and enmity.

Enmity.

I hated them. All three of them. Alistair and Elena had hurt me, insulted me, but Ollie had gone above and beyond. He had lied, exploited and sexually degraded me, then planted the woman he cared for into my life so she could mislead me and finish my marriage.

Alistair wouldn't have turned on me without Elena providing the impetus, and they wouldn't have met without Ollie's interference. The bastard. I wouldn't grant him the luxury of death because he didn't fucking deserve it.

The sign on the hotel said, 'Fifty-nine pounds per person, per night.' I stared at it until the garish red numbers merged into one, defined in the centre and blurred at the edges. Fifty-nine pounds per person. Per person. And therein lay the solution. I would deal with them one by one.

Somebody knocked on my window, breaking my train of thought. I hit the window button, and the window crawled open.

'Good evening.' The man wore a cheap white shirt and a badly knotted tie, which he touched self-consciously. I resisted the urge to tell him to learn how to fucking dress himself. 'I'm sorry, but this carpark is for hotel patrons only.'

He lurched back, narrowly avoiding the car door which I flung open. The ground felt like granite beneath my feet, the pollution-tainted air an unexpected tonic to my lungs. I skirted around the car and flipped open the boot.

'Would you be so kind as to carry my luggage.' I emphasised the carry; I didn't want the wheels dirtying. 'And yes, I packed it myself and it doesn't contain weapons or explosives.'

Yet.

I pointed at the expensive suitcase I bought with the expectation of the Maldives. What I actually got was Cape fucking Verdi. Al knew I hated shitty package holidays. As such, his suitcase never came off the carousel as punishment. He never did work out where the label went.

Without a word, the man hauled the case from my boot and carried it to the foyer, his body lopsided, his strained breaths hidden badly. Regardless, he complied with my request – probably realising I wasn't in the mood to be fucked with.

The hotel room had a grey mottled carpet, chosen to hide the stains, and an insipid print hung on the white wall above the uncomfortable bed. The bathroom had too many spotlights, a tacky shower cap, and tiny bars of soap. Still, the bed, bathroom and Wi-Fi fulfilled my basic needs, and the hotel accepted cash.

I laid on the bed and kicked my legs like a carefree teenager while I picked at my room service and surfed the internet on my newly purchased pay-as-you-go phone. The search items seemed random, but the words I scribbled on the complimentary paper were very significant.

The World Cup was in full swing, and the match itinerary would give the location of both Alistair and Ollie at these times. They watched every match together, alternated between houses, and I knew they were at Ollie's house for the last game. I scribbled down each night-time match and the kick-off time, followed by either an A or O.

My car would be too obvious if I used it; however, if I faked an intermittent engine fault, I could park it away from where I planned to stay and hire another under the guise of my car's unreliability. To qualify my excuse, I booked the car into the local garage for the 'repair' of the untraceable problem in a few weeks' time. Next, I phoned a hire car company and arranged a time for it to be collected. Finally, with the help of Google Maps, I located the perfect hotel and a nearby place to abandon my car until I needed it. I planned routes without traffic cameras and calculated travel times precisely. And then I thanked the internet for its help in my criminal plans and phoned Toby for a chat.

34

ELENA

The bench sat between an oak tree and a silver birch, exactly where Alistair had said. I took a seat on the end, crossed my legs and straightened my skirt. I took out my AirPods and waited. Alistair was late. A woman walked past with two little dogs on extendable leads, which darted and dashed and threatened to topple her. We exchanged a good morning. I picked up my phone and checked it, turned it over in my hand.

Definitely late.

'Hey.'

I raised my head. The first time Alistair and I met, I realised his expressions relayed the emotions in his head; no buffer, no pretence, no subterfuge. Right then, his eyes sparkled, feathers of smile creases around them. Alistair looked happy.

'I was worried you wouldn't come,' I said.

'I told you I would.' He scanned the bench before sitting on the end, farthest from me. His water bottle landed on the seat, followed by the phone from the pocket of his shorts and the earphones from his ears. A little wall of obstacles to separate us. 'Sorry I'm late. I planned to run, then I realised I couldn't...'

Because of the injuries hidden beneath his t-shirt. My belly stung.

'How are you doing?' I asked.

'Fine. They'll be gone in no time.'

My unconvinced smile met his weak one. Alistair told me I looked nice, though the flowery vest and linen skirt suddenly seemed over the top. I wished I'd forgone the lipstick.

What was I doing there? What was I even doing?

I re-straightened my skirt. 'It's lovely, here.'

'It is.'

Alistair stretched out his legs and crossed them at the ankle. The khaki fabric made his skin more golden and the soft hairs more blond. I wanted to touch him, yet I didn't. He told me the cycle path made the best bit of his run, especially where the river split and meandered, and it was always quiet, except at the weekends if it was a sunny day. Our words stopped. We both watched the river a short distance from our enclave.

And then Alistair said: 'I missed you.'

Feeling brave, I crossed the no-man's-land of aged wood and carefully arranged possessions and touched his arm. But only for a moment. 'I missed you too.'

We talked freely then; all awkwardness gone. I'd booked my car in for its first MOT and he'd bought paint from Homebase. Colourful paint to repaint the bathroom when he'd re-plastered in a week or two.

Alistair turned to face me, then bit his lip. 'I'm going to the Lake District for a few days. Would you like to come? I've told Celia she has 'til the weekend to get her stuff. It'd be a good idea if we aren't around.'

'Are you sure?'

'Is that a yes?'

I grinned. 'Erm, yes. I'd love to.'

We laughed about something or nothing and I told a terrible joke, then Alistair said 'shit' twice over. I followed the line of his sight, though I couldn't work out exactly what he referred to, having left my glasses back home.

'What's wrong?'

'Look who's coming,' he said. 'Of all the bloody people.'

I recognised Ollie as he neared, not from his face but from his frame, the structure of him. He held the lead of a small white terrier. Ollie stepped from the path and crossed the longer grass to the bench. He caught a bramble branch which pinged back and lashed a tree, smearing it with fruit which had barely set, let alone had the time to ripen.

He looked between us; both of us teetering on opposite ends of the bench.

'Aye up,' Alistair said to him. 'What are you doing here?'

Ollie put his free hand in his cargo trouser pocket. So many pockets to hide things. 'Could ask you the same question.'

Alistair pointed at his well-worn trainers. 'Running. What about you?'

Ollie pointed at the triangle-eared dog. 'Exercising my mother's dog.' He met my eye. 'What about you, El?'

'Walking.' I held up my AirPods to back up my dishonest claim.

'And your paths just crossed?'

'Yes.'

'Bullshit,' he said.

'Ollie…'

'Does he know?' Ollie snapped.

He glared right at me, excluding Alistair from this thing, whatever it might be. I said Ollie's name again, though it came as a plea. Please don't do this – not here, not now, not ever.

'Do I know about what?' Alistair said.

'About me and Elena.'

Everything stopped. The moment after an explosion in a movie. The moment before the explosion in real life. The bench creaked. I pinched the flesh between my eyes so hard that a throbbing feeling settled on the tip of my nose.

'Are you gonna tell him, or shall I?' Ollie said.

Alistair waited. Ollie stared. And my stomach, the stomach filled with butterflies and hopefulness so recently, hardened like stone.

'We slept together,' I uttered.

'I thought you might,' Alistair said to me. 'But you were both single and drunk. It is what it is.'

Thoughts trickled in my head, like sand in an egg timer. I could lie. I could lie and hope Ollie would back me, to lessen the harshness of the reality. Though one glance at Ollie told me otherwise. 'No, we were both married and sober.'

'I'll leave you to it,' Ollie said, bombshell dropped, feet already in motion, tugging on the dog's lead. 'I'll leave you to it.'

I resisted the urge to yell after him, berate him for ruining things between Alistair and me out of spite. Because, as harsh as it was, if Alistair and I had a future he needed to know.

'We didn't sleep together after the night at yours. It happened a few years ago.'

Alistair stopped scratching a plastic burr on his water bottle and turned his full attention to me. I moved on the creaking bench and prayed it wouldn't splinter and break, make me crumple and fall.

'Lucas and I went through a terrible patch,' I started, 'and what I did made it worse.'

I told Alistair everything about Ollie and me in a long, rambling torrent. About our friendship. About the pregnancy and Ollie leaving his wife. About the upset which ensued and how Lucas made me have the termination that probably meant I would never carry a child again. I told him everything.

Silence.

'Please say something.'

Alistair touched his bottom lip, stroked it softly, then got to his feet. 'I need to get my head around all this. I'll speak to you in a bit.'

He left.

The message came a painful two hours later: Can you be ready for eight in the morning? Can we leave the past where it belongs?

With eyes full of tears, I replied with a yes and a yes.

And I followed the words with a thank you.

35

CELIA

The next hotel was located one and a half miles from the layby on the dual carriageway. Luckily, due to the footbridge and a bridleway over farmland, I could run between the two points in ten minutes and the chance of encountering anyone would be small.

Wearing my most indistinguishable clothes, blue jeans and a grey hooded top, I drove the Polo down the busy bypass towards the lay-by. I indicated in good time, yet a fat-faced man driving a van nearly rear-ended me regardless. I parked a little way from the white static caravan and glanced around as I strolled over, avoiding the shards of red plastic, crisp packets and McDonald's wrappers littering the verge. No buildings overlooked the poorly lit area, and I couldn't see a CCTV or traffic camera. The place was perfect.

They had replaced the original caravan interior with a sectioned off area, most likely the kitchen, and a small cubicle which housed the toilet facilities. At the closest window, overlooking the road, hung an off-white 1980s net-curtain that made the place even more drab. A brown-haired lorry driver sat at one of the plastic tables, a ketchup smeared plate in front of him. He needed a shave.

'Hi.' A portly lady appeared from the sectioned off area. She wiped her hands down her apron. 'What can I get you, my love?'

I glanced along the small counter in search of a menu. The woman pointed to a chalkboard. Full English breakfast, two fried eggs on toast, sausage or bacon sandwich. I felt grimy and greasy before I'd touched or eaten a thing.

'Please may I have a pot of tea and a bacon sandwich? On brown bread.'

The woman exchanged a bemused look with her other customer. 'We only have white.'

Great.

'Then white will be fine.'

She tapped on a chunky buttoned calculator. 'Three ninety please.'

The man sitting in the corner looked back at his phone, having clearly been checking me out. I took a chair at the table alongside his, shot him my sweetest smile and said hello. He might come in useful.

The woman soon arrived with a stainless-steel teapot, a mug, and a jug of milk. Ten minutes later, the bacon sandwich and a bottle of ketchup landed on the table. I said thanks and chatted with her about the weather, the café opening hours, the roadworks on the motorway, and whether she worked full time. Then I apologised for keeping her from her work, a polite dismissal.

'Oh, sorry, I forgot,' I said. 'I'm in a bit of a pickle. I just left the motorway because my stupid car went into limp mode. It's the grey one parked on the end.' I pulled back the net curtain and pointed through the window. 'Will it be okay there until the dealer collects it?'

'I'd have thought so. The road is busy enough at night so it shouldn't get broken into.'

'Do you have security cameras on the caravan?'

She ambled away, shaking her head. 'No. Nothing in here worth pinching, love.'

I peeled the top layer from the sandwich, removed the bits of rubbery bacon fat, and added a few blobs of ketchup. And then I thought while I ate.

The woman worked in the café Monday through to Saturday, seven thirty until four, so she could provide an alibi for the vehicle if need be. Nobody would know if the car disappeared for a few hours one night and returned to the same spot, and there was no covert CCTV to fuck me up. Absolutely perfect.

I dallied over the last few bites of the bacon sandwich and sucked my fingers clean of ketchup. The man alongside me watched. I thought about fucking him. I thought about fucking him over. But instead, I settled for a lift into town.

Following the visit to the car hire shop, I flitted around the town and called into a few places. The first was a skanky corner shop from which I not only purchased milk, but another pay-as-you-go mobile phone. Next, I went to the nondescript hardware store which sold everything from dog baskets and spades to children's books; from there, I bought a small rucksack, disposable nitrile gloves, a red-netted bird feeder, and a travel pack of cosmetic containers that included a perfume dropper. My last port of call was the oriental food store. I filled a basket with rice, a tin of water chestnuts, soy sauce, prawn crackers, and peanut oil; I later dumped most of it in a bin.

The phone box on the high street conveniently accepted coins, so I called our house and then Elena's landline again. Just to be sure. Both of them had picked up the cold calls I'd made the night after I left and neither of them had answered since; it didn't take a genius to work out they'd gone away together. Initially, I'd planned to leave Elena out of the equation and just deal with Alistair and Ollie, but her taking the piss out of me sealed her fate.

A little later, I tucked the car I'd hired into a space between an Aston Martin and a black Range Rover. The gravel crunched under my feet, announcing my arrival at the grand sandstone hotel. Leaded windows and clipped bay trees flanked the entrance, and a suited man wished me a good evening before opening the door.

The hotel was an eight-minute drive away from my marital home: a journey along roads totally devoid of traffic cameras and almost devoid of vehicles. Behind the hotel, a short footpath led to a single-track road, at the side of which sat a disused quarry. The quarry would provide the perfect place to hide my Polo after I'd collected it from the lay-by.

'Good evening.' I smiled beatifically. 'I have a reservation for the next two nights.'

The receptionist asked for my name, tapped away, and then looked up from her ultra-slim screen.

'Please check your details, add your car registration number, and sign here and here.' She placed a stiff piece of cream paper on the desk and smiled. 'And I need you to confirm the credit card details.'

I scribed my name and ran my finger along the summary of charges. One hundred and eighty pounds per night, accounting for the single occupancy discount. Breakfast and evening meals to be added accordingly. With glee, I handed over Alistair's card details; he could pay, what with him having a job.

The room smelled of floral cleaning products and freedom. Original paintings hung on the wall, and tasteful cream soft furnishings adorned the dark-wood furniture. The luxurious carpet swallowed my feet. After a quick stretch, I ambled over to the sash window and peered outside. I could climb out of the window, tiptoe along the ledge, make for the roof of a single-storey boot room, then disappear into the sprawling grounds. With a little more effort, I could retrace the route in the opposite direction. For my plan to succeed, I'd need to leave the hotel without using corridors or shared entrances: I needed to come and go without being seen.

From my case, I removed the bag of toiletries and cosmetics, which I arranged on the glass shelves in the bathroom. I hung my clothes in the wardrobe and placed my underwear in the bedside cabinet. Buzzing with excitement, in a psychotic kind of way, I decided to make my all-important voice recording before I got ready for dinner.

I'd bought the digital voice recorder years before, but had never actually used it. It was a tiny thing, easy to use.

'Hi Alistair, it's me, Celia. I'm so, so sorry.' I held back a vindictive grin, knowing it might change the inflection of my voice. 'Please pick up. I'm sorry you had to find out about Ollie and me like this. I feel dreadful – I really do.'

I paused. Waited. Imagined him coming from the living room, sauntering along the hall.

'Please pick up. I am so sorry. I love you, Al. I made a terrible mistake. I've told Ollie I don't want him. Please give our marriage another chance.'

The woeful explanations and pleas for forgiveness continued for another twenty-six minutes, enough to fill the answer machine capacity. Quite frankly, I deserved a fucking Bafta, but I had to make do with a hot shower, a Michelin starred meal and an early night.

36

ELENA

We were staying in a log cabin, a real log cabin with a terrace overlooking a stream. Inside, comfy red sofas huddled around an open fire, and wood panelling covered the walls. I hung my handbag on a chair and wandered to the kitchen, where I stroked the neatly folded tea towel, then opened the cupboards in turn. A stack of mismatched sandwich boxes and an antiquated cheese grater filled one, and condiments and a plastic salt pot sat in another. I touched the counter to check the place was actually real.

'You like it, sweetheart?' Alistair asked.

'Yes.' I smiled. 'I love it.'

Alistair opened the French doors and stepped onto the balcony, where he leaned on the balustrade and stared out. He suddenly seemed distracted, distant to me. There hadn't been a moment of awkwardness, in the car or on our arrival, though suddenly it seemed to be between us and around us. I loitered, listening to the tinkling water, wondering what to do.

'I'm sorry.' His voice came quiet, the tone heavy.

'What for?'

'Everything.'

The overhanging trees dangled a shadow on the balcony, though I walked right into it to be close to him.

'I've dragged you into this mess. I should have told you I was married right at the start, and I shouldn't have come into your house. I definitely shouldn't have kissed you.'

I touched his hand and rested my fingers between his. 'You shouldn't, but I'm glad you did.'

'You've had enough to deal with without being stuck between me and Celia.' Alistair stroked my knuckles. 'I'm scared bringing you here might have made things even worse.'

'She doesn't know where I am. Anyway, we're here now. We might as well make the most of it.'

'Yeah. I suppose you're right.'

'Of course I am.' I touched the small silver scar that crossed his cheekbone, felt the dent and the rise. 'What are we doing, Alistair?'

He blew out a sigh. 'I'm not sure.'

'Okay, cards on the table. I don't think we should sleep together. Not yet. It's not that I don't want to – because I find you crazily attractive – things just feel too complicated. But I'm okay with kissing. I'd quite like to, actually.'

Alistair took my hand and moved me, putting me between the railing and him. I rested my hands on his forearms. I breathed. He pressed his lips against mine and my tummy flipped. He had the nicest lips, the softest kiss, a contradiction to his hard body, his masculine frame. Alistair tasted of Softmints and liberation – I think we both did – and liberated was suddenly how we seemed.

We decided to make the most of the bright evening and walk to the nearby pub. Light patches littered the tree-lined footpath, falling where the sunlight broke through the canopy. We held hands, kicked stones, and exchanged a consuming kiss before we left our shady tunnel and joined the road for the last hundred yards of the journey.

The Cumbrian pub had a Chiswick feel, aimed at the more affluent tourists I supposed. The original flagstones still covered the floor, but white oak replaced the old dark-wood bar, and every surface sparkled and shone.

'What are you drinking, El?' he asked.

I usually gravitated to wine, decent wine and plenty of it, yet my head swarmed with the indecision of a woman stuck between her past and her future. I felt different and new.

'Whatever you're having,' I said. 'Whatever you're having.'

'A pint of Black Sheep! Are you sure?'

I nodded, and he doubled his order.

We settled for a table in a quiet corner, a sturdy table with a smooth wax finish. He took the chair against the wall while I turned my back to the door. The beer tasted sweeter and more syrupy than I expected, and I rolled it around my mouth while Alistair watched. Something intense settled between us; something which both excited and scared me.

Alistair swallowed. 'I'm starving. I might get a bag of peanuts to eat while we wait.'

'I'd rather you didn't. Me and peanuts don't mix. I've got my trusty EpiPen,' I said, patting my handbag, 'but I'd rather not chance it.'

I told him about an anaphylactic event a few years earlier, courtesy of a pre-packed sandwich, during which I'd have died on the floor of a motorway service station if not for the epinephrine injection.

'I'd rather not chance it either – not now I've found you.' Alistair stroked the hollow sitting between his nose and top lip. 'We'll wait for dinner.'

Dinner was perfect; everything was perfect, really. Alistair and I hadn't known each other for long, though it didn't matter. We exchanged words, silence and expressions, and we held hands across the table, only unlinking fingers to eat and drink. None of my other relationships, fledgling or not, had felt as real. Lucas and I were pragmatic and shiny – magpies furnishing a barren nest. Ollie and I were frivolous and reactive – not that he'd ever admit it. Yet with Alistair, it felt like we'd loved each other before, as silly as that sounded.

I smoothed his ring finger with my thumb. No indent or tan line lingered there – unlike on mine, which still carried the evidence of my failed marriage. 'You really didn't wear your wedding ring.'

'No. Not since I caught it on a nail stuck in some masonry and dislocated my finger.'

Alistair smoothed my ring finger with his thumb. 'I'll wear a ring if we get married. Thought I'd put a pot in the bathroom to keep it safe when I'm on site.'

'I'd like that.' My tummy fizzled at the thought he'd considered our future. 'Though I wish things had happened differently – that you and Celia were long separated and we weren't sneaking around behind her back.'

Alistair drew a triangle in the salt sprinkled on the table. He followed his finger with his eyes, looking resolved. 'I don't care anymore. After all I've done for her, all I've put up with, she killed my cat and attacked me with a knife. I don't feel guilty. Maybe it was meant to be this way. Everything will be fine in the end.'

'I know,' I said.

Though the journey there, to the end, filled me with worry and dread.

The short stroll back from the pub gave time for the two pints of beer, Mediterranean lamb, and a lemon sorbet to go down. Back at the cabin, I ate Pringles until Alistair called me from his place on the rug – the modern rug which looked bizarrely at home in the dated wooden cabin.

'What DVD do you want to watch? Ocean's Eleven. The Da Vinci Code, Mission Impossible or Barney?'

'Isn't Barney the big purple dinosaur for kids?'

'Aye.' He chuckled. 'Lots of singing and dancing. I thought it'd be right up your street.'

'Bugger off.' I half sat, half fell beside him, and playfully slapped his leg. And then I froze. Alistair's wife had been violent towards him for many years, and I didn't know what demons I might have unleashed. 'I'm so sorry.'

'You will be.'

He pushed me down onto the rug and tickled me. Amidst my giggles and screeches, I made a pathetic attempt at retaliation and, forgetting his injuries, lunged for his stomach. Luckily, he pre-empted the attack and grabbed my hands.

Alistair kissed my nose. 'Perhaps you ought to wait until the stitches are out.'

My eyes flooded with sadness and tears.

'Hey, don't get upset. They're clean cuts, so they'll heal in no time. And don't be scared of messing with me, play-fighting, whatever. I'm not messed up.'

He pressed my hands into the rug and kissed me, slowly and purposefully, and I swear the earth actually shattered. He shuffled on top of me, opened my legs with his knees, and I smiled onto his lips. He kissed my nose again, and it was kind of cute.

'Alistair.' I put my hand over his mouth. 'I think we should stop. Things are frustrating enough as it is.'

'You're the righteous one. Not me.'

I huffed and regained my moral high ground, ruining the moment entirely. 'My friend at work specialises in divorce. I can pull some strings?'

'Get me an appointment for Monday and I'll file for the separation.'

I kissed him. 'Good.'

Alistair clambered off me and selected a DVD, The Da Vinci Code. I touched his back, where three little blood spots made a perfect line.

'You're bleeding, Alistair.'

He pulled up his shirt and craned his neck, not that he could see. By lying on top of me, propped up on his forearms, he'd opened the wound in the middle of the diagonal cut.

'Have I burst the stitches?' he asked.

'Very nearly. Don't lie like that again until it's healed.'

I dabbed the beads of blood with a tissue. They disappeared, then reappeared, bright red and imposing. Celia was hundreds of miles away, yet still she hurt him and came between us, making her point.

I'd never suffered from insomnia before, but sleep simply wouldn't come. My brain buzzed on high alert, noticing everything from the big to the small. The clock ticking loudly in the living room. An uneven overlap of the curtains. The questions whirring in my head. The Egyptian cotton sheets hung onto the cold, and the big bed bemoaned with emptiness – like my marital bed the day after Lucas left me.

Yet it was different this time.

Because I didn't want to stretch out and find comfort in being alone; I wanted to curl up and make space for another. Unable to stand having Alistair so close but so distant, I decided to head for his single bed. I switched on the side lamp and pulled my most sensible pair of knickers from the bedside table.

I tiptoed into the next room, where I found Alistair fast asleep in his bed. Tentatively, I lifted the duvet and slid inside. I laid down, put my head on the pillow, and draped my arm across him. Alistair sat bolt upright and raised his hands, searching the speckled light for the person who'd touched him. Shocked, I jumped back and landed heavily on the floor.

'Shit.' Alistair, his hands on his head, dropped on the floor beside me. 'Sorry Elena. Are you alright?'

I rubbed my coccyx and said I was fine.

'I'm so sorry. It's just… don't creep up on me when I'm asleep.'

My mind went there without the explanation: Celia took advantage of his vulnerability while he slept. I started to cry, overwhelmed by it all. Me and him, him and her, and the terrible things she'd put him through.

'I'm sorry, I couldn't sleep.' My nose streamed, along with my eyes. 'Sorry, I'll go back to my bed.'

'Don't do that.' He pulled me close, surrounding me with his arms. 'Not unless you take me with you.'

My bed no longer looked massive with Alistair in it, lying awkwardly on his side, but I wanted to curl up, pull in my limbs, and screw up my eyes. It was all suddenly too heavy, too exhausting, too hard.

Alistair touched my hair, twisted some around his finger, flicked up the end. 'Talk to me. What's wrong?'

He probably expected reserve, a mincing of words, but I babbled everything swirling in my mind. About the hurting. The manipulation. My anger. Alistair replied calmly, almost as if he observed rather than suffered. He said everything Celia did healed, given time, and he was tough, as tough as they came. He would never understand or forgive her, though he could let it go because she would 'get her dues'.

'What did she do to made you so tetchy in bed?' I meekly asked.

Alistair checked the back of his hands. 'Waterboarding. Pillows over my face. Hit me with a cricket bat. But the sexual stuff was the worst. Do you actually want to know this?'

I nodded, uncertain.

'She'd wake me up and threaten me into having sex with her. Then take the mick if I couldn't get it up. I've woke up with her sitting on my face. She's whacked me in the balls. Bit the old fella while I slept like the dead.'

He tried to make light, embarrassed I supposed, though I grimaced in shock, appalled. 'How did you sleep in the same bed as her!'

'I work hard, and I get tired.' He shrugged. 'And it wasn't every night – some good runs were longer than others. It sounds weird, but playing the game – like sleeping in her bed – usually worked. Until recently.'

'So, what changed?'

'You, I reckon.' Alistair circled his finger in my palm. Round and round the garden. One step. Two steps. 'I think she realised I'd fallen for you, panicked and upped the ante.'

I focused on the sound of the scrunching feathers in my pillow and the tickle in my hand, trying not to crumble under the weight of guilt. I'd made things even worse. 'Then why did she go when you told her to?'

'Because of the other guy. She's probably got a ship to jump to now.'

I had a suspicion, a wild one at that. Like the time I thought I smelled another woman's perfume in my car. I hugged him while I mulled over mentioning it, unsure.

I inched down my nightdress. 'Alistair, this sounds crazy, but could the other man be Ollie?'

Bemused, he leaned back, shaking his head. 'No. What makes you say that?'

'A conversation when he came back to mine. It's probably nothing. He asked if you thought Celia was screwing around. Asked if Celia had told me about anybody else.'

'He was probably after information for me – because he saw the photos.'

'Sounds plausible.' I hugged him tighter, and my southerly regions pulled serious rank on my brain. 'Alistair?'

'Hmmm?'

I grinned. 'What I said earlier. About us waiting. Things don't seem so complicated right now.'

We kissed, soft and slow, Alistair holding my face in his hands. Wanting didn't come close. I hooked my thumb into the waistband of his shorts.

'What's with the rush?' He smiled onto my lips. 'You get rid of yours, and I'll get rid of mine.'

My knickers went, along with my nightie. Alistair, kissing my neck, rolled on top of me. We touched and kissed. I wrapped my legs around him, drawing him closer.

'Ah.' He sat on his haunches, pushing his shoulders back. He groaned and rubbed his face. 'This might not be easy. I can't go on top or lie on my back. Or on the side with the hole in the shoulder.'

Frowning, he stared at the wrinkled sheet. I reached out, touched his folded leg. He met my eye, looking embarrassed and sorry.

'Alistair.' I slung my legs over his and lifted my pelvis, using his hips as leverage. 'Would this be okay for you? Please say if it's not. I don't want you to be uncomfortable.'

'It's very okay for me.' A naughty expression arrived on his face. 'Absolutely perfect.'

The lamp cast its soft glow into the room. He stroked gentle lines along my legs and circles on my hips and tummy. We couldn't kiss, which focused every sensation. I was captured and hypnotised and lost and found.

And, judging by the look in Alistair's eyes, he was too.

37

CELIA

My alarm announced the arrival of two-thirty a.m. I left the warm bed with the feather duvet, twelve cushions and a throw, and got dressed. My mind and body felt stilted, like I'd got up in the middle of the night for an early morning flight, and my hands quaked from the unbalanced blood sugar. Trainers on, I checked the contents of my new rucksack. It contained, amongst other things, a balaclava, a head torch, a filled dropper bottle, a bag containing a crushed red-skinned peanut, and the key for the French door in Elena's bedroom.

The sash window groaned on its runners when I wrenched it open. I stopped and waited. No lights came on in the nearby windows and no new noises could be heard. I tiptoed along the ledge, scouting around the whole time, slid down the roof and jumped to the grass. Keeping to the shrubby contours, I sprinted across the dark grounds. On reaching the hotel boundary, I clambered over the fence and my feet met with the bridleway.

I strapped on the head torch before I followed the path, avoiding the holes where I could twist an ankle. It would have been easier to use the hire car in the hotel carpark, but I needed that car to stay in situ, thus implying I'd been in my room all night. I jogged to the lay-by where I'd left my car, then drove into the village, where I parked a short distance from my marital home.

My journey needed to continue on foot.

The moon disappeared behind the clouds, making the sky look sinister, blanketing the lane between the allotments and our street with darkness. The head torch cast a bright but narrow beam, illuminating the tyre tracks and a hole filled with hardcore, leaving everything around it hidden. Something scurried in the bushes ahead and a tawny owl called ke-wick, ke-wick.

I stopped.

It sounded so loud, so obtrusive, that I hesitated, tingling with nerves. Elena was not a bad person, and maybe she didn't deserve what I had planned. The owl cried again, and another owl replied hoo-hoo-ooo. They continued to taunt me – a female and a territorial male – carrying on like I wasn't even there.

Cold seeped into me, despite it being a mild night, numbing my digits and my thoughts. I shuffled from foot to foot, breathed into my hands, and tried to regain some feeling in my chilled body. The clouds drifted past the moon and the sky brightened. The warmth returned, along with my hot, blinding anger. Nothing would deter me. They all deserved it.

I pushed through Elena's shabby hedge and approached the bungalow, brushing off the leaves as I went. I shone my torch into her bedroom, her living room and kitchen, to be sure the house stood empty. Using my copied key, I gained access to her house, put on gloves, and went to the kitchen. As I hoped, Elena hadn't cancelled her milk delivery, and two unopened milk bottles waited in the fridge where her neighbour had put them, their lids stamped with the previous day's date.

In the kitchen, I put the plastic sheeting and the bottles of milk on the floor. I made tiny dents and holes in the foil lid of one bottle to mimic the damage made by a pecking bird. Then, with utmost care, I removed the top from the second bottle using the pointed blade of the craft knife. Into this bottle, I added a blob of peanut oil and some fragments of peanut from the netting birdfeeder. I smeared a little milk around the top of the bottle to stick the foil lid back down. After a quick rummage on the mug tree, I found Elena's favourite mug. I put a drop of peanut oil in the bottom, smeared the rim for good measure, and returned the mug to its home.

I repacked my bag and double checked I hadn't left anything. After putting the milk back in the fridge, I locked the house, and returned the Polo to its place beside the caravan in the lay-by.

All the ends were tightly knotted. The CCTV trained on the hotel carpark placed me away from the scene and a legitimate source of nuts waited in Elena's house. Unfortunately for Elena, she no longer had her EpiPens, what with me finding them in her handbag the day we visited the coffee shop, not so safely nestled between a powder compact and a strip of paracetamol.

I made it back into bed before five.

All done.

38

ALISTAIR

I didn't want to let Elena go, not ever. The soft dip of her waist fitted my arm, and her silky legs wrapped around mine perfectly. Before Elena, I thought love was a thing of the past, never to have again, but that had changed. Me and Elena could love each other, and we would.

If we got the chance.

I watched her silently, not wanting to wake her. Her cheek balled against the pillow and a few sleep creases sat by her eye. She looked peaceful, but I doubted a few hours' sleep would be enough for her – she hadn't lived with the broken nights and early mornings like me.

We didn't go to sleep until the early hours. We had amazing sex, then we talked. We had amazing sex, then we talked some more. Elena said I didn't take the abuse because of weakness – I took it because of strength. I was strong enough to stay, strong enough to not retaliate. My opinion of me changed after that, not completely, more of a drift. I no longer felt like a man broken; a man not right.

Her blue eyes suddenly met mine.

'Morning, beautiful,' I said.

Elena made a 'ugh' noise, and I chuckled.

'Don't tell me,' she said. 'You're one of those really annoying morning people who spring awake, ready to go. Unlike me – who mooches around like a dawn corpse.'

I chuckled again. 'Yeah. I'm one of those really annoying morning people who spring awake, ready to go.' I drew a circle on the top of her arm. 'But don't worry. My dad is a morning person and my mum is like you, and they've been married for forty years. We'll be alright.'

I kissed her softly.

'Good.' Elena wiped under her eyes and then checked her finger ends, for smudged makeup I assumed. 'Sorry if I'm a mess. My hair's always manic in the morning. And I cried last night.'

'You look lovely. Stop fretting.'

Our next kiss relayed a million words and a barrow-load of emotions. She hooked her leg over my hip, and we were soon back to where we were the night before. Eventually though, my stomach growled and our rip in spacetime repaired.

Elena groaned and stretched and grabbed her nightie. 'I need to eat too. I'll make us tea and toast.'

I overtook her before the wardrobe and told her to get back in bed. With the kettle on, I put the bread in the toaster. Elena leaned against the doorway and watched. I opened the first drawer and rooted out a teaspoon. She padded over to me and kissed my back between the shoulder blades, right in the middle of my tattoo. She touched it with her fingers and then stopped – and I knew exactly where she was looking.

'Is the cut any better?' I asked.

'A bit.' She kissed my back again, and my shoulders pulled together. 'It's not as red. The stitches look like upturned spiders now.'

Which I hoped would dissolve like they said; I didn't like hospitals and I couldn't reach to pull them out myself. Twenty-six of them.

The kettle clicked, and a steam plume made for the bottom of the cupboard. 'Go warm the bed for me. I'll finish up here.'

I returned to the bedroom with two mugs of tea, a pile of toast, and a packet of custard creams. Elena ate a slice of toast from the edges and saved the best bit, the middle, until last. I folded a slice in half and went at it.

The sound of my phone ringing soon broke our happy bubble.

Oh, for Heaven's sake.

Celia.

'Hello.'

Not surprisingly, Celia threw out word after word, not giving me a chance to reply. Like usual, I let her burn out while I screwed up my face and glared at the ceiling. Elena stiffened against my chest, her breathing shallow, not rustling the sheets, and then she wriggled out from under my grip. She sat up and pulled the duvet as high as her chin.

'I want you to collect your things before I get back,' I said to her. 'Can't you collect them today? I'll be home by lunchtime tomorrow and I'd prefer it if you'd done it before then.'

Celia droned on and on, like she could sense my happy place and was determined to ruin it. I held Elena with one hand and tried not to crush the phone in the other. Celia wanted to come to the house when I got home. To sort things out.

'I don't know.' I scrubbed my face. 'Fine. Come round before the match. It's a ten o'clock kick off and Ollie said he won't be there till ten minutes before. Celia, you won't try anything stupid, will you?'

'No,' she said, 'I promise. And Al, about what I did. I'm sorry I lost my temper.'

Her apology washed over me like a surfing wave on a Cornish beach. I actually couldn't give a monkey's about what had passed. I took Elena's hand. My thoughts were about the future.

'You want to thank your lucky stars I've never lost mine.'

I ended the call and threw the phone on the bed; it bounced and hit the carpet.

Elena pulled back the duvet, wanting out, but I pulled her into my hug. 'Where are you going?'

'Getting up. This is such a mess. I've just listened to the two of you talking while we're in bed. Does it not seem totally wrong to you?'

I groaned. The woman I'd stupidly married ruined everything. 'Aye, but I don't care anymore. I've spent the last five years of my life miserable. I've been treading on eggshells, trying to do the right thing, and look where it's got me. El, you make me happy and I'm not giving it up because of her.'

Light pushed against the edges of the curtains and snuck in through a tiny gap where they met. Elena hugged herself, rubbed the goosebumps on her arms.

'Please come back to bed?' I kissed her shoulder. 'Don't let her come between us.'

'Okay.' Three pieces of toast were left on the plate. She chose the one from the middle. 'What's happening when we get home?'

'You're locking your doors and keeping your head down. Celia's coming over for her stuff. She says she wants to discuss the separation so she can have the papers drawn up.'

'Do you think she'll be okay about everything?'

I shrugged. 'I assume nothing where she's concerned.'

We'd been kicked back to reality. Both of us. Elena forced down a slice of toast, though I didn't. My appetite was long gone. Instead, I drank my tea and surfed the internet on my phone. I searched for the number of a locksmith and a security company who installed house alarms and CCTV.

'Can you book these for teatime tomorrow? I want you to upgrade your locks – windows and doors. Maybe get one of those doorbell cameras, too.'

'I think you're overreacting, but I'll do it anyway. And I thought we'd be home by lunch?'

'We will. I'll drop you somewhere else for a few hours. I don't want us getting back at the same time – in case she's hanging around.'

Elena brushed the crumbs from the duvet; some of them sprinkled on the floor, the others stuck on her hand. 'Whatever. I'm going for a quick shower.'

'I'll join you.'

Pine cones and needles covered the ground in the National Trust car park, putting trip hazards and prickles everywhere. Still, a van sold local ice cream, and the view from the top of the hill was something else. In the distance, the pikes touched the sky and, closer to us, the water shimmered. I'd visited The Lakes quite a few times, but I'd never visited Tarn Hows. Neither had Elena. Which made the place special and ours.

I slung my arm around her. 'Did you know that a tarn is a lake formed in a valley cut out by a glacier, and the name is derived from the old Norse word tjörn – which was a natural freshwater lake, surrounded by trees. So, in some ways, this place, Tarn Hows, is a bit of a con because it's actually artificial, not natural.'

Elena slapped my back and smiled. 'Come on, spit it out.'

'What?'

'Whatever it is you're using to raid Wikipedia.'

I pulled her neck into the crook of my arm, trapping her close, then I kissed her head, cheek, lips. 'I'll have you know, I read it in a guidebook in the cabin while you were shaving your beard – or whatever – in the shower before we went out last night.'

Elena slid on the loose hardcore, but I grabbed her before she fell. 'I haven't got a beard, you cheeky sod.'

I laughed. 'Not now, you haven't.'

Elena nudged me playfully and pretended to be cross. I scooted around, putting me down the slope and not towering over her. Her freckled skin glowed, and my insides warmed like I'd drank a full flask on a freezing site.

'You happy?' I asked.

'Yes.' Her smile touched mine. 'Very.'

Time didn't chase us as we strolled around the lake. We'd left our phones in the car, and I didn't have to think about putting out the bins or sorting the liability insurance or whether I'd put the top back on the skin glue. We roamed along, stopping to watch the tiny waves rattle the small stones, all colours and polished by old age. I headed off a few times to check out interesting trees and foxholes, while Elena stayed on the flat and watched the water. Eventually, we came to a fallen tree studded with vertical coins, some still shiny and some dulled by age. I rammed a coin into the wood and made a wish and handed Elena one so she could do the same.

'I don't need to wish on a money tree. I'm loaded,' she said. 'Okay, not strictly true. I made the mistake of visiting Ikea when I set up the house – so that put me five grand down on garlic presses and plastic tubs.'

I laughed, and she laughed, but she wouldn't take the coin.

'Don't wish for money,' I said. 'Wish for strength.'

With a huff, she stuffed the coin into a crack, closed her eyes, and tinkled her fingers along the cold lines of coins.

'It's like armour,' I said.

She snatched her hand away. 'I don't want to think about armour because it reminds me of war.'

I tried to apologise with my face. 'I hope, if I'm right about this other fella, Celia will go quietly. But if she doesn't, me divorcing her will be like a war. She'll go for my house and my business. Do anything she can to rubbish my name. It's not gonna be easy.'

'I know. I just don't want her to hurt you.'

'Or you.' I sandwiched her hand between mine. 'That's why I want you to keep your head down until she's well and truly gone.'

'Okay.'

Elena gazed across the water and to the distant mountains. Their faces were green and velvet, like my nan's old chair, only broken by rusty plants and silver rocks. All except one. It stood looming and dark. Yeah, that mountain reminded me of her. Looking down at us. Casting her shadow.

39

CELIA

The hotel lounge reminded me of Singapore. The polished marble floor caught the light, and white orchids were growing everywhere. The air held the subtle smell of wealth. Regardless, every distinctively aged or cosmetically adjusted eye followed me across the room. If the story broke – which it never would – those people would shake their heads and utter, 'Not her. She simply couldn't.' The petite lady with the shiny hair and the subtle pink lips would be deemed incapable of such things. Such was my rapport with life's pathetic jury.

I took the hire car from the carpark and headed to my marital home. With the sun dropping behind the house, the hall held a slight chill. Gloom tinged the air. A lamp sat on the side table, a chrome lamp with a tangle of arms and glass flowers, but I didn't switch it on. Nor did I kick off my shoes; I wanted to bring the outside onto the expensive beige hall carpet. I wanted to ruin and destroy. The ropes on my bridge hung frayed, the boards rotten and broken, and so I planned to take out a blowtorch and burn the fucking lot.

Alistair said nothing as he trod the path to the kitchen. He placed his phone on the table and dropped onto a chair, a different chair to the one he usually took.

'I've missed you, Al.'

'New top?' he returned, which I interpreted as how-much-has-that-cost-me.

'It's purple, and you know what they say when you see purple in a film.'

'What's that?'

'I'll tell you later.' Smiling like an archangel, I swung a carrier bag of supplies onto the counter. 'I thought I'd cook curry. I bought beer too – in case you fancy nothing in the house.'

Alistair looked exhausted, weary and drained, and I wondered whether my little bloodletting or his dirty weekend had taken the greatest toll.

'You alright? You look worn out.'

He rubbed his eyes, then scrubbed his face with his hands. 'I'm knackered. Got up at the crack of dawn, then spent all afternoon sitting at the computer, trying to work out how to do my accounts.'

'I can still do them for you.'

Alistair's jaw dropped, yet he said nothing, so I skirted around his disbelief with a comment about runny eyes and white onions.

I chopped the ingredients, mixed the spices, and fried off the chicken, which I then covered in coconut milk. I over-spiced the curry and added enough chilli to turn my nose into a tap – I wanted his palate distorted. All the while I talked to him, keeping things polite and bland, not wanting things to blow up in my face. I told him about the imaginary fault with my Polo and the hire car; I even talked to him about the World Cup, not that he responded.

'Where have you been?' Alistair asked.

'Staying at a Three Seasons budget place, though I checked into Bradley Hall last night. I'm only there for one more night, though.' I paused, gazing into space, before I snapped out of it and picked up some cutlery. 'Would you mind setting the table and carrying the rice to the dining room?'

I hurried ahead of him and placed the pan of curry on the table. 'I'll just grab my drink from the kitchen. Do you want another beer?'

Alistair turned the pan around and around: me poisoning him had clearly crossed his mind.

'Yes, please. I'll dish up.'

I took the bottle from him and headed back into the kitchen. Toby, what with caring for me and hating men who abused women, had kindly supplied me with an oral solution of diazepam, which I tipped into the empty bottle I then refilled with beer. I persuaded the metal lid back over the bottle top and pressed it around the glass the best I could. After a glance over my shoulder, I plopped his phone inside the oven gloves, which I tossed over the copper-bottom pans on the draining board and onto the windowsill. I flicked off the outside lights and returned to the dining room, making a show of removing the bottle top before he could notice the misshapen metal.

I perched on the opposite chair. 'I'm so sorry about everything. Hitting you and shouting at you. I visited the GP and I'm seeing a counsellor. I've realised I have issues with anger. No, I've realised I have issues full stop.'

I heard the counting inside his head. One. Two. Three.

'I admit my behaviour was abhorrent. Unforgivable. I panicked when you said you wanted a divorce, but I shouldn't have lost my temper with you.'

Glowering, Alistair pushed a heap of rice onto his fork. Yet still he held it back. My husband was the Aswan fucking dam.

'I still love you in my own way. I always will. But I know I've ruined everything. And I regret it, I really do.' The letterbox creaked open, and something dropped on the mat. The local paper probably. I hated the local paper – all stupid stories about re-homed pets and adverts placed by people trying to offload utter shit. 'Will you help me financially while I find a job and somewhere to live?'

'Aye. What do you want in the divorce?'

'Half of our savings and half of the house. I need enough money to start again. I'm not interested in your business or pension.'

'Fine.'

I didn't expect his lack of resistance. He owned the house, and I'd never contributed a penny towards the mortgage when he had one. He really wanted rid of me. I placed the knife and fork across my plate.

'I'm full and I need another drink. Do you want another beer?'

'No thanks.'

Alistair drained the bottle when I held out my hand to take it from him. I grabbed the neck, and he kept hold of the body.

'You killed my cat.'

Alistair directed his quiet words at the table, which the satin runner split into two asymmetrical halves. I'd never seen him so furious, so hateful, and a surge of anxiety filled my chest.

'Celia. I said you killed my cat. Have you got nothing to say?'

I swallowed so hard that it hurt. 'It was an accident.'

Alistair stood up, still holding the bottle. His eyes looked dark. His whiskers looked dark. The sharp shadow under his jaw looked dark. I'd never noticed the angles, the indications of his masculinity.

'Bullshit, Celia. You accidentally put slug pellets in her food?'

I tugged the bottle, but he didn't let go.

'Oh, for fuck's sake, Alistair. It was only a cat.'

He threw the bottle against the wall and green daggers of glass fell onto the carpet. A picture followed, a photograph of a sunset, sliced in half by an angry crack.

'Exactly. A cat which didn't deserve what you did.'

I backed up, past my chair and the one next to it. 'I thought it'd just make her sick, make a mess in the house. I didn't think it'd kill her,' I lied.

He stepped closer to me, his one stride matching two of mine. 'She suffered for hours on her own in the dark. Behind the shed, fitting and vomiting, in agony.'

'Then perhaps her dying was for the best.'

I touched the cold plaster, my hands at right angles to my body. He'd backed me into the fucking corner. My heart thumped, double the speed of the ticking clock.

'The cat didn't die. I told the vet to put her to sleep. I killed her in the end.'

'Just get another one. For fuck's sake.'

My shoulder bounced off his chest, so I pushed his arms, trying to get past him, but Alistair was a brick wall. Swathes of my purple top disappeared, covered by hands which dug foundations and wielded hammers. He held me tight, very tight.

Alistair stopped my attempts at escape, dodging left to right. 'Do you know how hard it is to keep going, hiding this shit. Bruised and burned. With broken fingers. Cut and scalded and spat at. Do you know how hard it is to lie over and over? To everybody and yourself.'

The heat came from him in waves, scorching my cheeks. I tried to move, turn away, retaliate, anything. But I couldn't move through the fear.

I didn't hear the kids mucking about on the street or the cars droning in the distance. I closed my eyes and...

Smash. Smash. Fucking smash.

The chair missed me by a slither. I screamed. Not that it stopped him. The table went next, plates and pans, dirty cutlery and wasted food. Alistair stomped towards me, and I fell into the corner, cowering. Waiting for the foot in my stomach and ribs; or the pain when I bounced into the wall.

He could kill me; he would kill me.

And then, with a pained shout, he shot away, and his hands hovered, unsure of their calling. But I knew what he wanted to do. He wanted to grab me and shake me and punish me for every last thing I had done.

My militancy had faded to a wide-eyed plea. 'I'm sorry. I'm really sorry.'

His eyes were fierce and unblinking. Like he was the predator, not me. Everything inside me quivered.

'I'm sor—'

'I don't want to hear it.'

Alistair stood still, hands motionless, shoving the air, putting everything he had into finding his lost temper before his lost temper found me.

'Make a list of what you want and give it to your solicitor,' he eventually said. 'I'll pack your stuff. This is the last time you set foot on this street. Come within five hundred metres of me and I'll have you prosecuted. I visited the police station the other night. Gave a statement and let them take photos. You messed up, Celia. Because you can't plead accidental injury or self-defence when you slice somebody across the back. It's ABH, and the best you can hope for is diminished responsibility. And I swear, if you do anything which I don't like, I'll not stop until you're criminalised and ruined. Now get out.' He backed up and pointed at the door. 'Now.'

Alistair still looked ready to blow and, if he flipped, he could batter me to death long before the sedative kicked in. I struggled to herd my shit-scared thoughts.

Collect your coat from the hall.

Reset the answer machine and grab the handset.

Leave.

With shaking hands, using Alistair's keys, I locked the front door after I passed through it. I tossed the keys into my bag, along with the window keys which I'd purloined earlier. He stood at the window, his hands in his pockets, oblivious to his newfound imprisonment. The triple-glazed windows were locked, as were the reinforced composite doors, front and back, and he couldn't call for help. From his vantage point, however, he didn't see me dial Ollie's number using the house phone. He didn't see me rub the handset on my trousers and then switch it off and he didn't see me bite back my tears or drop the ignition keys over and over.

That was close.

I shouldn't have killed the stupid cat.

40

ELENA

The contentment of our trip gave way to the gloomy reality of our return. My newly fortified home seemed less of a sanctuary, and the thought of Alistair and Celia, together in their house, filled me with unease. I flitted around for a few hours, unpacked and titivated, then decided pyjamas, milky hot chocolate, and an old film might make me feel better.

The first bottle of milk had a damaged foil top: the local blue tit had been at it again, and I didn't fancy a dose of campylobacter. I tipped the milk away and gave the bottle a quick wash before putting it on the draining board. The second bottle top remained intact and so I filled the mug with milk, heated it in the microwave, then stirred in several chunks of Galaxy chocolate.

I took a pew on the sofa and hit play on the DVD player. I lifted my mug. And then my phone rang. I swiped the screen and returned the mug to its coaster, silently thankful for the distraction.

'Livia. How are you?'

We chatted about work, food and alcohol, and whether we could schedule a few days at our favourite spa. She told me about a man she'd met, her gardener, though I didn't speak about Beelzebub and her legal spouse. A few sentences into a discussion about sex toys and my phone beeped. I checked the screen.

'Liv. My phone's about to die. I need to...'

I bustled around the kitchen and checked my travel bag, looking for the charger, before letting out a groan. In my mind's eye, I saw its white wire snaking around the alarm clock in the bedroom in the log cabin. My laptop displayed no battery too. I found the charger, unwound the connection cable from the sixty wires in the basket, and resigned myself to trickle charge.

Bang.

I clutched my chest and told myself not to be silly. The gunshot came from the TV. Celia didn't have a gun, and she wouldn't be stupid enough to turn up with a knife. Alistair was prepared for her. I opened a packet of biscuits and reheated the hot chocolate.

The crawling inside my lips began minutes later. I couldn't work it out, not at all, because I'd eaten nothing other than the biscuits and hot chocolate. My thoughts spun like the wheels on a runaway bike; faster and faster, knowing where I headed, unable to stop.

I got to my feet and rushed back into the kitchen, frantically scanning the room for my bag. I yanked open the zip and searched for medication to halt the anaphylaxis, though the two auto-dispensers had gone. Amidst increasing panic, I rifled through the contents of my bag before emptying it out on the table. The balled-up tissues, old receipts, and my purse landed on the floor. Gasping, I grabbed my phone. The screen lit up and then went black again, the battery still dead.

I raced to the bathroom, where I clawed the contents of the cabinet into the sink below. Those two EpiPens were missing too. I fell to my knees, unable to breathe or swallow, everything blurred by the tears. Even if I made it to the front garden and somebody found me, an ambulance wouldn't get there in time. I couldn't stand, and if I exerted myself the heart attack from my plummeting blood pressure would kill me before the asphyxiation. I was going to die. Die because I did not have an EpiPen. Somebody had taken my medication.

And I knew exactly who.

I thought about the lines of coins in the fallen tree and unfurled from the broken ball of a person. There were two shots of epinephrine in my work satchel, but I doubted my wheezing breaths and palpitating heart would get me up the stairs to reach it. Thirteen steps, I told myself. Just thirteen steps. I crawled on my knees and elbows, swollen tongue pressed against the back of my throat, spittle pouring from my mouth. I could hardly see through my swollen eyes, and I might be unable to locate the satchel or operate the device blind, anyway. But I did.

I lay with my legs raised until the swelling had reduced enough for my blood pressure to be safe. I took it slowly, my head swimming and my stomach knotted on the cusp of a retch. The allergen exposure must have been unfortunate, but the disappearance of the medication couldn't be circumstantial. I needed to get to Alistair's house. Celia wasn't angry and slightly unhinged. She might be a psychopath.

And Alistair could be next.

41

ALISTAIR

Hands in my pockets, my pulse almost normal, I watched her drive away. Peering around a smear of bird shit, I could see Elena's bungalow. I wanted to go over there, to tell her things were fine, but I decided to wait in case Celia came back. I turned to face the mess I'd made – the dented wall, the bits of glass. I leaned over to collect it up, but came over dizzy and exhausted. The mess would have to wait, though calling Elena couldn't.

In the kitchen, I blindly reached on top of the fridge, where I always kept my phone, but it wasn't there. I looked behind the kettle, shifted the dirty dishes, patted the pockets in my jeans. Rubbing my bleary eyes, I went to the hall. The phone wasn't on the windowsill or in my hoody – and neither were my keys. Maybe I'd left them all in the truck. I pushed the door handle but it didn't budge. Feeling suddenly drunk, I wove to the back door and found that locked too. Behind me, the landline phone cradle sat empty. Both phones gone.

My arms jellied, and my brain turned. I swayed back to the front room, and I thought I saw Elena through her window. Then she disappeared. I needed to climb out of the window, but the handle wouldn't budge. The bloody thing was locked. Along with every window in every room.

Trying not to panic, I returned to the dining room, where I stumbled into the serving bowl of rice. I grabbed a chair to hit the glass, though I could barely lift it, yet alone get my weight behind it, and the pane didn't even bounce. I'd had a long day, but the world shouldn't be shifting and I shouldn't be fighting sleep.

Shit.

Celia.

She'd drugged me and locked me in the house. I needed to get out and go to Elena's. I needed to smash a window. The toolbox under the stairs contained a hammer. My body circled over my feet, and I blinked the doorway back into focus.

The cupboard wasn't far.

I just needed to get there.

42

CELIA

I left our quiet cul-de-sac a nervous wreck. As a distraction, I focused not on what had gone wrong, but instead on what would go right. Starting with a rehearsal of the inevitable interview with the police.

'Could you please tell me about the events of last night?' the officer would say.

'Yes, officer,' I would reply. 'I left my hotel at around seven-thirty and returned home – I mean to the house I'd shared with Alistair. He'd asked me to come over to talk about marriage counselling and me moving back in. He was drunk when I got there, and in a terrible mood. Angry and shouting about Ollie. I told Alistair I was sorry and I loved him – that I wanted to make our marriage work.'

'Who's Ollie?'

The man who, evidence suggested, Alistair phoned and lured to his house just after I left. I would tell him Ollie's full name, along with his address.

'He's Alistair's friend,' I'd say. 'Until recently, Ollie and I were having an affair. Ollie has divorced his wife, but I refused to leave Alistair for him... do we really need to talk about this? It's all very raw. Things have been dreadful. Between me and Alistair. Between Alistair and Ollie.'

And there it would be. The prime suspect, his motive, and a situation of conflict. Done.

'Ollie didn't do this. I'm sure. He'd never—'

The officer would interject, probably by raising his hand. 'Could you tell me where you were between the hours of nine-thirty and eleven o'clock last night?'

'At the hotel. I left the house at around half nine and drove straight back there. I went to my room and tried to phone Alistair, to apologise again.'

'Did you speak with him?'

'No, he didn't pick up. I left a message on the answering machine.'

The officer would offer the nonchalant nod, like in the films. 'Is there anybody who could vouch for your whereabouts at this time?

'Yes, I'm sure there is. The receptionist – or a guest. Oh, and I'm probably on CCTV.'

'Thank you.'

He would snap his notebook closed and slide it into his pocket, like they did on the TV.

'Please catch the man who did this to my husband. He had his problems, but he didn't deserve this.'

'We have every intention of catching them,' he would reply valiantly. 'Thank you for your time.'

I'd learned my lines and honed my behaviour. It was just a matter of when.

The gravelled carpark was much busier than it had been when I had left. I scanned the two remaining spaces and ascertained their position in relation to the camera on the antique lamppost. I needed the Clio in full view, on every sweep, no omissions.

The immaculately presented man at the reception looked up from his screen. 'Good evening, madam. Is there anything we can help you with?'

'Hiya. I've decided to watch a movie tonight, what with there being nothing on but football.'

He told me about the on-demand button on the TV remote control and made polite conversation about a few films on there, which he'd enjoyed. I chatted and smiled, cemented a memory of me in his mind.

'Thank you. I'll call down if I have any difficulties. Goodnight.'

'Have a good evening, madam. Enjoy your film.'

Which I would. After another brief trip out.

I proceeded to the room at an amble, perused the local attraction leaflets, and looked at the artwork gracing the walls. I wanted to be seen by lots of people; noticed by lots of people. However, much to my disappointment, my encounters were limited to an old couple who I doubted could even see, let alone remember me, and a middle-aged man who walked past while I deliberately fumbled with the key card outside my room. The foyer CCTV and the receptionist would have to do.

Once inside the room, my actions accelerated somewhat. I needed to get back to my marital home, execute the last part of my plan, and leave just before Ollie arrived. With the tournament being held at the other side of the world, kick-off was at eleven o'clock. He would be there ten minutes before, on the nose: he wouldn't break his just-in-time habits.

I turned on the TV, scrolled through the titles, and eventually decided on Pride and Prejudice; a sensible choice. I changed into black yoga leggings and a long-sleeved gym top, and I exchanged the pumps for trainers. After propping the Dictaphone on the dressing table, I dialled home using my contract phone. After five rings, the answering machine picked up; I hit start to play the recording of my voice and placed my mobile phone alongside the voice recorder. The location icon showed on my phone, thus setting my alibi, along with the background noise of a TV which coincided with the digital records of the hotel.

I slunk out of the window, shuffled along the ledge, and dropped to the floor like a cat. The grass gave silently beneath my feet and the hedges masked my progress to the fence. I poked my toes into the railing, above an intricate swirl, and vaulted up. I slung my leg over the fence and dropped. Pain shot from my ankle, down into my foot. My looped shoelace had snagged in the ironwork and so I hung, with a leg on both sides of the fence, scrabbling for purchase.

Shit.

The rail dug in behind my knee, pressing into the tendons, sending spikes of pain into my muscles. I took a deep breath; eight inches of fucking nylon wouldn't beat me. I threw one hand and then the other and grabbed the fence like a hero on a cliff face. Sharp flakes of old paint dug into my hands, though I eventually yanked myself high enough to get free. I dropped to the floor, tied both laces in double knots and tucked in the ends. Once bitten and all that. Tentatively, I circled my foot at the ankle. It felt sore, but it took my full weight without protest. I would be down the bridleway and back to my hidden car in no time.

The Polo bumped over the potholes in the lane. I hated driving down the track, but the darkness and overgrown vegetation meant my arrival would go unnoticed. Being spotted would ruin everything.

I skulked along the path, squeezed through the gap in the beech hedge and dashed up the garden. I let myself into the house using the back door and shut it behind me. As I snapped on the nitryl gloves, I listened hard. There wasn't a sound. Not the television, nor the dishwasher. Even the grandfather clock in the hall had stopped ticking. I saw two red lights flashing on the answering machine when I returned the phone to the base station; my message had been received.

In the kitchen, I relocated Alistair's mobile phone from its hiding place to a spot on the counter. I then stuck my head inside the dining room. Alistair wasn't there. Beside the table leg laid his blue sock, twisted like innards in a dish. The second sock sat at the entrance to the living room. Socks were always the first thing to go when Alistair felt tired. He hated having his feet covered while he slept.

I found Alistair on the floor, fast asleep, with one arm draped on the sofa and the other bent beneath his body. His cheek pressed against a bobbly cushion and his legs ran the length of the coffee table. I watched him for some time.

He didn't flinch when I pulled Ollie's belt from the plastic bag tucked into my leggings. I ran Ollie's belt through my fingers, wishing I could feel its smoothness. I'd washed it with soap, soaked it in hydrogen peroxide laundry brightener, and wiped it with alcohol: my fingerprints were long gone. Ollie would add his fingerprints when he tried to assist his friend.

I threaded the belt under Alistair's chin and then through the buckle. His jaw snapped shut when I yanked hard. I kneeled on the rug, facing him. Alistair stirred, his movements lethargic and confused, before his face met the carpet with a thud. I stroked his puce cheek before snatching his head to the side. His eyes formed bloodshot slits.

'You really shouldn't have mixed the diazepam with alcohol,' I said sweetly.

He gurgled and gagged, and his fingers scrabbled on the belt.

'You see, Elena shouldn't have said yes to you and Ollie shouldn't have said no to me. Oh, yes, darling, I've been screwing your best friend, and he's about to turn up, put his fingerprints on his belt and be framed for your murder.'

I peeled off the gloves to avoid spreading fibres from the murder weapon and crammed them back in the bag.

'I told you not to fuck with me, Alistair. Did you honestly think I'd let you disappear into the sunset with her? While you were on your dirty little tryst, I laced her house with peanut oil. Unfortunately, she doesn't have her medication.'

I pulled her four EpiPens from my pocket.

Alistair heaved silently and his eyes closed. Poor Alistair. He was a kind man and he'd been a good husband. Just not good enough. I sat down and hugged my knees as his fingers slid along the belt, the life deserting them. A moment of calm filled the air and a hundred new bubbles escaped from the filter in the fish tank.

'Purple.' I kissed my fingers and touched his forehead. 'When you see it in the movies, it means someone will die.'

Hanging back, I peered through the window and watched Ollie's Range Rover pull onto the drive. I unlocked the front door and opened it a touch before rushing along the hall. And then I froze, my mouth agape.

Elena barged through the back door. She looked like death: pallid and clammy, with her hair stuck to her puffy face.

'What the hell is going on?'

The voice belonged to Ollie, pushing me from behind. The contradictory bastard had arrived five minutes early. I shoved Elena into the wall, and I ran into the night, my breaths feral and my chest on fire.

The car wheels sought out dregs of mud and splattered it up the wings. The gears screeched as I forced them, a gear too low, a gear too high, no gear at all. I could no longer return the Polo to the lay-by and sneak back to the hotel because I needed to disappear.

I wasn't going down for murder.

43

ELENA

The house seemed uncomfortably quiet. So quiet, I heard the whir from the freezer and the buzz from a TV on standby. The air sat heavy with the smell of leftover food – food waiting to putrefy and decay. The trodden back of my trainer pinched my skin, urging me on.

'Alistair? Alistair?'

I stumbled into the hall wall, sending a violet print flying, before falling into the dining room. A wooden chair lay on the floor, along with the jagged glass from a broken picture. Grains of rice lay scattered on the table, on a seat, on the carpet, crushed and trampled. An ominous feeling washed over me, leaving sickness and grimness in its wake. I turned and ran. Straight into Ollie.

'What's going on?' he asked, gripping my arms.

'I'm not sure, but I think she's done something to him.'

I rushed from room to room, not really looking, not wanting to absorb. Ollie followed, two unhurried strides behind, casual and half-bemused, telling me to calm down, telling me everything would be fine. Alistair wasn't in the kitchen, the downstairs loo or the snug.

'Elena, stop panicking,' Ollie said, his eyes on me, his hand on the living room door. 'He's probably in the bathroom. You check upstairs. I'll... Oh my God.'

I chased him into the room.

Alistair lay face down on the floor, one arm resting on the back of his head, the other splayed on the rug. A brown belt circled his neck, tied so tightly that his skin bulged around the metal buckle. Ollie moved fast and sudden, as if he couldn't slow himself down. He threw the coffee table out of the way and dropped to his knees. Ollie swore and fought with the jammed buckle and eventually threw the belt clear. He tried to roll Alistair onto his back, but halfway over his deadweight pulled him back.

'Elena, help me, for fuck's sake.'

My body froze, legs frozen, along with my thoughts. I covered my mouth and made a sound like a trapped animal. Ollie wrenched Alistair over and his arm slapped on the floor. His hand made a tense claw, the fingernails pale like lard, and his swollen eyelids made the eyelashes disappear.

Ollie pressed his fingers to Alistair's throat. 'God, no. Please, no.'

His elbows met his knees, and his shoulders started to shake.

'Please don't say he's dead,' I uttered. 'Please don't say he's dead.'

Ollie didn't reply.

The floor fell, taking me with it. He couldn't have been murdered by his wife. I wouldn't let it be true.

'Move, Ollie. And phone the ambulance. Now.'

I barged him out of the way and desperately searched for Alistair's pulse. I counted, hoping and praying, but I felt nothing.

Nothing at all. I grabbed his wrist and pressed down hard, under the tendons and around them.

Ollie's voice drifted further away, and my heart thumped, vibrating through me, tricking me into thinking my pulse belonged to him. And then a feint bump pushed against my finger. I didn't dare breathe. Alistair had a pulse, but not a whisper of air touched my cheek when I hovered over his mouth.

I tipped his head and pinched his nose, and then I sealed my lips to his.

One. Two. His chest barely moved. I inhaled deeply and breathed into his mouth again. Over and over.

'Come on, Alistair.'

I blew harder. My chest hurt with the effort, and his chest heaved with the strain. I sat back on my heels, one hand over his heart, the other stroking his hair.

'Please,' I sobbed.

Alistair's lips parted.

'Ollie.' My hand sunk, then lifted with the movement of his chest. 'I think he's breathing.'

The paramedics soon arrived, bringing with them questions I could not answer. I didn't know Alistair's date of birth, or if he had pre-existing medical conditions, took medication, or suffered from allergies. Ollie offered nothing at all. Not a word, not a glance. He stayed hunched up on the floor, staring into space, his folded legs surrounded by broken glass and red potpourri.

The medics worked around me, adjusting the oxygen mask, shining a light into his eyes, talking to him, trying to get a response. Their words made me dizzy and scared. Unconscious. Atypical responses. Low blood pressure. Bradycardia. Sedation.

Sedation.

'She killed his cat,' I uttered. 'She killed his cat.'

'Pardon?' the paramedic said.

'Celia,' I said. 'The woman who did this. She poisoned his cat and drugged me. She might have drugged Alistair. Or poisoned him.'

The paramedics exchanged a look. The situation had changed.

'Will he be alright?' I croaked.

'He seems to be stable. Let's take things one step at a time.'

Alistair looked very sick, grey lipped and swollen. His breaths were shallow, and he kept swallowing, gulping, almost gagging every time. The belt had left a purple-red mark around his neck and, closest to his jaw, the edge had broken the thin skin. He squeezed my hand, albeit weakly, and met my eyes.

'Can I ask you to move, please?' I glanced at the spinal board in the paramedic's hands. 'We need to get to the hospital.'

Reluctantly, I went to Ollie. Tears tripped off his chin and blood collected in his hands, pooling around the glass embedded in them.

'Ollie.' I touched his arm. 'Are you okay? You're bleeding.'

He shook his head, searching the air. I had never seen him so broken; I never thought it possible.

'He's gonna be okay. He's breathing on his own and he squeezed my hand.'

'It was me,' he muttered.

A trail of Ollie's blood ran onto his jeans. Like a tributary. A new tributary. It soaked into the denim, making the dark blue turn violet.

'What? But you weren't here. Only Celia. We arrived at the same time.'

'I drove her to it.' Grimacing, Ollie sobbed. 'I chose him over her. That's why she did this. I tried to make it right for him. What have I done?'

I could not process the implication of his words, and I didn't even try.

'There are more important things to worry about right now.'

The paramedics, having strapped Alistair to the spinal board, lifted him onto a trolley. I reached his side, talked to him, and he opened his hand to receive mine.

Alistair would be fine.

We both would.

44

CELIA

I pulled the Polo into the hotel carpark with my pulse drumming in my ears. I needed to hurry, and I needed Alistair to be dead, because he could tell the police where to start looking. Resisting the urge to run, I crossed the forecourt and strode along the corridors to my room. I locked the door behind me and told myself to get it together. Re-pack and re-plan. It was as simple as that.

I hurried into the bathroom, triggering the automatic spotlights, and swept my toiletries into my wash bag. Wherever I was going, I needed to be presentable. I'd need to befriend people and procure favours, most likely in exchange for my body. Again. I lobbed my toiletries and clothes into the case, checked the cash in the inner pocket, and tried to fasten the zip. The zip jammed on the seam, then snarled on a bra. I swore heavily, tore the bra, and eventually fastened the case. My mobile phone stayed on the ornate table, the voice recorder went in my pocket, and I left.

I collected my rationality as I drove to the outskirts of town. My Polo and phone were at the hotel, and it would take time for the Police to learn of the hire car. I also knew a man who might get me out of the godforsaken country. Things would be fine.

'Toby,' I said, when he answered the phone.

'Ceels.' His voice delivered the certainty that everything would be alright. 'You're on a different number. Is everything okay?'

'No. It's gone belly up. I need help.'

Toby groaned, like he always did when he stretched his arms. 'Take it you pushed him downstairs?'

'No, I did something much worse.'

'Go to Greenham quarry. I'll be there in ten.'

Witches' fingers and devil cloaks covered the industrial buildings in the dark quarry. I shuddered. The place was creepy, and I couldn't see Toby's Audi anywhere. I parked the hire car in the passing place and reluctantly got out. No light pollution reached the area, and the overhead clouds blocked the starlight. My eyes strained. Some headlights flashed along the road, so I jogged towards them.

Toby climbed out and hugged me briefly, and I breathed in the moment of calm.

'Have you killed him?' he asked nonchalantly.

'I hope so.'

'Get in the car and tell me what's happened. And I want the whole story Ceels, no bullshit.'

I dropped on the passenger seat. With the adrenalin passed, my legs were jelly.

'Okay. I knocked him out with the Diazepam then strangled him with a belt. A belt I stole from the friend coming to the house to watch the football. I wanted to frame Ollie for his murder, but he turned up early and caught me.'

Toby held up his hand, stopping my flow. 'Did you say Ollie?'

'Yes.'

'Shit.' He shook his head, hiding his face. 'Please don't tell me he's the same Ollie with the posh offices on Imperial Road.'

My head swirled. 'Yes. How do you know him?'

Toby pressed my hands between his. 'I've got something to tell you and you aren't gonna like it.' He blew out, his eyes trained on the insignificant interior light. 'I've spent months fucking up a job. Like, really fucking up a job, and you've catapulted it from a fuck-up to Armageddon.'

'You're confusing me. What job?'

'You. You were the job.'

The interior light faded and disappeared into the unsettling dark.

He gripped my hands tighter. 'Ollie employed me to break up your marriage, then dump you.'

'What? Why?'

'Because, I quote, "I want her to give my mate his life back and I want her out of my fucking hair". That's why I enrolled at your gym when I own a perfectly good boxing gym myself – so I'd bump into you.'

A branch tapped my window, testing the glass like an intruder looking for a way in. Toby told me everything; from the day he and Ollie met on the golf course, to the pages of information he handed over. Where I went and what I liked, the things he should say to flatter my ego. A private investigator had tailed me and, for a while, Ollie even had a tracker on my phone. He'd given Toby fifty-thousand pounds, with the promise of another hundred if I left.

I felt sick. 'So, you and me. Our time together was all a lie – because you were getting paid?'

'No. That's why I screwed up the job. I care about you. A lot. If I didn't, I wouldn't have risked my neck by scaring the woman.'

'And I care about you a lot, too.' I looked at our hands, blended together in the dark. 'Toby, about Ollie. We were having an affair.'

'That's not what he says. He reckons you had a drunk one-night stand and you've been obsessed with him ever since. Said you've been blackmailing him, threatening to tell the husband.'

Feelings came and disappeared, though I couldn't tell if the anger, hurt or disbelief were the most potent, the most devastating. I recalled my version of the story. Our affair lasted for years. I even had a key for his house. Ollie had lied. My words came desperate and rushed.

Toby said nothing.

The grey-speckled air hung in the space between our faces. I wanted to turn on the interior light so I could see Toby's expression. I wondered if he was scowling or frowning or if his eyes were hollow and sad.

'Toby?'

'I can't get my head round this shit.' He groaned. 'So, why did you decide to kill the husband and punish the rich dude?'

'The husband fell in love with somebody else and the "rich dude" raped me.'

Toby faced the window, swallowed, then rubbed his hair. I changed the way our hands fitted together and said his name. Toby turned back to face me, snapped out of it, his chin again high.

'Is he dead?' he asked.

'Yes. I drugged Al and strangled him. But then she turned up, fucking Elena. I'd spiked her house with peanuts and pinched her medication, so she should have choked on her tongue hours earlier. She saw me leaving through the back door as Ollie walked in the front.'

'And this Elena woman. Is she a good person?'

I pressed my knees together and curled my free arm around my stomach. The temperature had dropped in the car without the engine running.

'Yes.'

'Then you messed up. I was happy to kill your husband because I saw your injuries and you said he abused you—'

'I didn't,' I interrupted. 'You assumed it was him.'

'You misled me.'

He dropped my hand and started the car, and I felt the heat from the only bridge I didn't want to burn. I didn't want to lose Toby because I cared about him a lot, and the reality fucking scared me.

'You've killed an innocent man and tried to kill an innocent woman. I'll help you, then you need to leave.'

At Toby's insistence, I climbed in the car boot, where I stewed with my thoughts until we stopped. I heard the sliding of metal and the boot opened. My eyes took a few seconds to adjust to the light, and my cramped legs took a few seconds to straighten.

Toby held out a white all-in-one suit and threw shoe covers and a pair of gloves into the boot. 'Put them on and get your hair under the hood. I don't want your DNA in here.'

I did as he said, and he lifted me out. We were in a small garage; the car parked on metal ramps. Mismatched cupboards and cabinets lined the far wall, and to my left stood a small stack of boxes. The space smelled of cleaning products and fresh air.

'Are we at your house?' I asked.

'No,' he returned, fighting his way into a paper suit.

Toby said we were in a row of 1960s garages which nobody used because they were tiny and a distance from the terraced houses.

'I laboured for a bloke who owned a house in the terrace when I was young,' he said. 'When he died, the house passed to distant relatives. The garage wasn't on the deeds and I have the keys – so that makes it mine.'

Toby got a torch from a locker, dropped to the floor, pulled out some wooden slats, and rolled under the car. I crouched down and peered after him. An old pit sat beneath the car, enlarged from what I could make out. He passed me several sealed bags and a few small boxes, then inelegantly scrambled out of the pit. He replaced the boards as I looked on, puzzled and silent.

'Toby, you're not a small-time drug dealer, are you?'

'Never said I was.'

He handed me a plastic bag and told me to hold it open while he dropped the things from his stash inside.

'Five grand in cash,' he said. 'Two mobile phones – unlocked and untraceable. Three cloned credit cards.'

I nodded and pulled a taped-up packet from the carrier bag. 'What's this?'

'Ten grands' worth of uncut cocaine. I do my bit to get it off the streets if it crosses my path. Hardcore narcotics – the universal currency of scum – and you're gonna have to find some scum cos you need to disappear.'

'Do you know anyone who can get me out of Britain?'

He shook his head. 'No. It's out of my jurisdiction.'

'I'm sorry for messing up.'

'You should have told me the truth and let me sort stuff out.' Toby unzipped the suit and peeled it down, slowly and carefully, like a rescuer from a chemical decontamination or a forensic expert after the scene of a crime. 'And Ceels. Don't even think about messing with me. I've got more influence than the Prime Minister 'round here. You won't win. Same goes for Ollie. You'll only get hurt.'

I brushed the white bits off my leggings. My stomach felt soft and squidgy, like it did the night my father marched me to that rapist bastard's door. 'Will Ollie do anything bad to you? For taking his money and helping me?'

'I gave the money back ages ago, and no, he won't hurt me. Ollie's smart enough to only start fights he can win. You really underestimated him, Ceels. Messing with him was a big mistake.'

He pushed down my head and slammed the boot.

Toby briefly stopped at an unknown destination before he finally released me into his other garage. Not breaking stride after the events of the evening, he prattled on about buying eggs and led me into his hall. He switched on the kettle, then rummaged in the kitchen drawer.

'What's the plan, Toby?' I took a seat at the island.

He plonked a pair of scissors and a box of hair dye in front of me. Light-brown and permanent, guaranteed to cover grey.

'We're giving you a new hairstyle and dying our hair.'

'Why yours?'

'Because I walked into a CCTV covered shop and bought hair dye. Then I'll get the clothes Laura sorted for charity and kit you out with some new stuff. And then,' he paused for a yawn and stretched his arms skywards, 'I'm taking you to bed for a few hours before I take you to your car.'

'What after?'

Toby shrugged. 'You tell me. Where are you going?'

'The coast. Somewhere with B&Bs with chintzy curtains – owned by unobservant old people who don't ask for a credit card. I'll dump the hire car tomorrow, before the police start looking for it, and dogleg there using taxis.'

I skirted onto his lap and shoved my cup along the counter. Toby reached around me and got his ever-present iPad. He created an email account in a random name and signed up to the mailing lists on a few websites to keep the account open.

'Use the drafts as a drop box, Ceels. Make sure you tell me if anything critical happens.'

Toby leaned along the counter for a file bound by a stiff plastic comb. He handed it to me.

'What's this?'

'One of Laura's uni projects. I've been watching you, putting two and two together, and after tonight's little murderous rampage... Read it. I put stickers on the most interesting bits.'

I opened the file. The first pages caught in the binding, resisting my progress, but I read on hesitantly: Narcissistic Personality Disorder (NPD) and the Digression from Socially Acceptable Behaviour. The introduction summarised the personality disorder. It mentioned exaggerated feelings of self-importance, a lack of empathy, an obsession with admiration, and excessive anger when the sufferer felt aggrieved.

I glanced at him, confused. 'Toby, in case you haven't noticed, I haven't got the time to sit around reading school projects.'

'Read it.' A severe expression matched his serious tone.

I tugged my bottom lip and continued reading at the next place he'd stuck a pink post-it. Relationships. Unreasonable control and blame. Entitlement and envy. My nails dug into my skin. There were too many words, triggering words, words which made me want to kick out in defence.

'Sufferers are easily offended and react with disproportionate rage or long-term strategies of revenge. Are you implying this is me?'

Toby ran his finger over the last sentence. 'Stating the obvious, Ceels, you just tried to kill a woman because she fancied your fella and strangled him cos he wanted a divorce.'

My insides turned to sand, filtering down from top to bottom as though I'd become a massive egg timer. The next section said that NPD might happen following an extremely controlling, excessively critical or emotionally abusive childhood. Beside the paragraph was another post-it note; written in neat uppercase lettering were the words: father is a wanker.

Toby sat back, hands behind his head. He wasn't frightened of me. No doubt he encountered people who were scarier and more violent than me, and he could probably be scarier and more violent himself. His nonchalant reaction to the events of the night said as much.

'Turn yourself in and you'll get off with diminished responsibility. They'll send you to a secure unit instead of some high security prison. If you convince them you're better, you'll do fifteen years, maybe less.'

'Fuck that.'

Toby turned the file and scanned the text. 'You've got this NPD, no doubt about it.' He paused before reading aloud: 'Sexually seductive. Clever. Against genuine intimacy. Commonly partakes in affairs. Paranoid. Calculating and ruthless. Potentially homicidal. Guiltless. I mean, for fuck's sake, you killed your brother and—'

'I didn't kill him.'

Toby chuckled. 'Told, ya. Textbook.' He grabbed my hands and pressed them together inside his. 'You can get help. There are tablets and stuff.'

His fingers were soft, protective around mine. 'I think I'm past that, don't you?'

I kissed Toby. I kissed him like my life depended on it, because, what with him giving me a new image, cloned cards and narcotics to deal, if I got away with my crimes, it would happen because of him.

45

ALISTAIR

Is this real?

The words played over and over, as loud as klaxons in my head. I opened my mouth and tried to swallow around my swollen tongue. Everywhere I looked there were squares, squares with long lines and blurred edges. Wired divided the door window into thousands of squares, and a square sign hung on the wall. I tried to sit up, but the turning got faster. I fell back, and something plastic scrunched next to my ear.

'Alistair, don't move.'

Elena.

She studied bits of my face, not the whole, which didn't seem right. Her puffy eyes were pink, penned with red. She grabbed my hand, and I wheedled my fingers in between hers. They were puffy too, the flesh bulgy around the topaz ring she wore.

Somebody said my name.

The voice belonged to a man. I stared at him for too long, running his features through my brain; trying to place him. He had dark eyes, kind eyes, the type of eyes my sister would have said belonged to a person who knew things.

'What's going on?'

I struggled to talk. A hard lump filled my throat, and swallowing around it hurt. I touched the tape and pad on my neck, though I didn't know what it hid or how it got there.

'My name is Doctor Vashri.'

I scanned the hospital ward again. The blue-white lights behind the shiny metal grids hurt my eyes. I shuffled up the bed and winced.

'May I call you Alistair?' the doctor asked.

I nodded.

A curtain with blue diamonds surrounded the bed, like a stage backdrop for the metal stands in front of it, one with monitors and the other a hanging bag. A tube from the bag led to the plastic thing stuck in my hand. I touched it, and the needle moved under my skin.

'Alistair,' the doctor said.

Back in the room.

'You were admitted with neck and throat injuries and the effects of a benzodiazepine overdose.'

The doctor said too many words, and the sentences made little sense in my muddled brain. 'Benzo-what?'

'Benzodiazepine. Commonly known as Diazepam. How do you feel?'

'Tired, and my throat's killing me.'

Elena squeezed my hand. 'Celia did it, Alistair. I caught her in your house just before Ollie and I found you with the belt around your neck. You need to tell the police everything you remember so they can catch her.'

I screwed up my eyes. I remembered so little, hardly a thing. Pictures came and blocks of words came, but they didn't fit together, then they disappeared. The doctor strapped a blood pressure cuff around my arm. It got tighter and tighter and my brain bulged. My heart beat really fast. Elena touched my head and a lock of her hair fell forward. I followed it up and down, focusing on her.

'Do you feel well enough to speak to the police?' the doctor asked.

'I suppose so.'

The police officer shook my hand and told me her name was PC Green. A tuft of brown hair poked out from her ponytail, like a horn. Her mouth twitched with an uncertain smile: a going-through-the-motions smile. She sat down, opened her notebook, and offered a few pleasantries.

'At some point we'll need to tend to the formalities but, in the meantime, can you tell me what happened last night?'

The world began shifting again, and my stomach rolled the bile and emptiness. Elena placed a cardboard bowl on my lap.

'She came to my house and cooked dinner. Curry.'

'Who is she?' the officer prompted.

'Celia.'

'Your wife?'

The word blocked my throat, and I wanted to cough it up, like Fluffy did with a fur ball. 'Yes.'

'At what time?' PC Green asked.

I shook my head, unable to remember. I'd lost hours, hours of memories, and it scared me. This wasn't blacking out after drinking games after winning the league in college football.

'How much alcohol did you drink last night?'

I tried to replay the night, what I could remember anyway, second by second, line by line, until it became another pain in my hurting head. I remembered one bottle of beer, an IPA, but I threw a different bottle at the wall.

I threw a bottle at the wall.

'Not much. A few beers, maybe. I never drink much at home.' A feeling of disapproval surrounded drinking beer alone in the house. I'd got it from Mum, who got it from Gran because of Grandad's problem. 'What's that got to do with catching her?'

'I understand your frustration, but there are questions we need to ask.' The officer shook her pen, scribbled, then wrote something on her pad. 'Do you take Diazepam on prescription or otherwise?'

I might have been dozy and spinning like hell, but I caught her tone. 'No, I don't take anything. Do you think I took the stuff myself?'

'Excuse me,' Elena said, sternly. 'Why don't you save the incriminating/non-incriminating questions and focus on the more immediate issue of finding Celia?'

'Elena.' I shushed her. 'She's just doing her job.'

'Alistair, Celia tried to kill you! She drugged you and strangled you with Ollie's belt. If we'd turned up five minutes later, you'd have been dead.'

'Ollie's belt! How the hell did she get his belt?'

Elena ran her fingertip over the bumps of my knuckles. 'Alistair. They were having an affair. He admitted it last night. Ollie told Celia they were through, so she decided to kill you and make it look like he did it.'

I saw Celia's face, twisted and spiteful. She said she'd been seeing Ollie. 'She told me last night. I remember now.'

'With all due respect,' PC Green said to Elena, 'we need to ascertain the facts before the speculation.'

'With all due respect,' Elena bit back, 'if you'd met the devious cow, you'd realise my speculation is much closer to the truth than your implication that Alistair got drunk, took an overdose and tried to strangle himself.'

The police officer didn't bite. 'Does your wife have friends or relatives she might have turned to?'

I shook my head. 'No, and please don't call her my wife. Her father lives in Malaysia – she hasn't seen him for fifteen years – and her mother is dead. She has no siblings. No friends close enough to run to – not ones I'm aware of.'

She asked me if I knew where Celia was living, like a house or a hotel. I rubbed my face, certain I knew something, somewhere.

'Erm. The posh hotel. Bradley Hall.'

PC Green's writing disappeared into nothing. She shook the pen, then scribbled in the corner to get the ink flowing again. 'Right, we'll start there, thank you.'

'Don't waste your time. She'll be long gone,' I croaked, cleared my throat. 'Track her phone. Use the traffic cameras to look for her car.'

'We need a warrant for that. She's only wanted for questioning at the moment. I'll follow this up and be in touch.'

The room filled after the officer left. Filled with questions. Filled with secrets. I knew my marriage was built on lies, but I'd never realised the extent of them.

'What did you see?'

Elena sighed. 'Nothing really. She rushed out of the house, then we found you unconscious.'

'What did Ollie see?'

'The same as me. He walked through the front door as I walked through the back. We caught Celia in the hall.'

I closed my eyes and drifted into my head for a bit. My illogical thoughts landed like footballs in the back of a net. I piled them up, trying to make sense of everything.

'So, nobody could say I didn't do it to myself.' I screwed up my eyes as another ball flew in. 'She wore blue plastic gloves, so only my fingerprints would be on the belt.'

'And Ollie's. He undid it after we found you.'

'Then he could go down for attempted murder if she says he did it.'

'She can't say Ollie did it because I can testify otherwise.' Elena's jaw twitched. 'I think she planned to kill me, kill you, and have Ollie languish in prison for the rest of his days.'

'Kill you?'

'Yep. Ollie told her he divorced his wife for me. Turns out Celia had it in her head he divorced Suzie to be with her. So that, along with me and you, seems to have pushed her over the edge.'

'What did she do to you?'

'I think she put peanuts in my house and pinched my medication.' Elena scratched the starched sheet. 'I went into anaphylactic shock and the EpiPens were gone from my bag and the bathroom cabinet. I managed to get upstairs and get the one out of my court bag. I'm alright now – don't worry, the doctor said I'm fine – but I had minutes, Alistair. I thought I'd die.'

The obvious prodded my cloudy mind. 'She'll get away with this.'

'Probably. Unless they find my medication on her person, there'll be no way of proving she stole it and contaminated my house with peanuts. And when they catch her, she could say she told you about Ollie and you topped yourself.'

'They won't catch her, Elena. She won't be at the hotel. She's gone – and hopefully she never comes back.'

Elena looked scared and destroyed, and it was all my fault. If I'd never set foot in Elena's house or kicked Celia out of mine, none of it would have happened. Elena went from having her illusions trashed by her philandering husband to being almost murdered by a psychopathic neighbour.

'I'm sorry,' I muttered. 'If you want to run and never come back, I'll totally understand.'

'Not a chance. We're absolutely meant to be.'

I kissed her hand. 'Aye, we are.'

For better or worse. Richer or poorer.

Only upon death would we part.

Epilogue

YASMIN

I disappeared.

I became anonymous.

And then I became someone else.

In all honesty, I had always been the unreliable narrator of my own story, so I simply needed to start again with a new cast list and a new protagonist.

Yasmin, poor Yasmin. She gave the nasty man all that she owned in exchange for a new life in Britain. Her English was broken, punctuated by mental grasping and perfect Malay, and she'd never felt settled. Until she met Aida.

Like me, Aida looked twenty-two, despite being thirty. She had black hair and my skin tone, and she stood a little over five feet tall. We got talking in an Asian food store over a basket filled with fresh vegetables and rice noodles. Aida split her life between Britain and Jakarta, and she didn't have a contracted job. She was engaged to a man called Adam, and they wanted a housekeeper. Aida and Adam were the answer to my dreams, so I moulded myself to be the answer to theirs.

I liked Aida a lot. But I liked Adam enough.

Six months after the start of my employment, Aida unexpectedly disappeared. Adam later received an email, sent from an account he never knew she had, which said she'd met somebody else, and he needed to move on. He tried to call her again and again, but her phone was switched off. He had no luck with the email address either. Much to my surprise, he asked very few questions after that, other than, 'Will you stay on at the house?' and a few weeks later, 'Fancy joining me for a glass of wine?'

The rest became a tick-box exercise.

Over the next few weeks, I cut myself a heavy fringe, bought low strength reading glasses, and I took to wearing brightly coloured lipstick, just like Aida had. When a neighbour made a comment to Adam about Aida coming home, he didn't dispute it and neither did I. Because poor Aida forgot to take her driving licence and, unbeknown to Adam, her passport, bank cards and immigration paperwork too. This meant I got a new identity which would save us from our fears: his of my deportation and mine of a life behind bars.

It was a win-win situation.

I look out of the guestroom window in the house which I chose. It is spacious and stylish, and it has a great outlook, its location perfect. The river runs close to the garden, sweeping away the rain from the storms, and on the horizon is an enormous house surrounded by an eight-foot-high fence with a double garage and an unused paddock.

I will go back there. To Ollie's house. When I am good and ready.

I turn my attention to the ovarium on the windowsill, all planted with beautiful flowers. I know he's in there somewhere. I hate wasps, but they're easier to catch than bumblebees, what with them being unthinking, greedy little bastards. The last one died because I put it in a jar and shook it. I chopped the one before it in half, right at the narrow part where the thorax meets the abdomen.

But death happens. It's all about numbers. Population dynamics. Predation. Resources. Life's stupid mistakes. Though he would die because he had hurt me, and for that he couldn't go unpunished.

I will deny the wasp of freedom. I will provoke and exhaust it. I will make it suffer in every way. Its tolerance, however, will be remarkable – unlike those before it which simply curled up and died.

Yes, it turns out insects are just like people.

And you, Ollie, can get fucking ready.

ACKNOWLEDGMENTS

A big thank you to my husband, David, for tolerating my anti-social PC habits, for being reader number one, and more recently giving me the kick up the backside when I almost gave up this book stuff.

Thank you to my final proof reader (and editorial point-maker) Jenny. Who, not only pointed out the failed plot point (milk doesn't keep on the doorstep in summer), but also for sending me back to Google to clarify gerunds!

Thanks to the early readers and feedback: David and Judy, and the best neighbour ever Shirley – all who motivated me to go on and overcome my uncertainty. Thank you to Alice who did a sterling spellcheck before I put the book for submission.

Now for the writing group mention! Thank you, thank you, thank you. You know who you are. A little bubble of talent and brilliance and inspiration. My Celia story only lives because of your encouragement. You are the actual top team.

Finally, thanks to everybody who takes the time to read my book. You are the reason us writing people don't give up and go home. If you like it, a review on Amazon or Goodreads would be gratefully appreciated. Or a mention to a friend or on social media.

Anyhow, a big thank you and I hope you enjoyed it!

About the author

Kerry Birds was born in a small Derbyshire town where she was raised on a diet of pork pie and spring greens; she still lives in Derbyshire with her husband and two boys. She was introduced to fiction at the tender age of thirty-four and took up writing shortly after. She is a mother and an Environmental Chemist. Her hobbies include walking, reading, and wine.